'A jazz lick of a debut – fast-moving, offbeat, and shot through with a sense of cool.' CRAIG SISTERSON, KIWICRIME

'The ultimate movie buff's thriller… The shadow of *The Third Man* looms so large I could practically hear the zither music echo from the waters of the Thames.' DOUGLAS SKELTON

'*Fade to Black* is a smart and gripping cinematic mystery; a love letter to London's less familiar hinterlands and a multi-layered narrative that demands to be re-read.' GRAEME MACRAE BURNET

'From the first page of *Fade to Black* you're on the running-board of a fast moving novel that takes you smack into a parallel London…Mulins treats us to sharp and sassy prose redolent of '40s noir thrillers… *Fade to Black* is original and witty and goes like stink.' GREG LOFTIN, SAXON

'I rooted for Root Wilson,…a media man who has his fingers on the pulse of contemporary London. This book offers a fresh, contemporary twist in the genre…Razor-sharp prose and knuckle-dusting adventures. *Fade to Black* is worthy of a wide audience and deserves to become a cult classic.' ANNE AYLOR, *THE DOUBLE HAPPINESS COMPANY*

'Sharp, precise and witty.' GEOFF PAYNE, THINKTANK INTERNATIONAL

FADE *to* BLACK

STEVE MULLINS

CONTRABAND

Published by Saraband
Suite 202, 98 Woodlands Road
Glasgow, G3 6HB, Scotland
www.saraband.net

ISBN: 9781910192252
ebook: 9781908643269

Printed in the EU on sustainably sourced paper.

1 3 5 7 9 10 8 6 4 2

Chapter One

IN BLOOMSBURY I shook hands with a dead man.

I was waiting for a talk on expressionist imagery in *The Third Man* at London's newest cool gallery when the late Philip Hegley showed up. He announced his arrival by running into a chair he sent toppling onto its back. Then he managed to make an even bigger racket putting it back to sorts, dragging the legs screamingly across the floor. He opened his arms to the small audience in some kind of theatrical apology, looked around the room, then headed straight in my direction. He grabbed my hand and shook.

"I was hoping to catch you here, Root."

Hegley's head was bald and polished, his face hard, like it had lost its flesh, skin taut over bone. He kept a tight grip on my arm like he thought I might bolt.

Before I could respond – what do you say to the deceased? – he talked a staccato burst, offering a reckless spread of notions I couldn't possibly begin to take in.

"I shouldn't have done it, Root. Pure vanity, of course. But they took advantage. Yes, I should have put a stop to it. Foolish, foolish. I need to get on with things now. Difficult, of course. When you're supposed to be dead… "

Barely a minute later, this very tall man – I put the chap at around six-six minimum – arrived at the gallery. He came our way at a fair lick and I was impressed by how light-footed he was for his height. He stopped at our row and made to block an exit, so it seemed. I noticed he was very well-dressed – the stand-outs were his shoes which were absolutely sharp and shone with a patina that was almost antique.

Hegley finally let go of me.

1

"We need to talk, Root," he said.

He went over to join the waiting giant, then walked off towards the exit. The man – how was he able to walk so daintily? – kept clean step no more than a yard behind him.

I watched them leave, couldn't believe what had just happened. Well, it wasn't every day you met a dead man and got invited to a chat. What was there to say? Pretty much everything I knew about Hegley I'd put into the five-hundred-word obituary I'd written two years ago.

Hegley's had been the first, and to that date the only, obit I'd ever written, and though I'd certainly known who he was, it wasn't as if I was any sort of expert on him or his work. What happened was I got an urgent request from a *Guardian* editor. *Our regular on the filmmakers has come down with a bug. Anyone else who could do it is hanging in Cannes and, of course, no one had the thought to prep something on Hegley. He was only sixty, for Christ's sake. Do it for a pal, won't you?*

He was a vague kind of friend – I needed a lot of those to do what I did for a living – but I thought, why not, you never knew when you might be after a return favour from a daily. So I dug up what I could on Hegley on the Internet and then called a contact at *Sight & Sound*. He promptly sent over a bike with copies of articles covering the deceased in his cinematic prime, which would have been some thirty years earlier.

I took time to study the obituaries format and it seemed fairly straightforward, not a lot to it unless you personally knew the departed, or had some exciting anecdote up your sleeve. Well, I reckoned the genre needed a pep of sorts so I came up with a fitting style that leant heavily on the screenplay format I knew so well. I definitely managed to put a bit of life into the past of the deceased in the present tense.

The *Guardian* was happy with it. I got the regular fee. That was the obit over and done. And Hegley. Well, until I got to shake his hand in Bloomsbury.

* * *

The morning after the talk, I got up at six-thirty. As I dressed I chatted to Meaghan, tried to explain what had happened, but as usual I wasn't able to interest her in any kind of early-morning talk. As I closed the bedroom door all I could see of her was a blond head sticking out of a snarl of sheets.

I headed straight to the Thames, guessing the tide would be out, though I could never be sure of that. I'd once gone to buy charts so that I'd know everything there was about the high and low waters, but when I actually got my hands on them in the bookshop I realised they'd take the magic right out of the river, that I probably wouldn't have the desire to leave home early hours to go and see the known. So I kept my money, savoured the priceless realisation that sometimes no price could be put on wonderful ignorance.

The Thames Path at Bankside was empty when I arrived, and the water, which was way down, was deserted too. I enjoyed the quiet for a while until a broad-hipped barge came along to spoil it. I leaned into the railings to see it make a graceless way under Blackfriars Bridge and watched as the bubbles of its wake fizzled, then faded. I thought of the previous evening at the gallery, Hegley's appearance, his babble, the intervention of the light-footed tall man. Maybe I should've left the event straight away, tracked Hegley and his follower right out of the place. But the truth was I was absolutely stunned – who wouldn't have been? – so I'd remained fixed in my seat for the next hour. Of course, I was barely able to listen to the speaker bang on about *The Third Man*, Nietzsche, the nature of tragedy.

Now, down by the river, I could barely wait for the world to wake up so I could tell everyone about Hegley's return, as well as try and find out just what might be going on when the dead suddenly show up and are mad keen to talk to you.

The Thames had started coming in – its shifts always took me by surprise – but there was still enough of a strip of beach to make it worth my while opening the gate to head down a set of concrete steps and onto pebble. I fancied myself a modern-day mudlark, unable to resist a search for jetsam, and a while back I'd got wildly excited on coming across a metal leaping cat that had somehow made its way to the river from the bonnet of a Jaguar car. However, I was always happy with a stroll, with simply tempting the water's edge with my shoe. And I could never resist a patch of bare sand where, like a child, I would plant my foot on uncharted territory, leave the perfect heel, toe.

I left the river and made for Al's, no mere too-little-too-latte coffee shop but an old-fashioned buttery-walled cafe, the only one close to the Thames to be open at this hour. I always collared the table close to the window which let me gaze out onto the street through the brassy lettering on the huge glass panes. From there I could also cover the door, mark comings and goings, and was on nodding terms with a few of the regulars.

I spent twenty or so minutes with the tailend of the wholesale market crowd who'd worked the night through. They were the people – I now recognised the citrus man and the beadle – who devoured Al's full-English fry-ups and drunk what seemed to be full-measure pints of tea. I supped my cup of stewed coffee, took in the pub-like atmosphere.

I was still getting to know, and like, the neighbourhood and I often picked up something in the cafe that I could use in my work. Like the time I put that broadcast segment based on how the Bishop of Winchester used to run the local brothels with the working girls, the so-called Winchester Geese. The area was now my starting point for things London and I liked to think I was at the beginning of a project to get to know the entire city.

* * *

Meaghan had already left when I got home. I phoned Harry to offer a heads-up on Hegley, but I couldn't get through and had to leave a voicemail straight off the cuff. *You just won't believe who's washed up, Aitch. Call me as soon as.* I knew Harry wasn't the type to wait a long time to find out what was up, would ring back smart enough.

I sat at my desk waiting for the laptop to boot up when I heard a loud snap directly behind me. Another. I went over to the window and saw that one of the panes had a crack running from the centre right into a corner. Down in the road a man – in fact, the very tall one from Bloomsbury – was staring up at me. He crooked his elbow, launched something, and I flinched as it hit the glass right before my face and crazed the pane. He had a bloody good arm, that was for sure. I had no choice but to go downstairs and see what the hell he was playing at.

He was waiting for me, was so cool he even held open the door to let me out of my own building.

"Good of you to come down," he said. "My name's Nesh." He dealt me his half of a handshake.

"Root Wilson." I kept my mitts in my pocket. There was no way I was exchanging pleasantries with a vandal.

"Root's an odd sort of name."

"It was the best my little sister could do with Robert as a kid." I had no idea why I was sharing such a personal detail.

Nesh nodded like he understood perfectly. Again he was nattily dressed. His brogues shone to a gloss and they were decorated with bright red liquorice laces. His light woollen trousers carried a cutting crease. His silk tie was done up in an impeccable Windsor knot. And he was wearing a three-quarter-length black coat that had a nap to die for.

"What's your game?" I asked.

"We're not *playing*, Mr Wilson."

"Who's we?"

"An interested party."

"Interested in breaking windows?"

"It's just a means to an end."

"An end to what, exactly?"

5

"I simply wanted to let you know that you went to last night's talk, listened politely, spoke to no one, then left."

"And Philip Hegley?"

"Don't know such an animal."

"Me neither, I suppose."

"I knew you'd catch on. You're not the type to cause any bother, I'd say."

"What if I remember later that I actually did see and talk to Hegley?"

Nesh made a show of adjusting the knot on his tie. "Memory's a funny thing, for sure. But one thing you're not likely to forget is your broken windows."

I looked up to the first floor, could make out the cracks in the glass even from the pavement. When I turned back to face Nesh, he was already a good twenty yards down the road. He certainly covered ground quickly with that easy gait of his.

* * *

I went back inside. I now had Nesh nailed as someone who really didn't cut it as a villain – he was clearly all show, was far too refined to be a proper tough nut. And rather than scare me, he'd managed to fire me up about our director friend.

I raked through my files until I found the notes I'd used to put together the obit. I read the *Guardian* piece once more. My article amounted to little more than a grain of history – Hegley had been born, had made his films, passed away. I looked though his career cuttings but there was nothing that might help me work out how he'd managed to turn up still drawing breath. He'd supposedly drowned but I now I realised I needed to find out the exact circumstances. For, in true obituarist style, I'd only dealt that detail a glancing blow when I'd knocked up the original sketch.

I found a dry account of the coronary court proceedings in *The Stage*. Philip Hegley had turned up his toes rather dramatically on a Dover ferry making its way to Dieppe. He had been off to lunch in France with his agent, Roger Huckerby, who reported that the two of them had spent a quiet hour or so in the passenger lounge before Hegley had left to lift a leg. But he'd never returned to his seat. Huckerby went looking for him and did a few tours of the boat before reporting the disappearance to the crew.

It seemed as though the French authorities had been lax. The ship returned to England with Huckerby onboard and it wasn't until hours later that a search turned up Hegley's Harris tweed jacket folded in a bin, along with a farewell note tucked into the inside pocket. The British police contacted everyone on the passenger list. One woman remembered seeing someone of Hegley's description – bald, about five-nine – on the car deck during the voyage, while one man said he was fairly certain it was Hegley who had asked him for a light as they stood by the rail at the ferry's stern and had chatted briefly about what was showing in the West End. Hegley's body never did turn up and, after the requisite time period, a verdict of suicide was returned.

At the time of his disappearance, Hegley's career had been deep in the doldrums and he hadn't made anything new for the screen in an age. With that lengthy blot on the CV, there was little prospect of any finance coming his way to change his non-working habit. In short, the prevailing view was that Hegley was commercially played out as a director.

His films – he made five altogether – were generally recognised to be ahead of their time. They were dramas of a gritty bent, with Hegley prone to using lesser-known repertory actors. He was considered to have brought out the best in his casts thanks to the use of what he told the trade press was *rehearsed improv with a twist*. His players were forced to remain totally in character for an entire shoot and they reported that they usually felt utterly spent for months after. Some of them never worked in cinema again, and only a handful of stalwarts appeared in his films more than once.

There was high critical praise for the look and feel of Hegley's work. Authenticity was his byword and he went to huge lengths to achieve it. For one thing, he directed his cinematographer to scrape the coatings from the camera lenses so that he might capture *real* light. And he insisted on using a rare and expensive black-and-white film stock imported from Austria that had a broad spectrographic range and delivered startling contrast. In an interview with the *Telegraph*, Hegley said he saw his job as similar to a painter's – light was the raw material he mixed on his palette until he got exactly what was required for a scene. Devotees said they needed to see only a few feet of rolling celluloid before being able to identify it as his work.

The last of Hegley's films was his most critically acclaimed, though it also took a heavy fiscal fall. *Greene Land* was reckoned to be a tough fiction set in the London docks shortly before they went into decline and disappeared from the cityscape. I realised I knew almost nothing about it.

* * *

I'd arranged to meet Harry after work. While I felt it was OK for me to dismiss Nesh, I wasn't about to take a risk by involving someone else, and I'd always been especially protective of Harry.

She was already waiting at the Bunch of Grapes when I arrived, looked stunning as always. She liked to dress her way around the decades and this evening was wearing bright-red hot pants with wide braces that rose dramatically up from her waistline and over her white T-shirted chest. Her auburn head was a tumble of waves and curls.

As soon as she saw me, she took me on. "So, what's up? Surprise me with your surprise."

"Can I at least get you a drink first?"

"You know exactly what I want."

"That's for sure."

I ordered our favourite Belgian beers and we waited out their delivery in silence, though Harry was working on sending over her best glare. I wasn't about to put up with any intimidation – I knew if you let Harry best you just once in the gesture stakes you were dead meat for the rest of the session.

We raised our glasses.

"So?" she asked.

"Shouldn't we try and scare up a pool table?"

"Job done. We'll be on in ten minutes. Tell me what's up.

"Look, Harry, there's not that much I can give you."

"Come on, Bro, talk to me, why don't you?" Her face was tight with frustration. "It will feel soooo good."

"I'm going to write a biog of Philip Hegley."

"Hegley? How come?"

"Roger Huckerby, his old agent, called me out of the blue and asked me if I was up for it."

"I haven't heard anything about this on the grapevine," she said. "Tell me more."

"But I've signed an NDA."

"Oh, give me something."

"Huckerby told me he really enjoyed the obituary."

"How can anyone *enjoy* an obituary?"

"Maybe I have a knack when it comes to writing about the dead."

"So, you're saying this book is what all this mystery is about?

"In a nutshell," I said.

"What? Don't go around thinking I believe this for a minute, Bro."

"I need your help here, Aitch. Tell me what you think of Philip Hegley's work?"

"Why should I say anything when you're obviously not being straight with me?"

"Be a pal. I'll definitely give you more when I can."

Harry looked into her glass. "Well, I'd say he was a bit of a directors' director who strutted some good stuff on the lighting side. The look of some of his films is, frankly, totally amazing. Not just for their time, either. They still pop socks today."

"Something of a technician, was he?"

"Far more than that. He had this thing about multiple plotlines that were too much for audiences back then. Have you seen *Greene Land*?"

I shook my head, drank some, was enjoying listening to Harry begin sounding off on something she was clearly encyclopaedic about. She was currently a film production star, knew what was what, who was who. Not that it was any surprise she was flying so high, because even at uni she'd been mad, mad, mad about film, was top of the class and then some.

"Thing is, Hegley's too much of a social realist for me," she said, "though it's clear why the film's doing well posthumously. It plugs right into the Zeitgeist. I can't believe you haven't bothered to see it."

"Well, you know my feelings on British filmmakers…"

"They love it in Europe and on the East Coast," she said. "It's bringing in pots for the production company, and the fact that Hegley's content is part of my portfolio makes me stand out on the balance sheet."

"I didn't know that." Harry was turning out to be a great source.

"That's because you never ask what I'm up to."

"Come on, Aitch, you know I'm not one to follow the deals."

"Typical bloody creative."

"Guilty." I held up my hands. "But give me more. I can't believe Hegley would have approved of a smash hit."

"I think def he would've. I did meet him a couple of times and he was crazy for success. Thing was, he thought everyone who came to see him after his career troughed was going to somehow pull him back up. I was just another bloody graduate at the time. I couldn't do anything for him."

"Tell me more about *Greene Land*."

"Hegley was nuts about everything to do with the Thames. He came from somewhere in oriental England, even had a sort of writing hideaway by the coast. His big idea was always to do a Docklands drama."

"And it flopped."

"To be fair, the film only screened in a handful of London theatres. And in midsummer. It could only die."

"To rise like a phoenix on the director's demise."

"If you say so." Harry emptied her glass with one thirsty pull.

She pointed to the two guys finishing their game of pool. "We're on," she said.

Harry was short of time so we played a best of three. And she handed me a proper drubbing. It was in the third, when she was already two up with nothing to lose, that she really cut loose. I'd just gone for a safety and it looked like she needed to proceed pretty cautiously herself to make something of her next shot. Of course, she wasn't seeing the position through my meek eyes and went at it full of ginger, pulled off a two-rail kick that dropped her stripe coolly into the middle pocket.

"That was something," I said.

"Wasn't it just?" She showily kissed the tip of the cue.

Harry then proceeded to run the table, finishing off with an inside cut that not only put away her last ball but also, rather cheekily, saw the cue ball gently tap a solid of mine into the nearest pocket.

"I'm irresistible, Bro," she said.

Looking directly as I was at Ms Hot Pants, I had to agree.

* * *

Meaghan was at the keyboard when I got home. She was wearing her earbuds, so didn't hear me come in. I sat myself out of the way in an armchair, watched her play.

One thing Meaghan Terry had in profusion was poise. I relished the rhythm that ran across her shoulders, and I watched it rise into her graceful neck to end in the serene nods of her head. I couldn't see her face but I took pleasure in imagining the lines of her mouth tensing as she worked her way through the tougher passages. And I admired the finesse of her fingers as they picked out the keys. I was totally fascinated by the art of her bones and the gorgeous cloth of her skin. I completely adored the form of Meaghan, wanted to make love to her right then.

I hadn't seen her play for ages. She'd studied piano full on until she hit eighteen, then given up abruptly. She abandoned plans of becoming a professional and went on to study composition at the Royal. On graduation, she went straight into publishing, a move that seriously disappointed her musico parents.

Meaghan stopped, removed the buds. My gentle applause made her start.

"Have you been there long?" She tucked stray hairs straight behind her ears.

"I've been admiring the view a while. I wish I could've heard the music, though. What was it?"

"Who Can I Turn To?"

"I'd be a good audience, you know."

I couldn't take my eyes off Meaghan's glorious bee-sting lips. They'd always fascinated me, were beautifully and sexily at odds with the understated features of the rest of her face.

"You don't really like jazz," she said.

"I do when you play it."

"You're still listening to Pulp."

"You make it sound like I'm unfinished business."

"Hanging onto your youth a little, maybe."

"Is that what you think?"

"Isn't that why you see Harriet?" Meaghan could never allow herself to use the name Harry.

"I wondered when she might come up," I said. "You did say you were working late."

She gave me a spiky look.

"It was about work," I said. The way it came out sounded feeble.

"I bet you got your pool fix."

"A few dull games."

"Oh, let's not go pretending anything to do with Harriet is plain vanilla."

"You know, watching you play had put me in a great mood."

"Apologies for ruining your day. And I'm dreadfully sorry I became part of it so very late." Meaghan picked up the keyboard and packed it away in a drawer.

"Unfair. I tried to talk to you this morning before you left."

"You mean when you rattled on about some bloke or other? Hedley, was it?"

"Philip Hegley."

"Isn't he dead?"

"You remember Hegley?" I asked. "I've been asked to do his biog."

"I hope you said no."

"Why would I?"

The telephone rang and I picked it up.

"Root? Philip Hegley. Need to talk, old chap."

The line immediately went dead.

I put down the receiver. Meaghan was no longer in the room. I heard water running into the bathtub.

Chapter Two

I got to the Cutting Edge Studio, which sat in an old warehouse in The Cut, carrying a nasty headache. It came either from what I thought had been a tame drinks session with Harry, or from the tiff with Meaghan that had spoilt a night's sleep. She'd ignored me over breakfast, and as a way of making up for what she perceived to be my wrongdoing, I'd proposed a trip to the Cotswolds, reckoning we needed couple-time away in a place we both really enjoyed. She seemed cold to the idea, said neither yay or nay. I was still deep in the doghouse.

In the studio I organised myself. I placed paper and pen dead ahead of me on the table, stood the water bottle to my right, adjusted the seat, pulled down the microphone, raised it slightly, lowered it again. I looked at my single sheet of A4 with key words circled, linked with arrows, and felt I'd done good prep. I prided myself in getting the show on tape in one single take, was convinced it made all the difference to a broadcast.

I'd been doing the programme for close to eighteen months and had built up a decent following according to the latest audience metrics. The production company I jobbed for had six months ago secured us a slot on the BBC, and we were currently riding high on the Corporation's Digital London channel. I enjoyed putting together material for Auntie, fancying it now made me a bona fide radioman, the current embodiment of a tradition stretching back decades. For that reason, I always went into the studio spruced up. Just like the old-school broadcasters on the wireless, I felt that appearance mattered even when one wasn't going to be seen by the public. Today, I wore a lightweight charcoal Paul Smith suit with a delicate mustard pinstripe and a loudish Paisley shirt from agnès b. I felt pretty cool in the combination.

I looked at my scant notes one more time, felt the jerk of panic I usually got at this point, knew things were totally fine. I scribbled a few words, underlined others, put the pen aside.

My half-hour went by the moniker of En Root – the first suggestion at a name from my producer, Minona, had been Root's Toots, but I'd managed to veto that monster as soon as it reared its head. Basically, the prog was a grab bag of ideas local, the remit being to provide news, views and happenings in the capital. That meant delivering many a Londinium titbit along with my thoughts on the cultural scene, regular film reviews, excerpts from an exceptional novel, tracks from a music find. Recently, I'd started capturing short interviews with people believed to be on the ascendant. The last best thing I'd put together was a neat segment on Jaymo talking about his new music show and doing a Skin & Data remix specially for the programme that he dedicated to a few kids who'd recently been downed in a spate of stabbings on South London estates. It was exactly the kind of thing I was keen to highlight.

I readjusted the microphone, ran through a sound test – *five, four, three, two … Root one* – and got a nod from the blue-dyed head of Cushman the engineer, the only member of the team I wasn't on good terms with. He was ace at his job, a true iceman in a crisis, and he could spout endlessly when it came to the audio likes of sibilance, PPMs and crosstalk. Everyone knew he had it in for me, though no one could begin to explain why.

With fifteen seconds to go, I helped myself to a final pull of Evian, readied for the top of the programme.

Welcome to En Root. Atypical, topical, digital. This last week, I've been swimming around in our river – you know I like getting you to love what I love when it comes to the day-to-day machinery of this city. That's why I'm going to share something I found on the Internet. It's a quote from the authorities on recovering waterborne bodies. 'Thames Division have specially trained and equipped

OFFICERS, INCLUDING POLICE DIVERS, TO CARRY OUT THIS TASK. UNPROTECTED STAFF SHOULD ONLY BE USED IF IT IS OPERATIONALLY NECESSARY, FOR EXAMPLE, SHEER NUMBERS…' WHAT? SHEER NUMBERS? ON AVERAGE, THE THAMES CHALKS UP MORE THAN FIFTY DROWNINGS A YEAR. THAT'S RIGHT, ONE EACH AND EVERY WEEK. I DON'T KNOW YET IF THERE'S A DISTINCT PATTERN TO SUCH 'INCIDENTS' BUT I'LL STUDY THE STATS AND SEE IF THERE'S A SEASON WHEN YOU SHOULD DEFINITELY AVOID THAMESIDE ACTIVITIES. IN THE MEANTIME, HERE'S A TRACK FOR YOU. WHO COULD FAIL TO RECOGNISE THE EARLY BARS OF – WHAT ELSE? – 'CRY ME A RIVER'.

As the track wound down, my voice went back on air with an update on the upcoming mayoral election, then I segued into reviews of a couple of new-release indie film, and hopped to a piece about a taxi cab opera which contained a wad of vox pops. That was another show all tied up. It had gone well, just a minor glitch after an audio clip failed to fire, something that was easy enough to sort in post.

I left the studio and went off to a meeting with the hyper-fiscal, biz-suited Minona, and the two of us walked over to the members bar at the Tate Modern where we grabbed cappuccinos. We sipped our drinks out on the high-up terrace with its view of the Thames, St Paul's et al.

"How did it go?" Minona asked. She rarely sat in on recordings, said she couldn't see the point of eyeballing a rough-and-ready production process when all she needed to do was wait a while to enjoy the slick final product.

"I think we have ourselves a decent slot," I said.

"Excellent. The BBC wants to up the time."

My first thought was to give Minona a hug, my second was not to. "Terrific," I said. "By how much?"

"To forty-five minutes."

"Christ." My mind raced with ideas. Director and author

interviews, live music clips and more of the visual arts like painting, sculpture and cinematography. It'd be nice to up the political content to make the programme racier.

"The next show will be the last at thirty," she said.

"Now's the time to hire that researcher."

"It's something to talk about."

That was poor news. I knew Minona's management style and when something was on she would be overwhelmingly bullish. But she couldn't bring herself to be negative, and that meant anything which was unlikely to fly would be left to blow in the breeze.

"I should tell you, I didn't care for the piece with that Jaymo character." Minona did her trademark shoulder shrug, scrunched her face. I'd never seen her smile with any gusto though it was something that would do wonders – she came up quite pretty when in a good mood, had enormously attractive green eyes.

"I think the longer format cries out for that kind of thing," I said.

"And there was that odd segment you did on hot film locations."

"But we got positive feedback on both of those."

"It was so-so." Minona poured another sugar into her coffee, stirred it overlong. She looked at me in the way a mother might regard a small child who'd just made a foody mess on the tablecloth. "Who on earth wants film on the radio?"

"Come on, Min. It's a fantastic challenge."

"This is a commercial venture, not a feat of derring-do." She pushed her coffee away.

"You've never interfered before."

"The show just went up a gear."

"And now you tell me what to do?"

"You have to think of it as a compliment, Root. After all, you're our rising star."

I looked down at the river, spotted a police inflatable jouncing along, wondered if the crew had found this week's body.

* * *

17

Back home, elated by the programme upgrade, deflated by Min's attitude, I got to work updating my blog with the show news and finally posted the graph I'd written on the talk in Bloomsbury. I'd started putting together all kinds of content that I was hoping would become a trove of London-related film-centric material, and it was getting a good number of hits.

I added a call-for-info on Hegley. *Everything's welcome*, I said, *send me what you have and I'll decide its merit. No nugget too small.* Then I hyperlinked it to a couple of UK sites that were carrying stories on the director and his work.

That done, I checked my e-mail. I was about to delete a message from an unknown source but the address of the sender – greenel-and-at-yahoo – stopped me dead. I opened it and found a note from Hegley written in his breathless style.

Root. Can't risk the phone again. But e-mail tricky too. Simply have to meet. PH

I banged out a quick response, asked him to give me a time and a place. But my message bounced back undeliverable – Hegley must have already cancelled the account.

The deceased was certainly proving to be a live wire.

* * *

The DVD of *Greene Land* arrived with the post late morning. I still wasn't overeager to watch Hegley's last and best, even though Harry had given it decent marks. I trusted her judgement in most matters filmic but still thought she was terribly wrong when it came to British film. I was now honest enough to admit to myself, if not to Harry, that my critical ability vis à vis domestic output was pretty impaired, that it was, in fact, little more than the sum of prejudices formed by the dire flicks I'd watched on wet Sunday afternoons on TV as a kid and teen.

I wanted more than anything to come to *Greene Land* with an open mind, but when I sat down in front of the box I wasn't expecting to be able to get through more than about ten minutes of Hegley's feature before hitting the off button. My guess was that, for all its technical brilliance, it would prove nothing more than a grey old drama featuring the usual pale faces.

What actually happened was that I found myself completely overwhelmed. I watched the whole thing through. Then I saw it once more. I replayed what I thought were the key scenes. I made pages of notes. I wrote up my take on *Greene Land* online.

```
Silence.
The Thames is almost indistinguishable from the
land at Woolwich Reach as the camera describes a
steady pan across the waterscape. But what seems at
first a static picture comes to life, the surface of
the river a hundred veins of grey that constantly
weave, warp.
The land is moving, too. Ashen shapes form on
the horizon, then fuse into recognisable objects
- industrial stacks, gangly-legged electricity
pylons, waterside derricks - which gradually burn
into the scene.
The music, a simple understated jazz sax, flows for
a minute before breaking off suddenly as the bow of
a huge ship enters from the left and a steel-plated
hull fills the frame, slides by in very slow-motion.
The soundtrack is now the bellowing thrum of an
engine.
Fade to:
A market scene with an indistinguishable racket of
voices. People are trading fruit and vegetables,
loaves of bread, clothing, shoes, fabrics. Much
money changes hands at speed.
We move steadily at waist height through the
plugged aisles between the stalls, are bumped from
left, right, head on. The direction, if there is
```

one, is increasingly hard to discern. The voices about us are turning into painful cries.

Mercifully, the noise begins to soften as we find open space, turning into the calls of gulls. We are back again at the edge of the Thames. The river's at high tide, now with the dimensions of a huge lake.

Cut to:

Boocock sits in the Mozart Cafe, Woolwich High Street. The voiceover, male, knowing, tells us he's a four-book author. That his writing furrow is sixties' pulp. That his fictive world revolves around Brighton gangsters fighting it out on the racecourse for the punters' money.

Boocock's waiting for an old schoolfriend, Thom Greene, who called him a week ago out of nowhere, said why didn't Boocock drag himself out to East London. They could catch up, couldn't they, perhaps Boocock might help Greene out on 'a little something'.

Boocock remembered getting on with Greene, liked the idea of seeing him, wondered what it was Greene had in mind. Well, he didn't have a lot going on, so why not.

Boocock has a plate with bacon omelette in front of him. He jabs the food with a fork. He looks out through the large window of the cafe as he eats. Wark, a bulky, stiff-necked man, appears by the table. "Eating alone can cause cancer," he says.

"Is that a fact?" Boocock asks.

Wark takes hold of the back of the chair. "Mind if I…"

"I'm waiting for someone."

"Thom Greene won't be joining us."

"You know Thom?"

"Knew him."

Cut to:

The interior of the Shirley Ann pub in Peckham.
The lights go out in the saloon bar and the room's
solidly dark for a good ten seconds before a single
spot is thrown onto Les Lea. She's decked in silk
lingerie, suspenders. But she's no stripper. Just
a few chords into the first number and it's clear
she's a London version of Sally Bowles. Les Lea
sings 'Speak Low' and 'I'm a Stranger Here Myself'.
Fade to black.

I took the Tube up to Kings Cross and the library but couldn't
shake *Greene Land*. The dark rail tunnels didn't help, and each
sooty stretch shot me right back to the film. I'd never seen anything like it, and I'd consumed mile after mile of celluloid footage as a student. The night scenes were, quite frankly, some of the
most stunning cinematography I'd ever come across, the contrasts
blade-sharp. I'd wanted to reach out and touch the achingly deep
blacks, but at the same time was afraid to. I thought I knew something about the technicals of lighting but felt completely out of my
depth. In the high-key scenes, for example, I could only marvel at
what should have been, given the intensity of the light, dead sur-
faces, but they had somehow retained their full forms. As for Les
Lea, her skin never once looked anything short of pure alabaster.
She was a tough character, for sure, but the way she'd been lit gave
her a fragility that made you want to protect her forever.

Immersed in the film, I almost missed my stop at Kings Cross
and then made hard work of getting off the platform and up to
street level. The film had transformed the escalators and stair-
wells into a lunatic blend of angles that raked and criss-crossed
seemingly at whim as I rose. And when I wasn't being mechani-
cally propelled, I had to take one deliberate step at a time to walk

properly, to make any sort of progress.

It was only when I got myself outdoors and was faced with the slow-moving traffic of Euston Road, a broad spread of cloud-pocked sky above my head, that the world of Root Wilson returned to something like normal.

I still felt shaky though. My first rule had always been to take a good look under the bonnet of anything and anyone I got close to. And here I was nowhere near to even unlatching *Greene Land*. Nor Hegley for that matter. I had to find out what this man was about.

* * *

Dennis Tabard had called up saying he had a project for me, and for the first part of our meet at the cafe in front of the British Library I remained pretty much in a muzz. The steep prow of that huge boat from the opening scene of *Greene Land* kept pushing into my thoughts. The bass of the engine thumped in my ears. Then I got caught up in the broad Thames scapes, saw the crane behemoths emerge from the brume once more.

I forced myself to leave Hegley's world and to listen to what Tabard had to say. He'd called me out of the blue the other day, said he had some great ideas to pitch, that I'd be one happy man if I met him.

"Fact is, I'm a big fan of your broadcasts," he said. "Totally refuse to miss them."

"Glad you've taken a shine. I wish everyone was as enthusiastic." Minona's attitude still stung strong.

"I'll bet you have a good following."

"That's my hope every time I address the mic."

Tabard nodded, looked to be in deep thought. He was an intense individual with eyebrows that spidered across his forehead, and he pulled constantly at the wilful hairs with finger and thumb. He took a pen from his top pocket and began to draw, in a delicate script, box after linked box across a sheet of paper as he returned to his spiel. It turned out that Tabard's current gig was the Internet, that he was the chosen child of what he called *a hotdog media outfit by the name of Ferris* that had put together some kind of fund to endow a number of promising start-ups. He told me he'd come up with a solid business model that would deliver breakeven in under fifteen months on the back of paid-for click-throughs. Tabard drew a perfect circle around his handsome flow diagram, though it didn't help – I hadn't got half of what he'd said.

"Truth is, this business idea is a financial cert," he said.

Tabard slapped a hand on his papers as a stiff wind pushed across the courtyard, spun the table umbrellas. A score of plastic cups hopped along the flagstones, jammed up against the drinks stand. I could only guess that he'd wanted to meet up here at the library because he thought it gave his project some kind of academic cred.

"What I want from you is a set of audio recordings to stream from our web site," he said. "It will be what you're doing now on the radio but with visuals. And you'll get a couple of graduate researchers as well as top-notch photographers to help you out. Root, I promise you'll want for nothing."

"Sounds cool."

He cleared his throat. "We're after video shorts as well, possibly even something long-form, all for digital distribution. I know that's your thing too."

Tabard was certainly making the talk walk now.

"The idea is London in the making. And I've read some of those scripts of yours that have made their way to Ferris over the past months. You're the man with a finger on the pulse."

"Atypical, topical, digital," I said. "En Root, online."

Tabard looked easy for the first time. He grinned, tugged his eyebrow.

* * *

As I walked back up Euston Road, a red line of buses dragging its dieselly way beside me, I felt juiced by Tabard's proposals, not least by the promise of some kind of video work. It was exactly what I was after. I had previous on the scripting front, had worked for a while as a pool writer on a handful of detective shows, managed to get some of my plotlines and dialogue into *Life on Mars*. I'd also scripted a few documentaries as well as a some short dramas that had made their way onto TV just a little bit down the dial, had even worked as assistant director on a couple. The reviews had been mixed, but I had promise, most of the critics said. What I clearly needed was to step up to the next level but, though I made sure there were always some words of mine kicking around for people to read, I hadn't yet bagged a decent commission.

And now there was Tabard's online project, which highlighted the fact that I was operating on a shoestring for En Root where even a recent mild request for help had been nixed by Min.

I was so full of the meeting that it took a few stops on the Northern Line before I recalled my previous Tube trip when *Greene Land* had so stalked my soul. Now I had my land legs back and, while what I'd seen earlier in the day had surely drilled down deep, I didn't expect to find myself half so disoriented by Hegley's film when I viewed it again, something I was raring to do.

I got off the train at Waterloo, threaded a path of sorts through a packed station concourse, made straight for Union Street and Harry's place.

She inhabited the entire top floor of a converted depot not too many blocks from the river. Each time I went there it brought home the fact that Harry belonged to big business and lived the career life, while I had bought into the freelance existence that had me working on all kinds of tasks. She had ownership of an *absolutely smoking exec job* – her phrase – in the film industry, enjoyed all the trimmings, and whenever I rode the lift that took me up to Harry's dominion I told myself I could have had everything too if I'd stuck with the only permanent gig I'd ever had knocking out copy at an ad agency. But I'd have made a miserable rich guy, and I was more than OK with doing OK on the money front.

Harry now tended with care two thousand square feet of home

that boasted a generous acreage of exposed brickwork and a forest of original Thameside beams. She'd done a grand job decking out her gaff, had hired a local architect to come up with a wild-wall system that could be altered quickly by unlatching a few clips and rolling the partitions over the concrete flooring. Harry being Harry, she liked to change the layout regularly and whenever I dropped in it would take me a while to suss the latest design.

Harry was waiting for me at the door. Her hair was trussed tight in a yellow bandana and she was toting a pair of angular specs that looked right-on fifties. They suited her to a tee.

"Don't tell me," I said. "Audrey Hepburn."

"I wish. You too, probably."

"Oh, Aitch, I love you just the way you are."

"Cue the music if either of us could croon." She squeezed my arm. "You're a sweet man, in any case. Step inside, why don't you? The living room's to the right."

Harry had constructed a narrow five-yard-long corridor that opened up suddenly onto a vast space with floor-to-ceiling windows on three sides. The light was washing in even on what had become a deeply grey day, the sky flat and grainy as zinc plate. Distributed around the room were all types of old studio flags – the teasers, scrims and cookies cameramen used to create shadow – and they cast eccentric patterns across the floor. Plus there were funky lamps like the Baby Keg in spanking condition, a Dinkie Inkie I'd always loved, and a couple of Foco Spots. Most of the gear was ex-Pinewood and Shepperton stock she'd rescued from long-term storage, but she'd also culled a good many items on regular trips to LA and had them shipped over.

I dropped onto the sofa and took a sip of the iced water with mint leaves Harry had magicked up. "You were right about *Greene Land*," I said. "Hegley's some filmmaker."

"*Was*, Bro." Harry walked over to her Mac, pressed a key.

I stared at the screensaver, a still from *Paris, Texas* made up of a dozen or so bricks that kept on shifting, re-laying.

"You busy?" I asked.

"And some. It's budget time and you know I've never been a whizz with rithmatic. Bit of a numberskull, me."

"You're too modest," I said. "I've got some figures for you, though. My show's been boosted fifty percent to forty-five minutes."

"That's cracking news." Harry dashed over and gave me a lingering smacker on the cheek.

Her skin smelled a heady rose, vanilla and something alluring I couldn't determine. My guess was she was spruced for a date with another unpromising beau toiling for zillions in a media boardroom. The types she chose never worked out, and I would normally have made some kind of crack, but the aroma of Harry had gone straight to my head.

"What would you have given me if the show had gone up to sixty minutes?" I asked.

"Oh, cometh the hour, cometh the woman."

I took another slug of water. It tasted of her delicious perfume rather than of mint.

"I need more stuff on Hegley," I said. "Can you tell me how well *Greene Land* has done financially?"

Harry sat herself in an old director's chair opposite. "Hegley's upsetting industry norms. In the best way, of course."

"Running a healthy profit, no doubt."

"Profit's a rare beast in the film industry. *Greene Land* did zilch in the theatre but is flying on DVD. Hegley's early departure was a boon to the firm."

"Pity he's not around to make more films."

"Oh, but we have the technology. He was a total stickler and he used to shoot and reshoot. We're putting together new cuts of everything, coming up with different formats. And whoever's doing the editing work is a bloody genius."

CHAPTER THREE

The next day, I managed to get myself down to the Thames ahead of the dawn. I always like being by the river before the sun came up, regarded it as a kind of race with the light, which, if I won it, set a bully tone for the rest of the day. But as the morning came, Bankside looked far from its best, showing up drab with an aluminium mist hesitating around the heights of the City's loftiest buildings. The Nat West Tower was in serious danger of losing its turrets, while the Gherkin twisted upwards into a blanching gloom.

I wondered how Hegley might deal with this kind of landscape. He'd use filters to rid the scene of its blunting middle-greys, but that would produce serious grain problems and I couldn't imagine he'd put up with the resulting lack of lustre. Indeed, it was the silk that was present in every second of *Greene Land*, along with the blistering degree of contrast, that I now knew was so Hegley.

A boat came into view. No more than fifteen feet long, it bobbed downstream with an ugly black necklace of tyres lashed to its sides, sent out a frail engine sound that popped across the water. I could make out a silhouette at the wheel, fancied the man to be an old hand on these waters, maybe a one-time pilot who worked down in the estuary when ships still had decent girth and needed navigational help. I found it difficult to entertain the thought that he might be barely out of his teens, and from one of those tourist craft that littered the Thames during the day. Or worse, that he was crew on a party hulk that discoed until the early hours at weekends.

I looked over the railing. The river was down, though I had little idea whether it was close to turning, taking pleasure as always in my ignorance of the tidal shifts. I unlatched the gate, hopped down the steps onto the beach where the mud-glazed rocks were tricky to negotiate. The place smelled rotten and I had to pick my way forward, arms out at shoulder height, happy enough to be a picture of inelegance rather than come a cropper.

I felt the object through the thin sole of my shoe, thought at first it was a stone. But I could see straight off it was man-made. I prodded it with a toe, freed it from the dirt. I hooked it up with my forefinger, went to the river's edge, crouched down and rinsed it in the water.

As soon as the mud washed from the four gaping holes I recognised it for what it was. A pair of knuckledusters.

✳　✳　✳

At my usual table and with a mug of coffee at Al's, I cleaned up the find, using the blade of my door key to scratch away the corrosion that had built along the nasty-looking corrugated ridge of rings. I pulled the sandpaper strip off a discarded box of matches, used it on a small section until I struck metal. I gave the knuckledusters a brisk rub with a serviette, polished up a decent area of brass.

"Tell you what, Boss, I haven't seen a pair like them in a while." Al was at my shoulder, a tea towel wrapped around his fist like a candy-striped boxing glove. "They was made after the Great War from trench-knife handles, don't you know it."

"Just fished them out of the river."

I held out the knuckledusters and Al took them, let them sit in a palm the size of a skillet.

"Growing up down the Old Kent Road these wasn't scarce, Boss," he said. "There was always someone fancied hisself with a pair of dusters on a dark night. After a set-to, he'd be sure to chuck 'em as the Bill didn't look kindly on anyone using the old brass, you see."

"Perhaps that's how these got into the river."

Al tossed them in the air, watched them slap back into his hard hand. "Well, Boss, they're hardly likely to have jumped in for a swim."

He handed back the knuckledusters. I rubbed the bare metal with my thumb, wondered if someone like Nesh would carry a pair. I concluded he was the sort to pack a tight roll of pound coins instead. It was a simple question of style.

I dropped the dusters in my jacket pocket and set off for the studio and the day's recording session.

MALCOLM HARDEE IS DEAD. HARDEE, TAGGED THE PATRON SINNER OF ALTERNATIVE COMEDY, WAS JUST FIFTY-FIVE BUT HE MORE THAN MADE HIS MARK. HE SOMETIMES TROD THE BOARDS NAKED WITH HIS SCROTUM DAUBED IN LUMINOUS PAINT, AND I OFTEN HEARD AN AUDIENCE GROW IMPATIENT IF THIS ODD SHOW WAS LATE IN APPEARING, HEARD A CRY OF 'SHOW US YER BOLLOCKS, MALCOLM'. I NEVER ONCE SAW HIM TURN DOWN THE REQUEST. HARDEE HAD AMBITION AND ONCE RAN FOR PARLIAMENT, PULL-ING IN ONE HUNDRED AND SEVENTY FIVE BALLOTS. FOR SURE, WESTMINSTER WOULD HAVE BEEN BRIGHTENED UP NO END BY HIS PRESENCE. 'SHOW US YER...' HARDEE ONCE OWNED A COMEDY CLUB, UP THE CREEK, IN GREENWICH. THEN HE WENT OUT ONTO THE WATER AND RAN A BARGE PUB, THE WIBBLY WOBBLY, IN ROTHERHITHE. THE SAME DAY THE POLICE FISHED HIM OUT OF THE THAMES AFTER A VERY FINAL SWIM, A GROUP OF FRIENDS WENT DOWN TO THE WIBBLY AND POURED A MEASURE OF RUM AND COKE, HIS FAVOURITE FIREWATER, INTO THE RIVER. I PLAN TO GO OVER THERE MYSELF AND DRINK A DRINK TO THE MAN WHO LOVED TO MAKE PEOPLE LAUGH, LOVED THE THAMES. BE MORE THAN PLEASED IF YOU'D JOIN ME.

I felt some kind of loss with Hardee's passing. It had been years since I'd caught him on stage, but when Harry and I were at university we used to dash over to Up The Creek. We'd listen to standup and delight in the comics before they made it onto TV and dished out far plainer material. We always stayed for the final turn, had to run for the last train back to Charing Cross, the two of us searching for an empty carriage where we'd try and re-count as many of the evening's jokes as possible. She was always better at remembering and delivering the gags than I was and, in any case, was genuinely funny in her own right.

I'd called Harry as soon as I found out about Hardee. *Another light goes out for all of us, Bro,* she told me.

She had a way of getting to the nub.

*   *   *

I went along to Huckerby & Partners in an effort to find out more about Philip Hegley's day of disappearance from his agent. The office was in Broadgate, at the very heart of London's financial bailiwick where the architecture played off every kind of geom-etry, the sine and cosine constructions a reference, I reckoned, to the mathematical movements of stocks and shares.

The first thing I told Roger Huckerby as we sat either side of his enormous leather-topped desk was that the area didn't seem one a film-industry man might be expected to wash up in.

"Let me explain," he said. "We moved here just six months ago. I never was one for Soho, so when this space came up I was more than happy to move the firm closer to where the money actually moves."

Huckerby was a peculiar sort. I guessed him at around forty five and, while his chalk-stripe suit pretty much conformed to busi-ness conventions, his dyed jet-black manga-style hair that jutted at every angle didn't. I wasn't sure how to take him, wondered how on earth he and Hegley had got along.

"Let me add," he said, "H&P is branching out into film finance. It's a backward-integration strategy and I'm enjoying running with the City crowd."

"The chaps in the chips."

Huckerby fell into the back of his chair and belched a sharp laugh. "I'm looking for us to being H&P PLC in under a year."

"That's some target." I wasn't sure exactly what he meant but thought my response sounded like I was impressed enough.

"The curve's riding steeply upwards. The CAGR's fat and healthy."

"CAGR?"

"Twenty percent." He pointed at me. "That's decent growth whatever you want to call it."

Behind Huckerby was a huge picture window full of the glass-construction puzzle of the building opposite. I pictured him the star of his perfectly financed film that depicted the cut and thrust of his new backwardly integrated lifestyle, his manga dominating every scene.

"This isn't what I imagined agency life to be," I said.

"I doubt any of the others are anything like H&P. We've certainly outperformed the sector in the last six quarters or so."

"What's your secret?"

"We're making something of a killing on DVDs."

"Anything to do with Philip Hegley?"

"A cash cow certainly." Huckerby very carefully raked his hair into what appeared to be a preferred style. There was obviously method to what I'd first presumed to be hirsute madness.

"Shame he's not around to enjoy the financial success. Were the two of you friends?"

"Never met the chap. He was on my father's list."

"Your father? Ah, you two have the same name?"

"Yes. We were known for a while as Roger and Me."

"Were?"

"He retired to southern Spain.

"I'd like to talk to him."

"Remind me what your business is again?"

"I've been asked to write Hegley's biography." It seemed a sound idea to keep the story the same as the one I'd tossed to Harry and Megs.

"Need an agent?"

*　*　*

Meaghan and I drove out to the Cotswolds early Saturday morning, my old but heavily reliable red Beemer pulling gently along the M4, Pulp spinning on the player. Normally Meaghan would have asked me to change the music, would have wanted something more current, but she seemed happy for me to have my way, probably because I'd agreed to do the bulk of the driving. She'd offered, though, to take the wheel on the journey back once the traffic stickied up on the approach to London, as it was bound to at the close of the weekend.

We arrived in Chipping Camden not long after ten and checked in at the Cotswold House Hotel, advertised alluringly on the Internet as *more than just a place to stay*. It certainly cut the countryside mustard for us with its mellow Regency ambience, the huge bedroom and grand four-poster, warming fire in the grate.

Meaghan was entranced by the room. She did a gentle solo waltz across the carpet towards the window where she stopped and untied her hair. I watched it fall full and blond past her shoulders, and when she started to move once more it took up the rhythm of the turns of her body, made her look more graceful than ever. Whenever she danced alone, I thought, it was to the music she was so easily able to compose in her head. I often wished I could hear it because at times like this she disappeared into herself and, while she was engaging to watch, it was exclusive, made me feel I really didn't belong there.

Meaghan was on the point, I thought, of sweeping past me when she pulled up right at my feet. She leaned in close, kissed me with her lavish lips.

"Don't move," she said.

Her voice was satin. I wanted to be caressed by it.

She undid my shirt, gave each button an indescribable amount of time before unhooking it from its eye. And whenever a fingernail grazed my skin it was all I could do to stop from crying out. She bared me completely and placed a palm close to my chest, let me breathe into her touch for what seemed like hours.

"Follow me," Meaghan said. She took my hand and walked me to the bathroom.

"Turn on the shower," she said.

I did as I was told.

"Get in."

I got in.

"Watch."

Meaghan teased herself slowly out of her clothes, handling each garment like it might break. No woman I'd ever known undressed as exquisitely as she did. I was aching for her.

She stepped under the shower and wrapped herself around me. We made love eagerly under the run of water. We made love again in all good time on the bed. The universe of Root and Meaghan was as good as it could be.

* * *

We stayed the remainder of the day in Chipping Campden, happy to make discoveries, the smaller the more delightful. In the silver workshop on Sheep Street, we bathed in the heat from the smithies' gas torches, breathed in the metallic air. Meaghan led a finger down the list of names in the old visitors book, squealed when she spotted Frank Lloyd Wright.

"We're in the right place, Root," she said.

In front of the old silk mill, she read out loud the sign about Charles Ashbee and the Arts and Crafts Movement. She entered into a monologue about Ruskin and Morris that lasted the length of a slowly walked street. We agreed that the country could do with a good dose of Fabianism.

Meaghan was at her best when she was thoroughly taken by something, and I was completely engrossed in her. I was happy, too, that I'd managed to leave *Greene Land* behind in London.

We ate in the hotel restaurant, tore our way through the menu. Meaghan started with the scallop ravioli, I went for the pigeon, though when my dish came we joked that the poor bird was so small its mother was probably still pining the chick's premature departure from the nest. The waiter talked us into an enormous poached sea bass for mains and we had planned to skip dessert until we spotted the mille feuille with plums on the trolley. We decided to split one before we realised we were too greedy to share and ordered a second.

Back up in the room after coffees, we ran aground on the bed where I told Meaghan we might have to cancel any further relationship with food for the rest of the weekend.

I reached out to take her hand.

"I'm so stuffed," she laughed. "I don't think I could stand you even laying a finger on me right now."

*   *   *

Next morning we skipped breakfast and drove over to Rodmarton Manor. Meaghan had heard about the place at the silversmith's, was determined to continue the Arts and Crafts theme from the day before. I was happy enough to go along with it – this was, after all, her weekend.

We were due at her parents for early lunch and had to make do with a rather snappy tour, first of the gardens and its yew, beech and holly hedges, then of the house where we had time enough to admire any number of dressers, cupboards, bedsteads and, more unusually, a period tennis-racket stand. Meaghan said she wanted all of them for our flat and I enjoyed the idea of making it more of a home for the two of us than it had been to date.

We jumped back into the Beemer and dashed along the A40 into Oxford to arrive at the Terry family home bang on time for the meal.

*   *   *

After a blessedly light lunch we were sitting in the Terry study that teemed with books, most of them beautifully bound volumes of the very best English lit that Ben and Rachel had collected over the years. It was against that kind of backdrop that Meaghan's parents liked to get down to conversation after the bare chat they always offered up with food in the dining room. As I sat myself down in a leather armchair, I detected a hint of marijuana.

"How's life on the airwaves, Root?" Ben asked. He looked at me eagerly, was very endearing with his teddy-bear expression, well-padded torso.

"The show's being plumped up a bit. On the orders of the Great Beeb itself," I said.

"That's super news, isn't it, Rachel?"

Meaghan's mother smiled at me as she moved gracefully across the room – she and her daughter shared the gift of music in their movements as well as physical looks. She took a CD from its box and pushed it into a slot in the hi-fi.

"I have a recording session lined up for the BBC myself," Ben said. "They want some free jazz."

"Sounds great," I said. "Though I really can't get a handle on that stuff."

"I'm not sure it's always that gettable," Meaghan said. "But Dad does follow the Ornette Coleman tradition so you can clearly hear the blues and gospel influences."

"It has regular time," Rachel said, "and that helps. I have to say I sometimes have problems with all that silence in the more abstract material."

"Soundlessness can be unnerving for some." Ben stirred his tea absolutely quietly.

"And tempting when you have a horn or vocal chords all ready to blow," Meaghan said.

I always enjoyed such talks with the Terrys, even though most of the musical conversation travelled yards over my head. I didn't mind not understanding because they were all so delightfully informed, and I loved wallowing in their passion.

Ben had played alto saxophone professionally all his life and had often gone on long tours of the West Coast, travels that Meaghan said really informed his music. He'd also played on a few Beatles recordings when he'd needed to earn his wad as a session musician, a job entry that totally wowed me. Rachel was a jazz singer and, though she'd stopped singing regularly a number of years ago, she still got the occasional scat booking in and around Oxford. I'd heard her perform a few times and she had an impressive range, was quite well-known for her vocalese abilities.

The music of Tom Waits in the shape of 'I Don't Wanna Grow Up' hung in the room, and I noticed that both Ben and Rachel were keeping time with a left foot.

"How's the publishing business, Meaghan?" Ben asked.

"Busy."

I could see the tension grab Megs, tighten her like a string in a bow. The work issue never failed to bother her when we were in Oxford.

"What exactly is it that you're working on?" Rachel asked.

"There's a major Mozart event coming up, so there's lots of fuss around that," Meaghan said.

"Didn't you once mention Montreux? Now that'd be very exciting."

"Mozart's got a bit of a name, though," I joked.

Rachel and Ben smiled at me politely. Meaghan got up from her chair, started browsing the bookshelves.

"I have the beginnings of an idea, Ben," I said. "Tell me what you think. How about I get my hands on some of your upcoming BBC recording and slot it into the programme along with some of your brilliant history. I'll be a fish out of water trying to explain what you're doing with free jazz but I like a challenge."

"That's an admirable attitude," Ben said. "All right, you're on."

"Good man, Root," Rachel said. "It's always better to have given it a go than to have given up."

"And Meaghan will help out on the technical side, won't you?" Ben asked

Megs was no longer in the room, though I didn't see her leave.

* * *

There was a crisp atmosphere in the car on the way back into London, Meaghan barely responding to any of my efforts to get her to talk. I toyed with the idea of playing a few Cranberries tracks to get her riled, decided instead to play the latest album from The Former Dictators, a band we'd recently taken a shine to. I tuned in to the lyrics. *I'm certain, if you're uncertain. That it's a state of mind more than anything.*

At the signs for High Wycombe I said I was going to pull in at the next service station so Meaghan could drive us into London.

"Why did you have to boast about your work to Mum and Dad?" she asked.

"Boast? I thought I was politely answering a question."

"*On the orders of the Great Beeb itself.* You idiot."

"I was joshing a bit. Your father seemed to enjoy it."

"You do so like to play up your achievements. You're always bursting to tell my parents how well you're doing. Of course, they adore listening to that kind of thing."

"Maybe it's because you never talk about what you do that I feel the need."

"Yes, it's my fault you're a braggart. For Christ's sake, we all know you're doing dross."

"Is that what you think?"

"Who on earth cares what I think?"

"You're always so touchy. The other night you even managed to work yourself up over a dead film director."

"What the fuck do you know, Root?"

I drove up the slip road to the service station and pulled into the car park. I felt sick, hadn't seen anything as serious as this coming my way.

"I think I deserve an apology," I said. "An explanation. Something."

Meaghan got out of the car and I followed her into the building. She disappeared into the ladies. I waited fifteen minutes for her to come out and when she did she was crying. She hugged me tight and long. I thought she might never let go.

When we got back to the car park I saw that the Beemer was sporting a front-nearside flat.

"Shit," I said. "I hope the spare's OK."

I took a closer look at the damage, not that I knew much about the technology of inflated rubber. I couldn't believe it. Someone had carved a neat three-inch-diameter circle out of the wall of the tyre.

"The vandals are getting creative," I said.

Unsure whether I still remembered how to change a wheel, I opened up the back of the car and found the jack. Tucked into the screw, I saw a business card. The print said 'A E Nesh' and, in an immaculately thin script that could have been written with the edge of a razorblade, there was a message. *You shouldn't have gone bothering Huckerby.*

While the find was startling enough, the thought that Nesh must have been following us for the weekend was altogether chilling.

* * *

Meaghan went to bed once we got home. That was the last place I felt like being, so I sat on the couch with beer in one hand, remote in the other, and for a couple of hours I watched *Greene Land*. Even though I'd seen it several times through, Hegley's masterpiece – I was convinced already the word wasn't out of place – still managed to shake me with its dynamic opening scenes. And I realised that the sheer poignancy of his drama was also making its way under my skin, could bring a tear to my eye. I wrote a piece with my latest thoughts on the film, posted it on my blog at around four in the morning.

Woolwich Crematorium.
Boocock is a tiny figure at centre-screen. He walks away from us down an arrow-straight path and we

follow at distance for a good half-minute. The
camera pulls in, slowly first, then with gathering
speed. Boocock becomes ever-larger until we zoom
right in on his lower legs. On each step, his foot
hits the gravel hard, the sound that of a hammer
smashing pebble.

Boocock reaches a flower bed. The toe-ends of his
shoes extend to the edge of freshly turned earth.
There's a flawless silence.

Cut to:

A close-up of a rose, a rectangular plate on a
long steel stem planted by it. On the plaque just
two words. 'Thomas Greene'. The rose rocks in the
breeze.

Voiceover. We listen to Boocock.

"I'd been looking forward to meeting up with Thom
again. I hadn't seen him for years and his voice
on the phone – dancing with bravado, nothing that
man believed he couldn't do – had made me keen to
find out what he'd been up to. My life had been on
the wane, what with no steady girlfriend, never a
steady job, lack of a steady income, and Thom could
always be counted on to provide brio. I'm not the
fool many people reckon, though, and I never believed everything he told me. But I knew that whatever came out of his mouth was said with the best
intentions. He had the knack of telling you what
you wanted to hear, did Thom. Like, come out to
East London, help me out with a little something.

Boocock's monologue is interrupted by the sound
of footsteps. Not the cudgelling noise we heard
as he walked but a gentler, more deliberate tone.
We can't see the latest arrival though we know
for sure it's a woman. But we have to make do with

a static image of the rose and we wait for it to shift in the waft of air that must come at any sec-ond…it does.

The camera pulls back from the flower and a female hand enters from the right, hangs a ribbon from the petals.

Cut to:

A tightly framed medium-shot, full-length from the rear of the figure of Boocock, the woman a yard to his right. It's a beautiful still.

"I was a friend of Thom's," Boocock says.

The woman doesn't respond.

"You knew him a long time?" he asks.

"I wouldn't say that."

"We were at school together."

"Two little boys."

"We grew up."

"I never thought anyone would say that about Thom."

"Sounds like you knew him well."

"You start to find out things about men once you sleep with them."

It's the voice of Les Lea we hear.

Fade to black.

Chapter Four

Next day I was dog tired but still got up early and walked over to Bankside. I skimmed stones, lost myself for fifteen minutes trying to best my best score of a half-dozen hops. It was something I did when I worried, and I surely had plenty to think about. For one thing, Meaghan's behaviour on the ride back from Oxford was deeply troubling and she hadn't yet apologised for anything. She'd never laid into me so heavily before and I was trying hard to convince myself it had nothing to do with me, and everything to do with Ben and Rachel. But that didn't explain why Meaghan had made it so personal in my direction.

I also had to decide what to do following Nesh's slash attack on the Beemer. At first take, it seemed clear I should let the whole Hegley affair drop, especially now that I was spooked by the thought that the tall guy had followed us around the Cotswolds. I hadn't shown Meaghan the card, of course, and I'd made an effort to rant about hooligans as I changed the wheel. She hadn't mentioned it again.

I could go to the police, but I reckoned that was something Hegley wouldn't have welcomed, and I felt peculiarly obliged to him after having written his obit. Plus, now that I'd watched *Greene Land* again, I was positively hooked on the film, its maker and the ongoing mystery of his 'death'. I couldn't bear to let it go. It was a crazy admission – I wasn't a detective, for Christ's sake, had no desire to be one either – and Nesh's knife act surely demonstrated that he wasn't playing around. I could well be in real danger. As could Meaghan. I knew it was foolish, but I decided I had to find Hegley and get an explanation. As well as learn more about the man who had made that haunting film.

I was in the café soaking up market snip-snap – a nil-one home defeat for Millwall, a penny-a-litre increase in the price of diesel – when Harry arrived. I was surprised. She was no early riser and she knew how much I valued this time of day. She must have something on her mind to dare trouble my time.

"Sorry, but I really, really need to talk to you, Bro." She sat down, her eyes looking achingly red in a face totally washed-out without makeup. She wore a grey raincoat buttoned right up the neck and, on the whole, Harry looked disconcertingly unlike Harry.

"You've been at it again, haven't you?" I knew she was going to tell me about the guy she'd been rosed and vanilla-ed for when I was last in her flat.

"This time it's different."

"You said last time was different. Perhaps, though, it was just dissimilar."

Harry shook her head. "Please, Root."

"Sorry."

I stroked the back of her hand, the one that held tight onto a tissue. She gave me a smile so skinny it made me turn quite cold.

"How bad can things be?" I said. "I presume he didn't run off with all your money … or your virginity."

"Shut up." She pulled her hand away. "Sean has admitted to seeing his ex."

"Is that such a big deal?"

"He collects her dry cleaning once a week. Mows the lawn. Probably offers to worm the cat between heavy chores."

I laughed.

"Not funny…well, only a bit."

"So, he has a few domestic duties on his plate. Maybe it was in their pre-nup."

"He's still screwing her, Root."

"What? He told you that?"

"First he said it was a lapse. Then he admitted to another. And another. It's bloody serial. I can't understand why he would want to even touch her now and again when he can have me any time he wants." Harry sobbed into her hands.

I ordered her a coffee I knew she wasn't going to touch but I felt much better simply doing something for her. I sat back, waited for the drink to appear, for Harry's tears to end. There was a blast of male laughter from a table at the back of the room, an awful rasp of brakes from a market truck pulling up right outside the café, but it all washed over Harry.

The coffee turned up. I pushed it towards her and she picked up a spoon, began tapping the side of the cup.

"Drink up, Aitch," I said.

"I knew I could rely on you."

"The shoulder to cry on."

"Must be quite saturated by now."

"I've been well waterproofed."

Harry stopped rapping the cup, looked past me. I turned around.

"You still have those dusters, Boss?" Al was standing at my back, striped tea towel hanging over his arm.

"I'm restoring them."

"Give you a fiver."

"What on earth would you want with a pair of old knuckle-dusters?"

"I've taken a real fancy. Go on, hand them over for a fiver, won't you?"

"I'll think about it."

"Might go up to seven-fifty. Ten at a push."

"I'll let you know."

Al headed back to the kitchen.

"Did I hear him right?" Harry asked.

"I'm sure you did."

"What on earth are you doing with knuckledusters?"

"Protection," I said. "You never know who might be out to get you, Aitch."

43

*   *   *

At home I found a note from Meaghan. All she'd scribbled was *xsorryx* but she'd underscored it with a wonderful musical curlicue. It was enough for me – there was something about her writing, its organic whirls and curls that always got to me in the finest way.

I spent the rest of the morning working through a number of ideas on the laptop, some for the programme and others for Tabard's new website. I'd used some of the driving time at the weekend to mull the online offer, and had now decided to take it up, go the hotdog-media route. Minona's sheer meanness, along with her moves to proscribe the show's content, had clinched it and I was now determined to disturb the dust with her somehow. I read through my existing freelance contract, decided that producing audio clips for download wasn't broadcasting as described in the non-competitive clause. I was sure the studio wouldn't bother pursuing it legally, cheapskates that they were. I fired off an e-mail to Tabard, he sent over an agreement quick as fire, and I added my electronic signature, then shipped it back.

I was given a sharp deadline to work to with three items due for recording in a couple of weeks' time. The good thing was that I was overflowing with material for the programme, so the surplus could go into the Net venture. I had banks of research to lean on and the scripts never took a great deal of time once I got into the subject flow.

I turned to En Root, spent a couple of hours developing London cinematic themes. Just before I completed what had been a satisfying and productive session, I checked my mail, found at last that I'd got a response to the call-for-info about Hegley on my blog. The upshot of a rather meandering message was that the writer was claiming to be an actor who'd worked on a number of the director's films and wanted to meet up as soon as possible.

Could I do as soon as today?

*   *   *

That afternoon I got on the bus, stepped off at the last stop in Denmark Hill for a rendezvous with Theresa Noble. I rarely travelled that far out of central London and needed to consult the A-to-Z a few times to find the tiny pinch of a street she lived in among the slapdash spread of the King's Hospital campus. Finally I was able to slap the knocker of a drab two-storey Edwardian. I waited a couple of minutes before trying again.

The door opened.

"You're Root," Theresa Noble said. She presented her hand in a way that was obvious she meant it to be kissed. She was dressed to the hilt, wore a black evening gown that folded down her body in no-nonsense second-skin fashion. The hemline gave way to diamond-net stockings that turned around her calves and into three-inch heels. She *was* Les Lea.

I gave her hand a peck, stood back, admired the woman framed beautifully in the doorway. Les Lea must have been sixty or so by now but had seemingly been preserved in *Greene Land* mode – it was as if Hegley's impeccable lighting had the ability to stretch over the decades to Denmark Hill and give his leading lady some kind of eternal cinematic youth. And, totally impossibly, she was bathed in the most remarkable monochrome aura.

"Come in."

I heard her voice but didn't see her say the words. I was caught firmly in her lights and trailed after her down the hallway in thrall to the pure she of Les Lea.

The living room pulled me back to reality. It was lit by a single overhead lamp, its bulb casting too many watts for comfort, and ugly, hard shadows splayed from every object in its line of fire. One wall was glutted with framed photographs that were either overposed portraits of Theresa Noble, or shots of her in the arms of numerous grinning showbiz bods playing to the lens. I spotted one of her with Hegley in which he was kissing her on the forehead in a fatherly sort of way.

Theresa Noble pointed to the two-seater sofa. "Sit," she said.

I sat.

She handed me a tumbler chinking with ice cubes. "Take it," she said.

I took.

She splashed heady doses of whisky into our glasses. "I don't usually at this hour," she said.

"Don't stand on ceremony for me." I was relieved to hear myself speak, knew the Les Lea spell had been broken.

"Oh, I shan't."

Theresa sat herself close to me on the sofa and smiled.

I took a sip of my drink, winced. I'd never acquired the taste for Scotch.

"I'm writing a biography of Philip Hegley," I said. "Anything you can tell me will be a great help."

"I was his utter favourite." Theresa Noble cradled her glass. "Philip and I really understood one another."

"You were lovers."

"My, you're not slow in coming forward." She knocked back her drink.

"Tell me if I'm being intrusive."

"Ask me anything you like. I have no secrets when it comes to that man."

I put my glass to one side, pulled a notebook and pen from my jacket pocket.

"He and I were together on the very first day of our first shoot," she said. "We couldn't resist one another. We didn't try." She caressed her knee with a palm. "I was his muse."

"Is that what he said?"

"Oh, Root. A man won't tell you the things he feels. It takes the right woman to intuit them."

"And you were that woman for Philip Hegley?"

"The only. One and one made a wonderful two. The perfect pair."

"But you were never a proper couple, were you? I mean, you never married or anything?" I knew that Hegley had lived with his long-standing wife until she died five years ago.

"Let's not get caught up in the detail. We can leave the minutiae to others."

"Are you saying that Philip was the love of your life?"

She placed a hand on my arm. "You're a highly perceptive fellow, Root. How young are you?"

"My clock's ticked to exactly thirty."

"Just as mine had when we made *Greene Land*. A magnificent film. Philip knew it would be his chef d'oeuvre."

"Shame he's not around to enjoy the acclaim."

Theresa Noble smiled. "Oh Root. And here was me beginning to think you must know our secret."

Chapter Five

I met Harry at The Bunch of Grapes for a game of pool. I knew I'd be in trouble if Meaghan found out I'd seen her twice in one day, but my old pal had been so upset in the café that morning that I couldn't refuse her request to play *just an itsy best of three*. And I never had been able to resist Harry when she pleaded for something.

Near the close of what had been quite a tepid opening game – I was playing conservatively, wasn't taking any risks after the drubbing I'd received at her hands the other night – it was clear Harry was out of sports sorts. Early on, she had a great opportunity to cut an eight ball into the corner pocket, the kind of shot she would have gone for a hundred times straight, but she opted instead for an iffy bank, caught some accidental side spin and fluffed it. Normally, she'd have been livid at such an error, but all she managed was a shrug that had no heart in it whatsoever. I felt like going out and looking for that Sean character, giving him a seeing-to. She was so absolutely correct in what she'd said – what man in his right mind would opt for another woman part of the time when he could have the whole of someone like Harry?

Back at the table, I sunk my remaining balls and won without gusto. I watched as Harry racked up again in silence.

"Look," I said, "how about we stop?"

"Just play the game."

"Come on, Aitch.

"And make sure you do it to win."

I took Harry at her word, enjoyed a great run in the second game which I topped with a three-rail kick that hammered the target ball into the middle pocket. She conceded.

"Two down, none to go," I said.

"Rack up the third," she said. "I want to see if I can avoid my first-ever whitewash at your hands."

"Aitch, please…"

"Do it."

I did as I was told and my game was fair flying, the cue almost an extension of my arm, so intimate was I with it. I effortlessly delivered the pasting Harry so dearly craved.

She raised her glass to me, tears choking her eyes. "The best man won," she said.

"Clearly."

* * *

I heard Justin's laughter as soon as I cracked open the door to the flat, and I hoped Meaghan's brother would be staying to break bread with us – she was always a lighter spirit when he was around, and we surely needed that right now.

I went into the kitchen where Meaghan was chopping onions. Justin thumped out a few steps in my direction and crunched my fingers with those major mitts of his. He was a strapper, a good fifty percent bigger than me, looked larger still in those huge Arran sweaters he wore whatever the weather was up to.

"My friend, it's been the longest time," he said.

"Good to see you."

"Megsie informs me you're going to be an online star. Congrats to you."

"I'm not sure she should be telling all just yet."

"Ooops, I've divulged an industrial secret," she said.

"I forgive you," I said. "How could I not when you can make even slicing veg look sexy?" I kissed her on the neck.

"Flatterer," she said. "Tell me, Justin, do you think I should let him off for being out of touch the whole afternoon?" She washed her hands, flicked water off her fingers and into in my face.

"I had to go out of the hood," I buried my guilt of hanging with

Harry in a pull of white wine Justin had poured. "I went over to Denmark Hill."

"Whoa, that's deep, deep south," Justin said. "I feel giddy."

"You Hampstead hick, Justin." Meaghan pointed a knife at him.

"And happy to be condemned as such, natch." He took a slug of his drink, chewed it around his mouth before swallowing.

"Thanks for the note," I said quietly to Meaghan.

She smiled.

"What's this, a touch of the billets doux?" Justin asked. "I'm dead chuffed to hear you two still scribble I love-yous back and forth."

"Shut up," Meaghan said.

"I'll leave now if the two of you want to get close."

"Stay where you are, Justin." I topped him up from the bottle. "You're not getting out of our company that easily."

"If I'm to stick around, you have tell me what you've been up to, Root. Is something rotten in the state of Denmark Hill?"

"Not sure I can talk about it."

"Come now, I'm almost family. Bet you told Mum and Pops all about your work last weekend, dincha?"

I looked at Meaghan who stuck out her tongue. Then she smiled at me.

"I'm writing a biography," I said. "Some film guy you've probably never even heard of."

Meaghan slammed a bowl on the counter. "I can't believe you're going ahead with this Hegley thing."

"Philip Hegley the director?" Justin asked.

"The same," I said.

"Whoa, there," Justin said. "That chap was always poor news."

Brother and sister were looking at me like I was untouchable. "What's the matter with the two of you?"

"Dad did the music for one of Hegley's films," Justin said. "What was it called? Hold on… yes… *Greene Land.*"

"He wrote the score?" Everyone I knew seemed to be tied to Hegley in some way.

"Played on some of it too," he said. "Remember the opening?"

"Of course." I could hear the sax, see and feel the cold expanse of water again.

"Pops used to be a good chum of Hegley's," Justin said. "The shoot ended that."

"What happened?" I asked.

"He never even got his name on the credits."

"Let it drop, Justin, won't you," Meaghan said.

He pulled out his phone, messed with the keyboard. Meaghan turned her back on me, began wiping the counter. The sudden silence was almost raw to the touch.

"I met an actress in Denmark Hill to answer the earlier question," I said, relieved I'd found a place to go.

"Someone famous?" Justin asked.

"Her star's shining right now," I said. "Theresa Noble."

Meaghan left the kitchen.

"She played the stripteuse in *Greene Land*," Justin said.

"She wasn't a stripper. Les Lea was a performer." I was surprised at how strongly I felt the need to defend her.

* * *

Meaghan served up a poached salmon and the three of us sat around the table for a couple of hours finishing off the fish and its trimmings. Meaghan barely spoke, barely looked at me. It was hard to believe she could get so angry about a tiff her father had years back, especially when everyone knew Hegley had a reputation of getting almost everyone's back up. I would make sure never to mention him to her again.

I was happy when we headed off to the living room with another bottle of wine, hoped the change of venue might break Meaghan's silent spell.

"You still doing celibacy, Justin?" I asked.

"Sad but true. I think I've gone and overdone mourning my ex. I'll prolly never find a good lass now."

"There must be some eligibles at the *Observer*," I said. "I can't believe a newsroom is bereft of pretty females."

"I'm freelance and hardly there. I never meet women."

"Sounds like dating's not the easy street it was on the road," I said.

Until a year ago, Justin had been playing with the Halle and had always dealt us colourful stories of post-concert couplings between members of the string and horn sections. That's how he'd got together with Helen, a violinist, who'd then dumped him for someone more percussive. It was around that time he gave up being a pro musician, though, as I understood it, that had more to do with the lifestyle and super-high expectation on the part of Ben and Rachel than with his failed love life. He seemed content enough now being a music critic.

"Root, I know who'd be perfect for Justin, and vice versa, don't you?" Meagan asked.

"Can't say," I said. I was relieved that she'd spoken to me at last.

"Your best friend, of course."

"You mean Harry?"

"Harry? Hold on," Justin said.

"She's not a man, you fool," Meaghan said. "Her name's Harriet. And I can't believe Root hasn't thought to set the two of you up before."

"She's a bit of a high-flyer," I said. "A film exec. Always flitting across the Atlantic. Has a sad and sorry thing for high-flying media execs, too. Not sure she has any kind of musical bent either."

Meaghan threw up her arms. "You're a sorry salesman. Would anyone buy a girl from this man?"

"I was just pointing out…"

"A woman needs all the help she can get. Even Harriet."

"Why *even* Harriet?"

"I didn't mean even exactly."

"Steady on, kids," Justin said. "Don't get in a fluff over me. I can look out for myself."

"No you can't," Meaghan said. "And I feel it's my duty to help out. Root should too."

"And I will," I said. I grabbed the bottle, tried to fill my glass but there was no wine to be had. From beginning to end this had surely been Harry's day.

I'M SOME PLACE WHERE I CAN BUY FIVE LITRES OF FLAME CHECK FOR FORTY QUID, SPEND JUST SHY OF SEVEN POUNDS ON A TUBE OF GOLDFINGER PASTE – THAT'S A RUB-ON METALLIC COLOURING, BY THE WAY. GOLDFINGER OUGHT TO BE SOME KIND OF CLUE AS TO WHERE I'M STANDING. NO HELP? OK, WHAT IF I LET ON THAT I'M OUT WEST? DOWN BY THE RIVER? IN THE LOCKS? STILL NOT? WELL, CORD GRIP HOLDERS COST A BIT OVER A POUND IN THE STORE HERE. CABLE TIES ARE TUPPENCE APIECE. THE STANLEY KUBRICK BOOK SITS ON THE SHELVES NEXT TO A TOME ENTITLED *CARRY ON LAUGHING*. RIGHT, I'LL COME CLEAN. I'M AT TEDDINGTON STUDIOS, A LOT THAT'S BEEN IN FILM USE SINCE NINETEEN TWELVE, WHEN, STORY SHORT, A LOCAL OFFERED UP HIS GREENHOUSE TO A CREW WHEN THE RAINS FELL. SINCE THEN, ERROL FLYNN, REX HARRISON AND BURT LANCASTER ARE JUST A FEW OF THE SCREENERS TO HAVE MADE MOVIES HERE BY THE BANKS OF THE THAMES. HOWEVER, THESE PROUD STUDIOS HAVE SERVED THE TELEVISION GOD FOR MORE THAN FIFTY YEARS TOO – THINK *OPPORTUNITY KNOCKS* AND BENNY HILL, IF YOU CAN BEAR IT. YES, TEDDINGTON'S BEST KNOWN NOWADAYS FOR ITS POP ENT, WHICH IS WHY THE FACILITIES ON OFFER INCLUDE FAST LIGHTING RIGS, BLACK AND WHITE CYCS AND CHROMAKEY. BUT FOR ALL THOSE FANCY NAMES, IT'S VERY COMFORTING TO KNOW THAT TEDDINGTON STILL SELLS CABLE TIES. A FILM MAKER'S STAPLE IF EVER THERE WAS ONE.

The studio session – a patchwork of film segments I sewed together with music links – went well, though as usual Cushman, the engineer, hit me with a few gripes.

"You're too quick with the fade-ins," he said. Cushman always lowered his gaze when he talked to me and, because he came up a few inches short, I was forced to look down on his blue hairdo.

"Can't wait to start chatting is my problem," I said.

"Count to five once you start the fade." He tugged at a huge ring on his middle finger, twisting a silver tiger head fiercely around a knuckle.

"I tried that when you mentioned it last week. Doesn't seem to work."

"Then fucking try harder. You're ruining my soundscape."

I could always tell Cushman was truly miffed when he became possessive about the show. Now he was really tense and the muscles bulked in his neck and shoulders. He wasn't a slightly built guy, and I certainly wouldn't want to meet him on a dark night and get into a tumble.

"Maybe a quick fade-in isn't so bad," I said. "It could add a little frisson."

"Look, you do what you do, leave what I do to me."

"I'm just saying…"

"Don't. Fuck, sound is pretty much a black art, you know."

"Well, I apologise bigly," I said. "But why don't you go and work your special magic and I'll consider the fate of my fades for next time."

I headed for the lift. Cushman was still standing where I'd left him when the doors closed on me. He was probably afraid to move, show the nasty stain he was sure to leave on the carpet.

* * *

Minona had an office on the western side of the studio building that gave her a partial view of the Houses of Parliament and Westminster Abbey. It was the only window in the place that offered a great vista of London and no doubt she'd fought like a cat with the rest of management to get it. She always enjoyed putting one over on her rivals, and, while she generally trod more lightly on mere broadcasters like me, she often went in too heavy for my tastes.

Minona was on the phone gushing financials – ROIs, cashflows, EBITs – and barely took notice of my entrance except to point to the chair at the other side of her desk. I used the waiting time to tap out a couple of texts, one to Harry to see if she was in better spirits, the other a simple 'hi-how-goes-it?' to Meaghan. I got a quick return of serve from Harry telling me work was humming, so no time to think about life or loves, but *thanks for the pool work-out and looking forward already to winning the re-match*.

Minona ended her phone conversation without so much as a bye. "They're putting the squeeze on," she told me.

"You mean the magnificent men and their money machines?" The big company guys weren't in the building, perhaps not in London either. They were part of some enormous conglomerate I knew little about.

"I'm having to work on a re-financing package," she said.

"Sounds like we're short of cash."

"It's a question of shuffling resource. Nothing for you foot soldiers to worry about."

"Not sure you're right," I said. "Now that the programme's grown up, I'm working on doing some live content."

"Idea good. And?"

"We went up to Angel to record that ambient noise piece the other night and, when we tried to get in touch with the studio and do it like it was an outside broadcast, we failed miserably."

"Hold on, ambient noise?"

"Sounds of the city as art."

Minona shrugged.

"The only way I could reach them was on my mobile," I said. "Our kit's terrible. The tech boys say hardly any of the twigs – I mean aerials – work."

"Then bring in a different repair man."

"We need new equipment. I can't do first-rate job with third-rate gear."

"Don't be so damn milky." Minona riffled through papers on her desk.

"I'm trying to put a decent programme together, that's all."

"Take a look." She tossed a page my way.

The metrics were better than ever, up almost ten percent month-on-month, the best spike I'd ever delivered.

"Good stuff," I said. "But I bet you haven't called me in to shake my hand."

"I just wanted to share the numbers, light a fire under you after our talk the other day."

"I bet this still wouldn't be a good time to ask for a bigger budget."

"No need to get scrappy over a few percentage points."

"You told me I was a rising star."

"Then get out there and twinkle, twinkle," she said.

Chapter Six

I walked along the river to work off my frustration with Min, realising that I needed to get far more creative if I was going to make my dissatisfaction with her count. The vengeful thoughts occupied me as far as London Bridge where I'd planned to get on the Tube. But I pulled up short when I saw the jetty, realised a ferry was due to depart for Canary Wharf in just a few minutes. It seemed a much more agreeable way of getting over to my latest meeting with Dennis Tabard, so I headed down the walkway, waited a short while and then stuck out my arm to wave down the four-oh-eight as it rounded the bend dead on time.

The catamaran trip turned out to be a real treat, made me wonder why I didn't take to the water more often. I got myself a spot near the stern from where I felt the boat lift a couple of feet as the engine powered up in midstream. We laid a cream wake for hundreds of yards, blasted under Tower Bridge in the direction of the office towers on the horizon. I couldn't help but think of Hegley as we motored down the river. Had he actually jumped into the Channel the day he went missing? I stared into the water, hadn't the slightest desire to end my life but the pull of the Thames was strong and I could easily imagine the second or so of freedom I'd enjoy if I were to step off the boat. It would be so very simple.

I landed dry at my destination, made my way past a jam of wool-and-polyester-mix commuters making their way to the river. I picked up an espresso from a three-wheeled coffee cart, reckoning that a double-shot would serve me well for a meet that was set to be some kind of audition.

Tabard greeted me enthusiastically on the twentieth floor of the Canary Wharf tower, ushered me into his office with its expansive plate-glass vista southward. I saw the river curving spectacularly from the east, brushing Greenwich at the tip of its arc before pushing towards central London on a rising tide. A small sailboat was skating along the front of the naval college and I half-expected its hull to leave an indelible scratch on the surface of the perfect water.

"See the Observatory?" Tabard asked.

I nodded once I'd made out the dome on top of the hill.

"At night it sends a laser light goes right down to the water."

"The meridian," I said.

"High-tech version. I like it. It's exactly right for the times."

I watched the sailboat execute a tidy gybe turn on the river, still with the entire stretch of water to itself. "This is fantastic," I said.

"The way life is here." Tabard began playing with his eyebrows. "And we, and everyone at head office, are glad to have you on board."

"You saying they know me at HQ already?"

"Truth is, they're among your keenest listeners."

I knew Tabard was soft-soaping but didn't mind in the least. It made a pleasant change from Minona's sniping.

"Tell me, Root. What do you have for us?"

I stood with my back to the window to offer up my spiel, well aware that the theatricality of the setting could only bolster my performance. I told Tabard about the piece on contemporary architecture's contribution to the city landscape, said I already had permissions to use images from a photo show, I Shot Norman Foster.

"Like it," he said.

And I explained there was an item I wanted to do on the new Routemaster buses that would involve a virtual tour. Plus a story on weather reporting on the different London Underground lines where we could really work up the graphics.

"Boiling ideas, Root," Tabard said. "Let me know what resource you need."

I took a few pages out of my bag, handed them to Tabard.

"What's this?" he asked.

"You said there might be video money somewhere. I've worked up a few treatments for you people to look at."

"You're a good man," Tabard said. He wore the satisfied look of a guy who was most at ease when drinking champagne and was right now holding a glass full of the stuff.

*　*　*

I left the office and was half-way down the escalator at Canary Wharf station when I got the text from Hegley. *Meet me at six, globe theatre, ph.*

It was already after twenty-to when I boarded a Jubilee Line train and I knew I couldn't make it for anything close to Hegley's appointed time. There was now no signal for my mobile so I couldn't get in touch with him. The carriage was rush-hour full and we made slow progress towards London Bridge, with ever more people cramming onto the train at each stop. I tried to stay close to the doors but the press of passengers forced me back into an aisle – it would be hard to get off snappily.

At the station, I tried to run up the stairs but it was impossible to make quick progress through the crush, my efforts at hurrying seeming to slow me even more. By the time I was outside, I had just a few minutes to get to where Hegley was probably already waiting. I decided to leg it, reckoning a cab wouldn't help me get there any faster, even if I could manage to hail one.

I came a cropper right away on traffic-packed Tooley Street when a dispatch bike swerved to avoid my dash through the pedestrians and his shoulder bag caught me in the back and knocked me off balance. I tumbled hands and knees onto the pavement. Two guys helped me back to my feet and I just about managed to shout some kind of thanks as I took off again.

It was after six. How long would Hegley wait? If he really wanted to see me, surely he'd give it a decent shot. I rang him, couldn't believe it when I got a network busy message. The mission was looking doomed.

It was quarter-past by the time I got to the Globe. It wasn't a great place to meet as hundreds of tourists packed in around the building. My ears caught French, German, Spanish, and as I milled around I must have seen Hegley twenty or so times before I admitted I was kidding myself. I called his number once, twice, three times. He didn't pick up. I sat down on a step with a gaping hole in the leg of my jeans, a badly scraped and suddenly very sore knee.

* * *

I didn't realise how much of a belt the tumble had delivered until next morning. By the time I got to the BBC at Portland Place, I could scarcely bend my leg and my walk had become little more than a geriatric shuffle. I was happy to sit in reception and wait for Justin to turn up and spent an almost enjoyable time cursing Hegley as the cause of so much pain.

Justin showed up, striding in off the street in a too-tight crumpled brown cord suit. He gave me a tight hug.

"Good morning to you," I said once he'd set me free.

"Backatcha, my friend. And I think it is good, too. I was just chatting to Megsie and she's convinced me about Harriet."

"You mean Harry. And you haven't even met her yet."

"Megsie has a good feeling. I want you to arrange something."

"Don't get your hopes up. Harry is pretty particular when it comes to men."

"Megsie said the same thing but reckons she could be up for a change."

"I see," I said. "Tell you what, let's find your father." I led Justin by the arm towards the lifts.

"You're limping," he said.

"That's what happens when you go chasing shadows."

* * *

We found Ben Terry already recording with a bass man and drummer in one of the studios, and we sat next to the engineer to watch them play from behind plate glass. They were a tight trio, even I could tell that, and Ben's fingering alone was a delight, his hands full of years of accumulated craft. He looked far less teddy bear-ish now that he was strutting his stuff, blowing into a mute and producing a grade-A tone. And alongside him the bass player was busy threading a pacey rhythm, while the drummer was doing an ace job pegging the skins.

They recorded a boogie-woogie-style number, followed that up with what Justin told me was a take on Ellington's 'Mood Indigo', before wrapping it up.

We went into the studio, introduced ourselves to the band.

"I thought the Beeb had asked you to do free jazz, Ben," I said.

"That's next up. We've got ourselves a double-header today, Root. We just finished a few items on Soundies."

"Soundies?"

"They were films that ran on little projectors in diners in America in the forties," Ben said. "People dropped a coin in the slot to watch a three-minute music clip."

"They showed absolutely everything," Justin said. "Big band, blues, jazz, gospel, whatever. They were the music videos of their day."

"Cool," I said. It would have been ideal fodder for En Root if only London had had Soundies.

"We just put down some up-to-date versions of Soundies tracks," Ben said. "The BBC wants to distribute them as Podcasts."

"I'm doing a piece on it for the paper," Justin said. "MTV eat your heart out."

"What will they do with the free session?" I asked.

"Regular broadcast," Ben said. "But they do tell me that's rather old-fashioned nowadays."

"Come on, Pops, don't do yourself down," Justin said. "You've always tried out new things."

"Like working with Philip Hegley on *Greene Land*," I said.

Ben unscrewed the reed from the sax's mouthpiece, held it up to the light, tossed it in a bin.

"You didn't enjoy doing the film?" I asked.

Ben said nothing.

"Root's doing a biography of Philip Hegley," Justin said.

"It's a 'no comment' from me," Ben said. "And you can quote me on that."

"I just want to find out all I can about him," I said.

"Let me tell you everything you need to know," Ben said. "You can say as many things as you like about Philip Hegley, and they're all true."

* * *

When I got back from Ben's session I took another look at *Greene Land*. I had the bit between my teeth when it came to Hegley, had been annoyed, not to say painfully sore, after missing my meeting with him for the sake of a phone connection. And I was piqued at Hegley for all this cloak-and-dagger business – I'd tried calling him on his phone a number of times in the past few days but he never answered. However, after another helping of the film I forgave him. The astounding technicals were a given now, though there was no way I was in danger of taking them for granted. I was beginning to appreciate the startlingly realistic acting, with each and every actor seeming to live their role. I'd read that Hegley always took his players on long retreats before a shoot, got them to remain totally in character. Other directors had surely been doing similar kinds of things at the time, but Hegley's gatherings took the practice to another level and reports of love affairs and fistfights had filled the arts columns of the papers. The retreat for *Greene Land,* though, was infamous, as one of the actors had almost strangled a fellow thesp who ended up in hospital with serious neck burns, it was said. I believed it too. In the film's fight scenes it looked like true punches had been thrown, had fully landed. The look of pain on the characters' faces was pure.

I'd have given anything to have been on one of those retreats.

The Mozart Cafe.

A top-shot of an almost-empty cup. It sits gently
in a man's hand, the tea in the bottom swirling
until it comes to a rest. It's set in motion once
more, comes to a rest. We hear plates clatter, cut-
lery rattle, the even chatter of voices.

Cut to:

Boocock at a table, the upper serif of the C in the
'Cafe' painted onto the window shadowing across a
cheek. He puts down the cup, looks at his watch.

"Don't tell me you're still waiting for Thom
Greene?" Detective Wark is standing at Boocock's
side. He's holding a pair of leather gloves that he
slaps repeatedly into a palm.

"You have a habit of just turning up," Boocock
says.

"A peculiarity of mine."

"It must be useful in your line of work."

"I'm everywhere at once."

"Means you can finger villains at will."

"That's quite melodramatic. You should be a writer."

"How clever of you."

"Mr Stranks here's a reader of your works." Wark
jerks back his head to indicate a man standing a
yard and a half behind him.

A rapid cutaway, no more than second, gives us a
look at Stranks, currant eyes in a doughy face.

"What are you up to in Woolwich?" Wark asks.

"I'm here for Thom."

"Paying respects, I suppose. That why you were at
the cemetery?"

"Are you following me?"

"I told you. I'm everywhere."

The camera gives us another quickfire look at
Stranks. He laughs loudly.

"You have a fan, inspector."

Stranks, a tight fist suddenly at breast height,
moves at Boocock. Wark blocks him.

"Steady," says Wark.

"That's right," Boocock says. "Keep the dog on the
leash. You never know who he might yap at."

"He doesn't bark. But has a damn good bite."

"Are you threatening me?"

"A warning. Thom Greene was a criminal. Drop him."

"Steal the odd crate of cigarettes off the docks,
did he?"

"You think very small, Mr Boocock. Your friend
would've had you for dinner."

Boocock's on his feet, lunging at Wark, but Stranks
is suddenly between them. He catches Boocock in the
gut with a tidy punch. Boocock drops back in his
chair, pain folded across his face.

"Be nice not to see you again," Wark says. "Stranks
here will make sure you get to the train station
safely."

"Some nasty animals on the loose out there,"
Stranks says.

I sat at my computer working on my blog, dealing with the
latest batch of e-mails from Theresa Noble. Ever since my trip to
Denmark Hill, she'd been busy sending me around a dozen messages a day, most of them containing pastes from articles about
herself or Hegley she'd found on the web. By now I had her down
as someone who rarely left the house, probably out of fear that
the city's pollution would destroy her perfect complexion. She was
utterly determined to remain the character that had come to define
her and to continue to live her affair with Hegley, I'd concluded,

and that was why she spent hours on the Internet looking for any item that would sustain her belief that, not only was she Les Lea, but that her lover was going down in history as one of the British cinema greats. As far as the last item was concerned, I didn't think she was so crazy.

Theresa Noble's final mail of the day, though, woke me up. I'd told her about Roger Huckerby Senior taking off for retirement in Spain and his peculiar son's failure to give me contact details. A call-for-info about the father on my blog had yielded nothing so far and I was beginning to wonder whether it might be worth offering cash to Junior, given his penchant for finance. Theresa Noble, though, had assured me that she could get me the info given a little time and, sure enough, she'd come through. *Roger Huckerby is living in Marbella*, she wrote, a*nd, Root, you owe me. Not big time. But* good *time.*

I was sure she wasn't joking and I wasn't completely unafraid at the thought of the debt being called in at some point.

I phoned Spain right away but the phone just rang on, no answering machine kicking in. I imagined Huckerby and his wife napping in the back bedroom, needing to escape the afternoon heat, unconcerned about goings-on back in Old England. I'd have to try the next morning, catch the Huckerbys before they went out to an unruffled lunch down by the Med port, something they did every day for sure.

There was another call I had to make, one I couldn't put off any longer. Meaghan had been on my back ever since Justin had been round for dinner and she'd come up with the whizz idea of pairing him with my best pal. Now, every couple of hours she got in touch with me for some spurious reason and, before hanging up, generally offered up a *by the way, spoke with Harry yet?* It was the only time I could ever remember her dropping the name 'Harriet'.

I hadn't actually talked to Harry for a while, didn't know for sure whether that was the way things had panned out, or because I was deliberately avoiding the issue. Why wouldn't I want Harry to meet Justin? I was the one who'd been on at her for years about poor mate selection, had told her to go for the right sort just once. And here was Justin, a decent type, no doubt about it. I could see them getting on like the proverbial burning house. And he hadn't exactly been hit with the ugly stick, had he?

I couldn't face having the conversation. I wussed it and sent her a text instead, was as upbeat as I could manage in telling her that there was some handsome, talented male she really ought to get to know. I was relieved when she replied from New York, said she wouldn't be back in London for a few days yet but would be up to meeting soon after she landed.

I was looking forward to chatting to Meaghan over dinner, slipping in the line that I'd managed finally to get in touch with Harry and that, unfortunately, she was over in the States, though we'd be discussing all things Justin as soon as she returned.

CHAPTER SEVEN

Next day I was back down at the Canary Wharf offices trying to keep my eyes off the Thames – it was a beautiful morning and the water was catching the sunlight, throwing it back metallic. It was easy to envy Tabard and his hotdog-media life for the view alone.

I'd already knocked up a draft of the Routemasters piece and sent it through to a tech-savvy guy called Tariq, a recent graduate who, I'd been informed, could do astounding things with Illustrator, Flash and all manner of digital tools. Tabard had pointed out that copy which worked on radio and the printed page might well not fly on the Internet, though once I'd done my session with Tariq – *my best ever hire, this pup's going someplace* – I'd see how the Web opened things up for whatever content I wanted to bring to it.

At the heart of my piece were the efforts of the Save The Routemaster group to retain a handful of the old red buses for the capital's roads. Transport officialdom had designated a couple of so-called heritage routes that would keep the vehicles tracking past the Albert Hall, Trafalgar Square and Tower Hill, but that wasn't enough for the Savers who were calling the plans a sop – rightly, in my view – and were lobbying for north-south passages too. My story on the Routemasters also offered up telling tech details on the vehicle for the 'raks – a nineteen-fifties chassis-less sixty-four seater, with an extra thirty inches added to the bodywork the following decade to provide additional seating for eight, etcetera.

Tariq had torn into the job, crafted some stunning pages. I sat next to him as he pulled images of buses from God knew where, peppered the text with hyperlinks. I could see what Tabard meant about having to deal with the Web – what I'd done was fine as a linear structure but a reader linking, going off everyways wouldn't care for such a leadenfooted approach. I needed to seriously rethink.

While I made notes, Tariq worked up a few cartoonish buses and imported them to the page. The sketches were fantastic – Tabard's pup had needed just a few simple red lines to render what were clearly nifty Routemasters raring to go. He explained that he planned to animate a fleet of them, would turn them into an interactive infographic that would be some kind of short-form game to attract the punters.

"I have a few other ideas I want to knock around to get more eyeballs," he told me.

* * *

After my blistering session with Tariq, I met Tabard for lunch on the patio of an Italian eatery. We sat in the long shadow of an old dock crane, watched a while as a circle of screaming gulls snagged bread tossed for them onto the water by diners.

"What did you make of Tariq?" Tabard asked.

"Impressive kid."

"Fact is, he just soaks all this stuff up. My suspicion is he knows far more than any of us." He tapped his skull. "Absolutely gigs of memory."

"He's made me think, and that's no bad thing."

"We're all going to grow with this project, Root. You'll see. It'll soon be time to give up the day job." Tabard tugged on an eyebrow.

"I still love radio." It was very true. Not even Minona could knock the passion out of me.

"Something I want to tell you." Tabard forked up a tangle of tagliatelle and gobbled it down. "I read the treatments you gave me, but they're bigger ideas than I need. I passed them up the Ferris Media chain and the film-production guys want to talk business with you."

"You're kidding?"

"The word is that the Rootmaster just might have a feature on his hands."

I was knocked out by Tabard's news. I spent what must have been a good hour strolling aimlessly around the Canary Wharf development, crossing, re-crossing bridges, mounting and descending flights of stairs, found myself a couple of times stuck at the bottom of the huge basin that formed the Tube station entrance. I couldn't believe a major player was interested in my words.

I wasn't about to go home and work until I regained some kind of control of my thoughts, so I kept on walking. I went back to the ferry landing, footed my way by the river, happy for a while to take in breaths of cool air straight off the water. Was Ferris really prepared to give me a shot at making some kind of film? I passed a couple of housing developments, edged along a few old wharf buildings, before the pathway cut abruptly inland. Was I about to ink a real deal? I headed back towards Canary Wharf, did laps of the docks in the hope that a measured approach might slow the mind.

On the last of the watery tours, I almost walked into a huge cast-iron marker buoy parked on the quay outside the Museum of London Docklands. It was enough to lure me through the doors and I ended up working my way through an old sugar warehouse and a huge spread of history. My eyes were charged with hundreds of beautiful maps and illustrations and I gawked at a breathtaking balloon's-eye view of a Thames latticed with ships' riggings, the river bung-full of livery barges, wherries, smacks. I peered into wooden viewing boxes to watch nineteenth-century rarees – illuminated peepshows of ancient monuments, ferocious animals, exotic landscapes with palm trees, camel trains. I had to laugh. They were, of course, the Soundies of their day.

I watched a film about the first few days of the London Blitz as fire-brigade figures ran hoses, fought endless smoke and flame. It was an amateurish work, badly edited, but I got caught up in the heroic narrative, enjoyed the flickering footage that delivered a distinct vintage.

I looked at my watch. I'd been out at Canary Wharf for about six hours, really needed to get back, do serious labour for the next day's En Root recording.

On my way out, I saw a couple of huge, medium-format prints. At first I thought they were photographs of rigs but then realised they weren't oil derricks at all. In fact, they seemed no more than huge steel drums raised above the water on spindle-legs, looked as though they'd grown from seed in clusters from the sea bed like so much metal mustard and cress. According to the blurb, they were the Maunsell Sea Forts, built in the Thames in the forties and armed with anti-aircraft guns to tackle German planes, doodle-bugs flying in from the east. They'd been abandoned after the war, reoccupied twenty years later by a battery of broadcasters. The Knock John fort had played home to one radio station – *this is the voice of Radio Essex on two double two* – while another, Shivering Sands, harboured Screaming Lord Sutch and Radio City.

Here I was facing my Thames broadcasting ancestors, and I knew exactly what had to be done. I'd hire a boat to take me out to the Maunsell Forts. Yes, I'd go with a cameraman, shoot them, and make the hulking likes of Knock John look absolutely Hegley-style beautiful.

BERNARD HERRMANN'S THE ONE TO BLAME IF YOU JUST GOT HOT AND STICKY LISTENING TO THAT CLIP – WHICH, IF YOU DIDN'T RECOGNISE IT, FEATURED THE SQUEALING STRINGS FROM *PSYCHO'S* SHOWER SCENE. AND LET ME TELL YOU IT'S HERRMANN'S FOUR-NOTE BRASS DEVICE THAT MAKES EVERYONE SO FEARFUL IN *CAPE FEAR*. PLUS, HE ALSO CREATED THE SAX SOLO IN *TAXI DRIVER* THAT SO EVOKES THE SLEAZE OF GOTHAM. THINK OF THE SOUNDS OF *CITIZEN KANE* AND *VERTIGO*, TOO, AND YOU'LL REALISE THAT HERRMANN FILM-SCORED BIG TIME ON THE WEST COAST. IT WAS ORSON WELLES WHO BROUGHT HIM TO HOLLYWOOD, GOT HIM TO WRITE FOR *KANE* – YES, THOSE LOW WOODWINDS IN THE OPENING ARE HIS – BEFORE HITCHCOCK GOT HOLD OF HIM AND

THE TWO OF THEM STARTED A LONG HOOK-UP. WHAT'S IMPORTANT TO KNOW IS THAT HERRMANN WENT AGAINST THE GRAIN BY AVOIDING THOSE TYPICAL FULL-IN-BOTH-EARS ORCHESTRAL ARRANGEMENTS, OPTING INSTEAD FOR SIMPLE MOTIFS THAT HE REPEATED THROUGHOUT THE FEATURE – THOUGH WITH MINOR, BUT GENERALLY MAJORLY UNSETTLING, VARIATIONS. HERRMANN REMAINED HITCH'S FAVOURITE MUSICKER UNTIL THE DIRECTOR REJECTED THE SCORE FOR *TORN CURTAIN*, THOUGH SOME OF THOSE NOTES LATER GOT PLAYED IN THE *CAPE FEAR* REMAKE. INTERESTINGLY, HERRMANN ALSO MADE IT ONTO CELLULOID IN *THE MAN WHO KNEW TOO MUCH*, PLAYING A CONDUCTOR IN THE PIT OF THE ROYAL ALBERT HALL. AND NOW HIS MUSIC'S BACK IN LONDON AT THE BARBICAN WHERE I CAUGHT UP WITH IT LAST NIGHT. MY RECOMMENDATION IS THAT YOU GO ALONG THIS EVE AND LISTEN TO THE BBC CONCERT ORCHESTRA TAKING ON HERRMANN'S HITCHCOCK SCORES ONE MORE TIME. ONE PIECE OF ADVICE – BRING ALONG THE SHOWER CAP.

I rattled off the show in the studio pretty comfortably given the lack of prep. Even Cushman wasn't able to gripe about my lack of dexterity with the fades.

I snatched a couple of minutes on the receptionist's computer to check my e-mail and read a message from Theresa Noble who'd picked up an item on Roger Huckerby Senior from the online version of the *Costa del Sol News*. And all his Iberian demise ran to was a single, two-line graph noting the death of a retired Englishman in a car accident on a notorious stretch of the N-340 just east of Marbella. Theresa called it *tragic, so tragic*, added that *something had to be done*. I hadn't a clue what she meant.

I put a call in to Roger Junior's office.

"Sorry to hear about your father," I said. "I never did get to meet him."

"I was all set to fly out to Spain in a couple of weeks. Now they're shipping Dad this way."

"Your mother wasn't in the car with him, was she?"

"No, the old man was on his way to Malaga on business."

"I thought he'd stopped working."

"He liked to keep his hand in with some of the older clients. Quite a few of them live on the costas… Damn, this isn't good news for the company. A lot of people still see him as a mainstay."

That was more PLC than TLC, I thought. But maybe this would wreck all of Junior's big biz plans.

"You know, we might yet turn this to our advantage," he said. "A decent celebrity turnout at the funeral will draw the media. That could mean lots of goodwill for H&P. Didn't you mention you were on the radio, Root? You'll do something on him, won't you?"

*   *   *

I'd arranged to meet Harry in the bar of the Baltic, a bar-restaurant over the road from Southwark Tube station, and was surprised to see she was already there when I arrived. The Harry I knew was perpetually strapped for time, always managing to build up a terrific charge of late meets during the course of a work day. But here she was, feet up on a banquette in a nice nook, garbed in a bright red flapper-style dress, matching cocktail in hand, the whole of her very well-lit by candlelight.

"Well, you are preceding yourself." I pecked her on the cheeks. "Did New York instil good habits or something?"

"No way the Big Apple will change a bad variety like me."

"You're hardly rotten to the core, Aitch. You just need to ripen a little."

"Enough of this," she said. "Fetch me another drink. It's a fruits of the forest, or something. And when you get back, I need to bitch."

"What have I done?"

"I just need your ear. Hurry up."

The barman took so long to make the first cocktail – he had a dressy move for pouring the liquor and pestled mint leaves with great care in a huge stainless steel mortar – that I plumped for a beer. Harry would be rocking with anger if I stayed away much longer and she already looked primed to go off.

"What's that you're drinking?" she asked.

"I didn't want anything fancy."

"Well, sit yourself down, Mr Simple."

I threw myself into a chair and started on my beer.

Harry launched into highly convoluted story – she wasn't good at sticking to the knitting when roused – but I picked out the main threads and the gist of it seemed to be that she'd just found out her company had bumped her off all things Hegley. To date she'd practically been running the star director's show, cutting deals with distributors around the globe, goading the gofers to trawl through the endless lengths of extra footage so the company could haul more lucrative DVDs to market. And, it turned out that not only had they pulled the Hegley rug out from under her, they'd shifted Harry over to Guy Ritchie.

"This is strange, Bro," she said. "It's like I'm being punished."

"Could it be some kind of promotion instead?"

"Come off it. Hegley's a prestigious account."

"And Ritchie?"

"Oh, please." She took a gulp of her cocktail. "I'm supposed to be a top dog. And what they did was send me to New York then castrate me in my absence."

"Go over their heads. Talk to someone at the conglomerate."

"That'd be professional suicide."

"Maybe you can make something of Ritchie. Someone needs to."

Harry another took a huge slug of fruits of forest. "I could sleep with the boss, I suppose."

"Really?"

"Oh, Root." She turned big-time teary.

There was no way I could leave Harry in this state. And Meaghan was at a party up in Camden with Justin waiting for me to arrive with my best friend in tow. Plus, I hadn't yet mentioned that particular plan to Harry. As I watched her search through her bag for a tissue, I decided the only way I could hope to come out of this smelling anything like some kind of sweet flower was to make her fall for Justin before she'd even met him.

* * *

At Al's early next morning, I was feeling pretty pleased with myself. The previous evening had panned out much better than I could possibly have imagined. I'd talked Harry to a dinner table at the Baltic and, after an hour or so of borscht-eating and a more-than-half-share in a bottle of wine, she'd got the bitter taste of the demotion out of her system and, for a while, was happy to kid again. That was when I got to work on the fab features of Justin – *brilliant musician, fantastic journalist, salt-of-the-earth kinda bloke, doncha know it, wouldn't mess a gal about, plus those hands...* Harry was grateful for the escape, said she couldn't wait to meet him.

Several hours later, when he offered to give Harry a lift home, she gracefully accepted.

Sitting at Al's, though, I realised couldn't begin to think about what might well be the beginning of that social item to be known as Harry and Justin. So I left an almost full cup of coffee on the table and went home to change into a dark suit and scoot on up to Highgate.

Chapter Eight

At Huckerby's funeral, I had the smallest hope that Hegley would show his nose, even though that would be a huge risk on his part with so many people around who knew him. There was always the possibility he'd appear in disguise, I thought - but come on, this was real life, not some cheap novel.

I skipped the service, waited at the gates of the cemetery. It was a beautiful morning, warm with a crystal of a sky, the sun breaking stunning shadows everywhere I looked. Certainly not burial weather.

The hearse pulled up and I watched four men in top hats strung with trails of black ribbon pull the coffin out of the car, hoist it onto their shoulders and carry it down the gravel path, their footsteps so practised they made barely a sound as they walked. It was a strong scene.

The bearers were followed by a straggle of some hundred or so mourners. I scanned them – still looking out in foolish hope for Hegley – and it was odd to see so many film and TV mugs of the kind that were not quite nameable, a cast of character actors eternally seeking that big part. I did recognise that Stranks character from *Greene Land*, the inspector's sidekick, and those currant eyes looked more than ever lost in his face thanks to a hairline that had receded some distance from his forehead. He'd heavied up with age but still seemed someone not to mess with.

Junior led the pack, crassly sporting his hideous hairdo and a loud striped suit, a buxom wife hooked on his arm. The pair of them looked like a caricature gangster and his moll. I had a real dislike for this Mr and Mrs Huckerby and was sorry I'd never met Roger the First – I'd liked to have commiserated with him about his sad offspring while enjoying a Rioja in the shade outside some Spanish bar.

Theresa Noble was there, though it took me a while to recognise her in her conservative outfit. I was pretty certain she saw me, even though she didn't acknowledge it.

I stood back and watched the proceedings. As the ceremony unfolded, it sunk in that this whole procedure was to do with death. That was to say, it was life and it was as real as it ever got. Why was I, an intruder, here at all? And what was I doing chasing after Hegley, the dead man walking? It was absurd. It was a totally madcap venture. And I knew that once I left the cemetery, it would be the end of the affair. In truth, I was relieved it was over.

Theresa Noble came over to me once Huckerby had been dispatched.

"Roger deserved better," she said.

"I thought it was all done rather tastefully."

"I meant the way he died."

"No one's immune to accidents."

"You don't believe this happened just when we were on to him."

"What do you mean, on to him? I'm only writing a biography."

Theresa turned her back on me, headed for the gates. I felt she'd been sent over to say what she'd said simply to test my resolve in dropping this stupid Hegley business. As I'd just proved, I couldn't have cared less about this great 'mystery' any longer.

"Good you could make it." Junior shook my hand enthusiastically. "Decent showing."

"Everything you hoped for."

He raked his fingers carefully through his manga. "Are you still working on that Philip Hegley book?"

"It's up in the air."

"I was wondering if you knew someone. My father was on his way to meet a chap in Malaga. Could be an investor. The police found a business card of his among Dad's pocket litter."

Junior handed me the card. It said 'A E Nesh' and, in razorblade handwriting, '3pm, Café Andalucia'.

"No contact details," he said. "What kind of calling card is that?"

* * *

I felt chill standing next to Huckerby's fresh grave. I didn't really want to stay but couldn't bring myself to leave either. I began examining the floral tributes, saw scores of names I didn't recognise. I found a single yellow rose planted upright in the soil, a tag swaying in the breeze. I read it. *Oh, Roger, mea culpa, mea culpa. PH.*

* * *

I went straight home after the funeral, pushed the DVD of *Greene Land* into the player and watched scenes at random. I deliberately pushed them out of sequence and soon confirmed what I'd suspected for a while. Each segment had been constructed so that it was self-contained, and there was no need for the viewer to have seen the preceding footage to make sense of one small part of the whole. It was a wonderful moment for me. I got a huge kick and at the same time felt I had a better handle on Hegley, though I'd have been pushed to say exactly how if questioned on it. What I did know was that I was back in the game.

```
The facade of the Shirley Ann pub in Peckham. A
trademark Greene Land shot. The camera holds steady
for thirty seconds, recording no movement. It's an
image of stills quality. There's absolutely no am-
bient noise.
Cut to:
The saloon bar, lights blaze along with the mu-
sic, a crashing banjo song from Lonnie Donegan. The
place is full, the camera butting through a mass
of people, distorting faces grotesquely with its
wide-angle lens. Cavernous mouths, tortured lips
squeeze out hideous laughs. The music, the gruesome
```

crowing is simply too much…

A striking silence.

Cut to:

A mid-shot of Boocock standing with his back against the bar, propped on one elbow. He's drinking a short with ice and lemon. The music, Donegan still but with calmer chords, feeds in once more, the crowd noise now a mere hum.

Cut to:

A close-up of Boocock taking a sip of his drink. The shot is breathtaking. Behind him is a horizontal line of optics. The rectangular white labels on the upturned bottles stand in awing contrast to the black wall behind. They're clearly teeth.

The lights go down. Donegan's voice is killed. We hear applause, the opening bars of 'Cabaret', a woman begins to sing. We recognise the voice of Les Lea, wait to see her. But the camera remains trained on the lime-lit face of Boocock. We will it away, our eyes wanting Les Lea. But they're disappointed, have to content themselves with Boocock's unblinking look until the song closes.

Cut to:

Boocock waits in the corridor. He's smoking. He looks at his watch, throws the cigarette to the floor, crushes it underfoot, lights another. He looks at his watch.

Les Lea steps through a door, sees Boocock and tries to walk past him. He catches her by the arm. "I want to know about Thom," he says.

"What's to know? He was just another man."

"You don't believe that."

Les Lea laughs, shakes her head. "You're a romantic. You want me to say I was in love with him."

"Tell me you weren't."

"I hated him."

"Doesn't mean you didn't love him."

"You're a fool."

"I've been called worse."

"What is it you want?" she asks.

"I told you."

Les Lea laughs again. "Oh, I see."

Boocock shakes his head.

"You're a knight," she says. "You imagine yourself rescuing me from my grief. Such gallantry."

"I didn't come here to be mocked."

"You're chasing the wrong woman."

"I'm not chasing at all. I think I have my catch."

Fade to black.

Getting another fix of *Greene Land* and writing up my take online made me late for the studio. There was still scads to do for the upcoming broadcast, the show's extra fifteen minutes weighing emptily but heavily over us. We spent ages putting together an audio bed for Ben's session at the Beeb, only for me to find it difficult to do the voiceover. The fact that Cushman was glaring at me through the glass wasn't helping, but the irregularities of free jazz were making it impossible to put rhythm into the delivery. It was as if the story was being bounced off the walls by the dissonance, while the long silences were making a mockery of having a bed at all. I recalled Meaghan pointing out in Oxford that such hush could make you want to blow your vocal chords. That's exactly what I was feeling in the studio after what was now five straight hours with the cans over my ears.

I stopped the session, heard Cushman mutter something off about how I reckoned my shit smelled so sweet. I got on the phone to Justin, asked him if he could come over, straighten me out. *Chuffed to,* he said. *See you laters.*

The team and I pushed the jazz down the roster, polished off a few easier segments, including an interview I'd done with Boris Johnson where I had to re-record my part of the mayoral Q&A. The London boss had been tetchy about an odd property deal and it had thrown me for a while. I recorded some of the questions again in an assured way, was grateful the show wasn't live.

Justin arrived, was absolute velvet to work with. All we had to do was play him some of the morning's aborted recordings, run through snatches of his father's session and he was up and very much running.

"It's highly stripped down but the bass line's actually pretty standard," Justin said. "Best thing we can do is punch that channel up."

"Sounds good to me."

"And we can make the sax warmer and richer to match your register."

"Fine … if you say so."

"Don't worry, my friend." He grinned. "I'll totally sort it out for you."

I left him with Cushman, bought a coffee and went for a walk by the river. The Thames was at its most exciting, high and running quickly upstream. I spent a long while watching the water break white in fragile crescents at centre stream, could feel the strength of the tide even standing way back on the bank.

By the time I got back to the studio, I was ready to take on the job once more. Justin had done his stuff and played me the new bed. It was a beautifully fluid mix, even made Cushman smile. From there on it was easy – I did my bit in a single take, was relieved to wrap it at last.

* * *

I stumped up for a pint afterwards at the Charles Dickens.

"Cheers, Justin," I said.

"Mercy buckup to you, Root. I'd forgotten how much I enjoyed working in the studio."

"Ever have the urge play again?"

"Actually, I've been invited to do a short sesh at The Spitz."

"Great, I'll come with Megs."

"I'm well fired up. You know, since I met Harriet, things have been on the up."

"Is that right?" I hadn't been following the proceedings since pairing the couple in Camden. I'd failed to return Harry's many calls after the party and a few days later she'd gone off on some film boondoggle on the Continent. I stared into the beer I now had little thirst for.

"I think I'm going to end up owing you Moby-sized," Justin said. "Harriet's definitely someone I can rock with."

* * *

I left Justin at the bar, was planning to dodge a scheduled meet with Minona, but she snagged me with a text just as I was passing under Blackfriars Bridge. I footed it back to the studios where she was waiting for me in the lobby.

"Knotty session today, I hear," Minona said.

"Seemed like that because it usually runs so well. The crew's been spoilt."

"Not finding the new format too onerous, are you?"

"Is that what you're hoping?" I asked.

"Come on Root, I was only joking."

"It's my time of the month, that's all."

"All right, what's your beef?"

"Same as always, Min. Lack of resource. Lack of respect. An all-round lack, in fact." I was beginning to realise how totally hacked off I'd become with Minona.

"Ah, you want some mothering," she said. "You like to hear how much you're really needed, don't you?"

"I already know you simply can't live without me."

"What you don't realise is that I go easy on you. There's a lot of pressure from above."

"Must be tough," I said. "Though my programme's doing well enough to stand on it's own feet, thanks."

"Oh, get with the programme, won't you? Don't forget I gave you your chance to get on air."

"Well, thanks for everything."

In a rush of blood, I gave her a huge hug, lifted her off the ground. I held onto her for a few seconds. I let her down, found it hard to look her in the eye again.

When I did, she wasn't at all wearing the weapons-grade stare I'd expected.

Chapter Nine

I planned to spend much of the weekend at the Raindance Film Festival, was more than ready to let my body soak up as much celluloid as it could take. There was just one problem. While I'd gone to the event every year for the past decade, it had always been with Harry, and this time she couldn't make it, had to be in LA. And to top it off, she was taking Justin along as some kind of consort. *You'll have to put up with an empty seat next to you, Bro, but I know you understand...*

I wasn't sure I did, or wanted to.

The first film largely passed me by as I sat for an hour and a half in the dark feeling sorry for myself. I knew I was being foolish and afterwards gave myself a hard time – it wasn't in the slightest bit professional and what I needed to do was get down to the job of hunting for material for the show.

I was also at the festival in an official capacity, having a few months earlier read through a hill of scripts as I judged for the Reel Talent Award. My task now was to sit with my fellow judiciary, plus an audience of around fifty additional souls, to see the results, and I ended up quite taken by the winner, a short about the use of music to cure amnesia. I gave myself a pat on the back for being part of the process.

In the foyer afterwards I did my shake-hands-with-the-film-makers duty and handed out warm compliments before rewarding myself with a Smirnoff and apple juice. I was feeling better.

I went back to the bar for a second shot and ran into Abdi. The two of us had graduated together and he'd then plumped for the hardcore side of the business, vowing to make films, and films only, for a living. We weren't major chums or anything but we did see each other on and off at various dos around town, always made a good time of catching up.

"How are things, Root?" he asked. "I tune in to the show when I can."

"Life's good. The BBC bumped me up fifteen minutes."

"Hey, that's crisp. I'll raise a glass to that."

We clinked Smirnoffs.

"Corporate video market still buoyant?" I asked. "Or have you been forced into making rom-coms?" Abdi had managed to stick to his career guns, though he'd needed to stretch his definition of film over the years to pull in a liveable income.

"I've just closed a long stretch doing videos for some firm that feeds off the NHS."

"You must be quids in," I said. "We all know how the government loves to chuck cash at that side of things."

"That lovely money's going to produce the script I've been working on for the past half-life."

"You finished it?"

"Yes, and I'm absolutely ready to shoot. We roll next month in Rotherhithe."

"That's my neck of the woods nowadays. I'd love to see you in action, Abdi."

"Give me your e-mail and I'll send over a PDF of the schedule. Be good to have Root with us."

"I'll do a piece for the programme, get you some PR."

"Nice. I'll take all the puffery there is if it helps me get a distributor."

We continued our work on the drinks, missed the evening film and ended up in an Indonesian restaurant chewing riijstafel. We went on to a basement bar somewhere at the bottom end of Soho where we stayed until early hours knocking back port and brandies.

Abdi asked me about Harry, wanted to know if she was still the highest of flyers. I told him she'd attained such altitude she was in bloody orbit, wouldn't be surprised if she didn't finally come back to Earth in Hollyweird. I blacked out an image that was beginning to emerge in my head of her in the States with Justin.

"I never completely understood why you two didn't end up a mating pair," he said.

"One of life's unexplainables, Abdi."

I took a cab home, somehow never made it to the bedroom. When Meaghan woke me next morning I was lying on the sofa and using the kilim rug as a blanket.

* * *

I put in a full Sunday at Raindance, not even the trace of a hangover to hobble me. I arrived early enough to catch a morning feature called Hitler's Hit Parade, a disturbing doc about Nazis set to upbeat wartime melodies. It was something akin to The Producers without Mel Brooks, without even a glint of humour. Poor selection on my part.

I grabbed a pizza lunch that I chowed down at some tourist stand near Leicester Square and was back at the cinema for a showing of the finalists for the Raindance Short Film Prize. I quietly found myself a seat at the rear of the cinema. The first few films weren't so hot, and I began feeling the effects of the previous night's alcohol and dearth of sleep, while my lower back was giving me gyp from couch slouch. If I'd had just a grain more energy, I'd have slipped out of the show.

But the next film, something called Ness, dragged me back to life. The opening shots of Dungeness nuclear plant – perfect geometric forms rowelling the Kent clouds – were exceptional. The following visuals of the lighthouse were absolute gems. I thought I'd recognised the signature by then but it was the footage of the fishing boat tilted on a pebble beach miles away from the breaking sea, the long take of a beautifully feathered English skyscape that confirmed it. The screen turned black and we heard the only piece of narration in ten minutes – *Dungeness, dangerous coast*.

Out in the lobby I spotted Abdi.

"Did you just see the shorts?" I asked.

"A mixed bag."

"What did you make of *Ness*?"

He laughed. "Bleeding obvious, Root."

"What is?" I enjoyed having to tease it out of him.

"Philip Hegley. At first, I thought someone was simply doing a take-off. But the way it ended, well, that was totally the acid test that someone's dug up the real thing."

I leafed through the handout, found the listing for *Ness*. The director was one Lionel Naysmith. AKA that rough nut Stranks from *Greene Land*.

*   *   *

At Al's next morning, I enjoyed a comfortable sense of satisfaction. I'd sussed some of what was going on, and, for the first time since the Bloomsbury encounter, dared to believe I was maybe even ahead of the central character.

Back at the festival, Abdi had quite naturally believed someone had banged together a few thousand frames of Hegley and had tossed it into the Raindance hat for a lark, wanting to get a rise. However, it was clear to me that the man himself was back in the ring, practising his craft once more and doing it deftly. But he hadn't covered his tracks. Nothing wrong with using Naysmith as a front but that old trouper had now appeared on my radar screen twice in just a few days. It was evident that it was Naysmith who'd planted the flower at Huckerby Senior's funeral and that he was doing the bidding of his master. All I needed to do now was to track Naysmith down and I'd have a direct line to Hegley.

Perhaps I would make a good gumshoe after all.

I left the cafe, walked though the market drinking my on-the-go coffee and kicking the odd stray Brussels sprout down the aisles. I knocked back slugs of my drink like it was bourbon. I wondered if I should buy myself a sharp hat, one with a nice wide brim that would enhance my image as a modern-day sleuth.

My phone rang. It was Huckerby Junior.

"I want to hire you," he said.

"What would you want with me? I'm just a broadcaster." The thought briefly occurred that perhaps he was after my detective skills.

"I listened to your programme the other day," he said. "Let me tell you this, you're a pro."

"Thanks, but I don't see how I can help you."

"I also looked up your obituary of Philip Hegley. It was a great piece. I want you to write my father's."

"But they've all been done." I'd scoured the papers after Huckerby's death, read short obits in the *Guardian*, *Times*, *Indie*, *Telegraph*, also discovered a few column inches in the *Mail*.

"I want you to compose one for H&P."

"Why would you want an obituary?" I finished off the coffee, crumpled the paper cup and tossed it a good twenty feet into the dead centre of a rubbish bin.

"My father should have a decent write-up of his professional life."

"What would you do with it?"

"Run off a quality print. Distribute it to everyone in the sector. Post it on the web site for download. Maybe make an audio version to stream."

"You think it's good marketing, that it?"

"Can't be faulted. It pays respect to the founder and bolsters the H&P image."

"It's a little out there for me."

"Don't say 'no' now when you might want to say 'yes' later. The pay will be City grade, don't worry."

"Let me think on it."

"I'll call you tomorrow."

I caught a Brussels right on the end of my toe, whacked it hard to burst against a wall. A career as corporate obituarist beckoned.

* * *

I was a half hour behind schedule when I arrived at the National Film Theatre bar thanks to a phone conversation with Minona that carried on far too long. She wanted to talk numbers again. There'd been changes in the budget that meant she'd had to spend days, evenings, poring over spreadsheets. The developments had little to do with me and I wondered why she'd called until she brought up our spat in the lobby the other day. I hadn't acted professionally, she complained, shouldn't think I could get away with that kind of behaviour in public. I ought to dial it down. I was about to apologise when she added, *though I understand that men like to touch the fruit before they buy*. She hung up.

At the NFT, Theresa Noble was tucked into a corner by the window nursing a whisky. The look she gave me said she was already partly toasted.

"Sorry for the delay," I said. "Business."

She looked at her watch. "I can't be angry at you, Root. Not when I'm so happy to see you."

Theresa was togged up in an expensive-looking alpaca coat, and had on a pair of silk limo shoes that made me wonder how she'd ever made it as far as the bar. She held out a hand and I kissed it graciously.

"The funeral was difficult," Theresa said. "I barely knew Roger but the whole thing reminded me of Philip's service." She took a handkerchief from her handbag, ran a finger along its lacy edges, placed it back in the bag.

"Have you spoken to him?" I asked.

"As soon as I heard about Roger, I booked in for a seance. I needed to know what Philip thought."

"And what did Philip think?" I couldn't believe I was asking the question, but I wasn't able to break it to her that her beloved was still alive and popping up all over London, shooting shorts even. When I'd first met her out in Denmark Hill, I thought she'd known Philip wasn't dead, had been on the point of telling her about the meeting in Bloomsbury. Then she explained about the medium, talked quietly about the voices from the other side. So I said nothing. And right now wasn't the time to slug her with the truth, was it?

"He thinks Roger was murdered." She sipped from her glass, savoured, swallowed. "Just as Philip was."

"Hold on, you never said you thought Philip Hegley had been rubbed out."

She winced. "I didn't until Roger was done in. But now the last person to see Philip alive is no more. That's suspicious."

"What does Philip say about his death?" My line of questioning was getting weirder for sure.

"Oh Root, the departed don't know the nature of their passing." She put her hands to her face.

I leaned across the table, squeezed her forearm. "Can I get you another drink?" I asked.

Theresa showed me her face. Her mascara was beautifully intact considering the streams of tears.

"You're rosy, Root. Very rosy." She took hold of my fingers. "I shall have a whisky if you'll join me."

I went over to the bar and when I got back with the glasses I saw Theresa had spread a handful of black and white photographs across the table. I looked them over, realised they were stills from *Greene Land*. There was a great one of Hegley where he was crouching down behind the cameraman, aping the stance of his lensman. Another shot was of Theresa made-up and on stage at the Shirley Ann, crooning into a stand mic she was pulling towards her at a rakish angle.

"You have a great voice," I told her.

She laughed. "You're a flirt, Root."

"No, it's fantastic."

She laughed again. "I can't hold a single note, silly. I mimed everything."

"Then who did the singing?"

"A pro. The wife of a friend of Philip's. Her husband's a blowing cat."

"A what?"

She grinned. "A musician. Ben Terry plays jazz saxophone."

"You mean, Rachel Terry sang on *Greene Land*?"

"You know her?"

"A little." I saw Meaghan's mother rigged out as Les Lea, could hear her belting out a number.

Theresa pointed to one of the prints on the table. "This is Arthur Roney."

"He played Detective Wark." I took a sip of the ginger ale I'd told Theresa was whisky and splash.

"Roney and his boyfriend, Lionel Naysmith, endeared themselves to Philip by keeping everyone in line during the shoot." She pushed the photo away.

"You weren't fond of Roney and Naysmith."

"I've nothing against shirtlifters but I can't imagine what Philip saw in them." She gathered up the pictures, slid them into an envelope. "Roney told him to stay away from me, for the good of the film."

"And you're still angry."

"I shall ignore that for the sake of our friendship." She stood. "Now, you pull yourself together while I go and freshen up."

Theresa did remarkably well to move gracefully across the room considering the altitude of her footwear. While she was away I took the photos from the envelope, sifted through them and put a few in my bag.

Chapter Ten

Meaghan and I went over Shoreditch and had dinner at an Italian restaurant near The Spitz.

"I haven't seen Justin on stage for ages," she said.

"Pity your parents weren't invited."

"No need to wind me up."

"I was just saying."

"Well, maybe just don't." Meaghan scraped the tines of her fork along the edge of a plate.

"I'm really keen to see Justin," I said.

"He has amazing fingering."

"Surely not as good as his sister's."

Meaghan squeezed my leg under the table. "You're in frisky frame of mind."

She was right. I was feeling pretty chipper. I was getting quite a kick out of this detective thing. It surprised me a little, as I'd never been one for the whodunits that seemed to engross so many people. But, then again, I'd always taken great pleasure in putting together disparate things, making them into something of a piece – that was, after all, the way I earned a living. This affair with Hegley had lit a fire under me once more and I thought that if I could solve it, then it would sort out a good part of my life at the same time. That sounded rather odd, but it was exactly how I felt.

"Something's up at work," Meaghan said.

"Would that be good up or bad up?"

"I had a meeting with someone from head office." She picked up her wine, her fingertips following the strokes of the cutglass. I was entranced, hadn't been kidding about her fingers. I'd always found her hands one of the sexiest things about her, something that helped me enjoy life in the key of Meaghan.

"He was talking about promotion," she said.

"That's great. What's the job?"

"It's not so much the position, more where it would be based."

"I'm not sure I'm up to moving to the provinces."

"There's nothing provincial about it. It's Vienna. He wants me to go and visit the office."

* * *

We made it over to The Spitz well before Justin came on, caught the tailend of a male-female duo on guitar and xylophone. I wasn't that taken by what they were doing but when Meaghan praised them technically – something to do with their chord progressions – I started liking them more, notched the act up a few pegs.

Justin came on and did a half-hour set with a bass player and pianist. Maybe because of his largely classical background, I'd assumed he'd serve up something straight, traditional even, but the handful of numbers his trio delivered turned out to be a colourful mix of styles and I especially enjoyed the funk-type rhythms.

Justin had an easy style, didn't seem a bit rusty, and was warm and open as a performer. I'd always liked him, and now I reckoned him a very impressive bloke.

He joined us at our table after the set, getting a kiss from Meaghan, a healthy handshake from me.

"How do you feel?" I asked.

"Totally wiped. If you told me I'd been up there for four hours, I'd believe it."

"But I bet you feel good," Meaghan said.

"Utterly peachy. But look." He held out his hands, had terrific shakes.

"Is that what you were like in the Halle?" I asked.

"Not once. In an orchestra, you're invisible. Here you almost sit in people's laps. I'd forgotten how terrifying it was."

"So, no more gigs for you," I said.

"You're kidding," Meaghan said. "This is just the beginning."

"She's right, my friend," he said. "I can't wait for the next. I can play far better, don't you know."

* * *

Justin asked for a ride as we left The Spitz.

"You want us to trek all the way up to Hampstead?" Meaghan asked.

"I'm going your way. You can drop me on Union Street."

"What's waiting for you there?" I asked. "You after spending a few hours in a club?"

"There's a certain lady," said Meaghan.

"She's only just come back from the States and couldn't make the gig," Justin said.

I hadn't even wondered about Harry's absence that evening and realised I'd barely given a thought to the new romance I'd helped create. I obviously hadn't cared to see any great distance beyond the end of my nose when it came to Harry and her love life.

* * *

Naysmith met me outside his home at the gates of the Jam Factory, the old Hartley's place at the foot of Tower Bridge that had been converted to flats and live-works. He had an odd handshake – it was solid enough but his index finger was bent wildly out of shape and pushed hard into my palm, making me want to quickly let go.

It had been easy tracking Naysmith down. One call to Equity got me his agent's number. And then I posed as the producer of Abdi's film, left my name and number. Naysmith himself rang back in under five minutes, said simply he'd been expecting me. I suggested I pop down to his place ASAP given that I lived in the neighbourhood.

The two of us took the lift to the top floor of one of the redundant factory's redbricks and we walked into what was nothing more than a huge glass rectangle that took in views of all London's compass points. To the east, Canary Wharf's cloudbusters flashed redlight warnings that were matched in the south by the Crystal Palace mast. At ninety-degrees clockwise, I could see the wheel of the London Eye, make out a few crenellations from Westminster. The crowning glory, though, was the dead-on eyeful of Tower Bridge to our north.

"Must look killer at night time," I said.

"Beats TV."

I followed Naysmith into a large room with glass walls and concrete flooring. A half-dozen butterfly-form stools crouched together. There was an enormous limed-oak desk that was so organic it looked like it might move off under its own power at any moment. And I stared at a squatting kidney-shaped, glass-topped table.

In one of two plush airplane-style armchairs, sat Arthur Roney. "Discerning eye you've got," he said.

"It's a design feast." I shook his hand.

"Can't stand. Wrenched the back on set."

"A stunt?"

"Sex scene."

"I'd never imagined it so risky."

Roney winced.

"Seat," Naysmith said. He pointed to the second armchair.

"I fancy one of the stools."

"A Yanagi," Roney said.

"I'm honoured." I was close to making a fool of myself, felt able to say only stupid things in the face of Naysmith and Roney. It wasn't just their taciturn manner, they were also rather stiff bods who looked like hardnut versions of Gilbert and George. I'd taken the trouble to find out that they'd made careers playing dubious working-class types, had followed in the footsteps of the British cinematic likes of Arthur Seaton, Vic Brown and Joe Lampton, exactly the kinds of characters I had great antipathy towards.

"I saw you at the funeral," I told Naysmith.

He nodded.

"You left the flower."

"Respects," he said.

"From Philip Hegley."

"We did the necessary," said Roney.

"Hegley thinks he's to blame for what happened to Roger Huckerby," I said. "I have to see him."

Roney shook his head. "Tricky."

"It's been hit and miss between us," I said.

"Unlucky," said Roney.

"Too much miss."

"Perhaps so," he said.

"I keep on trying." I was in danger of becoming as staccato as this theatrical pair.

Roney shook his head, a gesture mimicked by Naysmith.

I felt a keen draught from the air conditioning. The whole place was cold and uncomfortable, though the two men before me had on sleeveless Tees, cut-off shorts.

"For fuck's sake, why don't you phone him right now?" I said. "Just tell him … well, tell him I'm here."

Naysmith took a step forward. I could see the tension in his cheeks that were suddenly veined, shiny as marble. I guessed he might still be able to pack a hospital punch.

"Philip's in Spain," Roney said.

"In Marbella?"

I could tell from the surprise in both Roney's and Naysmith's faces that I'd guessed right.

"We'd like to help," Roney said. "We'll talk to Philip when he gets back."

"When's that?"

"You'll be informed," Roney said.

"Just you make sure you stay in the postcode," Naysmith told me.

I couldn't make out whether that was meant as good advice or if it was pure threat.

* * *

I was waiting for Harry in The Hospital Club in Covent Garden, the first time I'd get to see her since the party in Camden. I'd barely spoken to her in the meantime, felt nervous at the prospect of meeting up and having to talk about Justin.

The place was a club for media types and had next-gen TV studios, a classy cinema, a games room where I sometimes played the odd frame of pool with Harry, plus a hip restaurant. Right now, I was sitting in the Bellini Bar with its blue Rorschach-Paisley wallcovering, was sipping some expensive, exotic mineral water. I wasn't feeling in the slightest clubbable.

My apprehension at seeing Harry was compounded by my frustration at how badly I'd handled things at the Jam Factory. On the face of it, Roney, Naysmith and I were on the same side, so it had seemed unlikely I would have left the place with a warning ringing in my ears. They didn't appear to be good enemies to have, especially with old currant eyes being of a twitchy disposition.

Harry arrived in the bar twenty minutes later than advertised, was definitely back on form on the lack-of-punctuality front. She took off her coat, was wearing a fabulous sixties-style tartan dress with a hem that ended way shy of her knees, and boots that streamed up her calves. She would have looked great on the set of *Blow-Up*.

"Penny for 'em, Bro."

"My head's full only of bargain-basement stuff, Aitch," I said. "Where've you been? Hanging with Mr Ritchie?"

Harry found an armchair, got the waiter's attention and ordered – what else? – a Bellini. "Thanks for rubbing it in," she said.

"Sorry, funny old day."

"Then why aren't you having good old fire water?" She pointed to my glass.

"I have to work later this evening. And write my blog."

"Still tackling half-a-dozen jobs at once?"

"Bare minimum." I drank my drink

"How's the Hegley biog shaping up? Not that I believe that story for a minute, of course."

"It's proving elusive."

"Found a decent narrative?"

"How about 'Philip Hegley's alive and well and making shorts'?"

"That'd be a coup," she said.

"I see myself as the guy who has to track Hegley down before the bad guys get him."

"You're moving heavily into fiction." Harry crossed her legs, was all boot and high thigh from where I was sitting.

"It's because I bumped into Abdi at Raindance," I said.

"Haven't seen him for a dog's age. What's he up to?"

"About to start shooting a feature."

"Good for him."

"Also, he told me he was concerned we never became an item."

Harry smiled. "Sweet."

"I said you were in love with someone else."

"You did?"

"Are you?"

"Depends who's asking," she said. "Abdi?"

"No, yours truly."

"In that case, quite possibly. If things keep moving this quickly, Justin and I could end up getting hitched."

I managed to force out some kind of laugh.

"Tell you what," she said. "How about a double wedding with you and Meaghan the second couple? That way, you and I end up related."

* * *

After I left The Hospital, I was in poor frame of mind despite the fact that I was ferrying down the Thames. I'd invited Harry to play a couple of games of pool at the club in the hope that focusing on the simple rules of a simple game would rid me of my bad mood. But she turned me down and disappeared, even though she'd barely taken the top off her Bellini. Perhaps she couldn't wait to see Justin. I hadn't asked.

I got off the boat and headed towards Canary Wharf, wasn't looking forward much to the meeting. But I perked up in the office when Tariq gave Tabard and me a demo of the Routemaster pages. He'd done a bang-up job linking my revised text to the photos and to his sharp animations. In one clever sequence, users could get avatars to jump on buses at stops like the Tower and Buck House where the Routemasters would open up like doll houses to show their insides, revealing a mixed bag of passengers along with conductors catchily singing, *fares please*.

"Fantastic," I said.

"Fact is, we're already twenty percent ahead of our ad budget," Tabard said.

"When does it go live?" I asked.

"In two weeks. The launch party's on Brick Lane and all the big wigs, including the film guy who wants to meet you, will be there. Bring the missus, Root."

Chapter Eleven

The beer garden of the Shirley Ann pub in Peckham.
A fifteen-second long-shot of two men facing each
other across a table.
Cut to:
Boocock drinking a half. The other man holds a G&T
in two hands. He's in his late fifties, wears a
trilby.
Cut to:
The long-shot. The beer garden gives onto a busy
road with its drift of trucks, buses, black cabs,
cars often blocking our view of the two drinkers.
Cut to:
An over-the-shoulder shot of the G&T man's face.
We see now he has a pencil moustache that he often
strokes with his forefinger.
"They say you were a friend of Thom's, Mr Baron,"
Boocock says.
"He was a regular here."
"Like you."
"We regularly talked business." Baron takes a sip
of his drink.
"What sort of business?"
"The private kind."
"Did Thom work for you?"
"We were partners. In imports."
"They say the stuff just walked off the boats."
"They say a lot."
"Are they right?"

"It was strictly on the up."

"How did Thom cop it?"

"Canada Water. A nasty affair. The chains snapped, see. The pallet dropped a good thirty feet before it hit him. It was obvious he was an immediate goner."

"You saw it?"

"I only knew it was Thom when we dragged the pallet off. Messy. You wouldn't want to see the like."

"But he *was* dead."

"A dramatic end. Like one of the characters in your books."

"You've read them?"

"I'm a real fan of *Pier Pressure*."

"Not my best."

"Never pays to underestimate yourself."

Cut to:

The long-shot. There's a huge gap in the traffic. Boocock and Baron continue talking. Then a hearse travels right to left, followed by a cortege of slow-moving cars.

Fade to Black.

My head was still busy working through the images of the Shirley Ann scene on the way out to Abdi's shoot. I enjoyed the fact that we were forced to watch a personal conversation from afar, that we had to strain to listen in, that this construct made us want to catch every word more than ever. And the passing traffic created another physical barrier, the noise serving to stymie any possible eavesdropping. For me, the hearse was a beautiful full stop, a reminder of the passage of Thom Greene's life. I was moved.

I'd watched the camerawork closely too because, after seeing Hegley's short at Raindance, Abdi had decided he wanted that particular look and feel for his new film and had given a job to Greene

Land's director of photography Bob Crasker. This gave me a great chance of finding out more about what had become my favourite film, and about Hegley.

It was still early morning when I arrived with my audio gear at the Gunwhale Estate out near Surrey Water and the Rotherhithe Tunnel. It was a depopulated seventies council property and Adbi had successfully pleaded with the local authorities to give the last couple of blocks a stay of demolition for four weeks while he completed a shoot set almost entirely on location.

I found the crew crowded into the old caretaker's office, and someone immediately pushed an instant coffee and a heavily sugared doughnut into my mitt. Abdi had gone off with the cameraman checking out spots for scenes, would be back shortly, I was told. I took the opportunity to do some scouting of my own, went cup and pastry in hand on a Gunwhale walkabout.

The estate was bleak. The duo of one-hundred-and-fifty-yard-long barrack-style buildings faced up to each other across a narrow passage, shutting out much of the daylight. They also managed to funnel in a nasty kick of wind off the Thames. The concrete blocks lifted up to six storeys, would have been mirror images of each other but for the scores of satellite dishes that had been planted like thorns along the landings. The place had evidently been abandoned by the residents a while ago – most of the windowpanes were broken and rags of curtain strained through evil-looking glass shards to snap at the breeze.

"Root!"

I spotted Abdi waving, hurrying towards me with a powerful-looking, grey-haired guy in his sixties whom I took to be Crasker.

Abdi grabbed my hand. "Damn good to see you," he said. "Root Wilson, this is Bob. We're out spotting."

We shook greetings. Bob had in the corner of his mouth the stub of a bulging perfecto cigar that looked not to be lit.

"I hope Abdi's being nice to you," I said.

"He's silk compared to most."

"Follow me, Root," Abdi said. "We've absolutely found some great stuff, haven't we, Bob?"

He nodded. "I'll have to drop out here, Abs," he said. "I need to get back and do some prep."

"This way," Abdi told me.

I followed him into a stairwell and we climbed two flights until we were blocked by a series of two-by-fours nailed across a door frame. Abdi yanked a few of them away, then eased through the space. I squeezed after him and chased him up several flights stairs until I came out breathless on the top landing.

"The council would go positively crazy if they knew we were here," Abdi said. "But we can't possibly pass this up. Bob and I now have this idea of opening with a tracking shot of the protagonist pacing between the buildings. I see it running easily a good minute. Then there'll be a super-extreme close-up."

"Very Hegley."

Abdi smiled. "Come on, we need to start shooting soon."

We walked along the landing until we got to the northern end. The view was spectacular and we could see across the Thames to the towers at Canary Wharf – they were there to reach out and touch.

"This is a gold-plater of a location," I said.

"Pretty crisp." Abdi pulled open a small wooden door and started to climb a steel ladder. "Go steady."

I was glad of the warning as the way up was sticky. A couple of rungs were missing, most of the rest rattled in their mounts, and the ladder rocked from side to side on each step. I finally pulled myself up into a loft right beneath a low-pitched roof, Abdi lighting my way with a torch.

He swung the beam around and lit up what looked like a bedsit right under the eaves – there was a double mattress, a kitchen table and chairs, a two-seater leatherette sofa, even a dressing table with mirror.

"These are fresh footprints." I coughed. The dust hung thick in

Abdi's beam, smelled about a hundred years old. "It's unbelievable."

"I'm going to rewrite a couple of scenes and get this in," Abdi said. "It's an absolute gift."

Abdi shone the torch onto a brick chimney breast someone had spraypainted. There was a single silver word. *DETH*.

* * *

I spent the morning knocking back pints of instant coffee, watched Abdi and crew manage to shoot just two short scenes. The first had little more than one of the actors banging on a window and shouting through a letter box, but took a couple of hours to get right. The second boasted a couple of shaven-headed toughs smashing in a front door with a mediaeval-looking battering ram that fell to pieces when first put into action. It was a moody, a film fake, and had to be given first aid. A foot-length of gaffer tape and a half-dozen nails did the business.

Everyone broke for lunch and Abdi took me to a boat cafe he'd found down by the river. "I want to be good to my friends in the media," he said.

The moored boat was a Thames barge called The Gripie that had been refurbished and looked in top shape with its furled brown sails, richly waxed woodwork. We nabbed a table right up by a glossily painted leeboard and ordered food.

"What did you make of this morning?" Abdi asked.

"Bob knows his stuff."

"Having him and this location is a real dream."

"I'll do an item for the show," I said. "Helps us both out. Anything else I can do, just ask."

"There's a scene this afternoon. The actor phoned and says he's stuck on a set way outside London. So we're one short."

"You're surely not thinking I'll do it, are you?"

He stared at me.

"Look, I'm no performer," I said.

"You're a broadcaster. A legitimate public figure."

"Perfect face for radio, as they say."

"Don't go shy on me."

"I really don't think so, Abs."

"The part's scarcely a step-up from being an extra. And think how good it will be for your programme."

"I'm not sure." I knew, though, that he was totally right.

"Come on, Root. It's non-speaking."

"Well, as long as I get to keep my clothes on."

He laughed.

*　*　*

When we got back from lunch, wardrobe went to work, dressed me for the scene in a soiled white T-shirt and blue jeans out at the knee, along with a pair of shabby black Converse. Makeup painted my face, mussed my hair.

Abdi walked me over to the set, a single room in one of the abandoned flats.

"This hasn't been at all scripted," he told me. "We need to improvise, given the nature of the scene."

"Which is what? You haven't told me a thing." I was beginning to feel nervous, knew I should've turned him down.

"It's very straightforward. There's a tart waiting for you in the room. You're the punter, see. All you have to do is go in, have quick sex, then leave pronto."

"Funny."

"Honest."

"There's no way…"

"Come on, it's not as if you have to be bollock-naked," he said. "All we're asking for is a bit of simulation. It'll be just a few seconds in the film."

"Abs… "

"Here, stick this down your pants." He handed me a wedge of sponge. "Protects both parties to the act."

"Christ, I haven't even met her."

"Which is why we went to lunch. I didn't want to risk you seeing her. The fact that you haven't clapped eyes on this woman before will be a terrific shot in the arm for the scene. You walk into the shot, you do your man stuff and you go."

"Bloody hell, Abs."

"I'll tell you what," he laughed. "Go in there and if you don't fancy her in the slightest, pretend you're doing it with Harry."

I felt sick.

* * *

I stood by the door. Held my breath. Heard Abdi shout *action*. I couldn't move. I thought of Roney and his sex scene. Surely if *he* could. But he was an actor. I wasn't. I wanted to be back in the studio. Safe. Fuck you, Abdi.

Then I *was* moving. I was walking into the room, blocking the camera, the crew. I saw her. She stood with her back to the wall. Had on a skin-thin yellow summer dress. I walked over. I unfastened my jeans. I dropped them to my ankles. I lifted her dress, lifted her. I pressed her against the wall. She tied her legs around me. I certainly didn't think of Harry. Here I was with Theresa Noble.

* * *

Abdi clapped me hard across the back when it was over. "Crisp," he said.

"How come you signed Theresa up?" I asked. "You picking over Hegley's bones?"

"Once I got the idea for Bob, I decided to do the homage thing."

"You should've told me."

"Watch this space because there's more to come." He slapped me on the back again. "Thanks for your help, Root."

Everyone moved on to the next set-up, leaving me alone in the room. Theresa's fragrance was there with me, though, a hard, cheap scent she must have picked up for the role and used to get in character. I could also feel a soreness in the small of my back where she'd clawed me through my shirt. I rubbed my neck where she'd taken a bite.

I made my way back to wardrobe, changed into my clothes. I went outside and found a pool of sun, drank more coffee, ate half a packet of chocolate digestives, even cadged a cigarette – the first I'd lit up in years – from one of the sparks. He told me he enjoyed my scene, said he recognised my face from TV, *The Bill isn't it?* He asked what else I'd been working on, didn't seem worried by my lack of response to everything. He strolled off into the long space between the buildings. I watched him, a couple of cables coiled over a shoulder, toolbox in hand, until he slipped into a doorway.

Theresa arrived. "Root," she said, "now I *know* you like me."

Chapter Twelve

I watched the crew set up the last couple of shots of the day, which involved a simple chase up a flight of stairs. It took close to two hours to hook up the lamps to get the mood that Abdi and Bob were after. Abdi was as fastidious about the look of the film as I'd have guessed, fussing over the slightest false shadow. His director of photography, though, was on another level entirely. He was absolutely painstaking, metered every centimetre of the set, got on the crew's back to make changes that to my eye made not the slightest difference. I should have expected nothing less, though, from a Hegley crony.

The first shot was straightforward enough. Randall, a thin, long-legged black kid wearing a bright red knitted hat, ran to the foot of the stairs, hung there half a second to check behind him, then doublestepped up and out of the frame. Five seconds later he was followed by the protagonist, a character called Freddie, who pretty much threw himself into the stairwell, was up away in one fluid movement. Freddie was played by Alan Smithee, a one-hundred-percent method man. I'd watched him earlier practising the move on a different set of stairs, always with the full run-up, and the accumulated sweat from that kind of fanaticism had been making life tricky for makeup.

Abdi reckoned the first take excellent. "Just one more for safety."

Randall and Freddie ran through the scene once again, to my mind a little less impressively. The whole show then moved up one storey.

Bob, though, wasn't at all happy with the lighting in the new location, and each time he metered, he swore to himself. He kept pulling a notebook from his shirt pocket, jotting down figures with a stub of a pencil he wore under his watch strap. He found a slab of wall that wasn't entirely covered in graffiti and sketched out a representation of the scene on grubby whitewash, drew a number of diagonal lines, daubed the whole construct with numbers he took from his book. He worked his way through a handful of equations, checked them over with a forefinger and marched over to the crew who then worked the lamps in a new configuration.

Bob took out his light meter, declared himself happy, though the look on his face hardly seemed to agree.

The shot, which had the two actors coming out at the top of the stairwell, needed six takes. It was clear Freddie was tired and he caught his foot on the last step, falling into a sprawl on the concrete. That seemed to gee him up and after that he carried the stairs quite comfortably. Randall then hurt his calf, everyone concerned he might have pulled it, but it was a cramp that was eased by some massage work from one of the wardrobe girls you could see he had a thing for. Another take was ruined by a plane that suddenly screamed low overhead. We waited a while until the world settled. Abdi then managed to get two for the can.

The set began to dissolve.

I watched Bob destroy the drawing he'd made on the whitewash with the heel of his hand. He scratched a few more notes in his book, tucked it back in his shirt pocket, slid the pencil under his watchstrap.

"Good day's work?" I asked.

"Fair. I knew we'd have trouble towards the end. Everyone was overtired and things were getting loose."

"Even Freddie was less than steady."

"Yes, even Freddie."

Bob picked up the camera and I offered to carry the lens bag. As we walked, talked, I got him to agree to an interview for the programme.

Back at HQ, while he stashed his gear, I fired up mine, did a sound check and was ready to roll.

"You happy with the shoot so far?" I asked him.

"Happy as you can ever be. I think it's a good script and I see eye-to-eye with the director."

"That usually a problem?"

"More often than I'd like."

"How was it on *Greene Land*? Did Philip Hegley live up to his reputation?"

"He was a perfectionist."

"Which caused difficulties?"

"Sometimes."

"What about the overruns? The costs were out of control, weren't they?"

"We did what we had to."

"You were after prime picture?"

"Neither of us would compromise."

"Did you know what you had was special?"

"It was clear that it was good."

"A masterpiece?"

"That's an important word. It's not for me to use it."

"The critics have. Especially about the photography."

"I'm proud of what I did."

"I'm a huge fan of *Greene Land*. The look's terrific. How did you decide on it?"

"Well, let's say it's simply *The Third Man* and then some. We ratcheted up the contrast. We tightened the angles as far as they'd go."

"Why *The Third Man*? Was it some big artistic influence?"

Bob looked at me as if I were an idiot. "Because *Greene Land* is a remake set in the London docks."

I ran a few of the scenes from *Greene Land* through my head, matched them with my memory of the older film. That's exactly what it was. And I hadn't bothered to look for it because of my huge block when it came to British film.

I FOUND OUT RECENTLY THAT HARRY LIME DIDN'T PERISH IN THE VIENNESE SEWERS IN *THE THIRD MAN* AFTER ALL. INSTEAD, HE LED A LIFE THEREAFTER ON THE THEATRE OF THE AIR. OBVIOUSLY, THE FACT THAT A FILMIC CHARACTER LIKE LIME HAD A CAREER ON THE RADIO IS INTENSELY INTRIGUING TO ME. AND SOMETHING I FEEL I SHOULD'VE ALREADY KNOWN. THE RADIO SERIES WAS CALLED *THE LIVES OF HARRY LIME* AND THE PROTAGONIST NEVER PRETENDED HE WAS DEAD, HE JUST MAINTAINED THAT HE HAD PRE-VIENNA STORIES WORTH SHARING. AND LIME IS SWEETER ON THE AIRWAVES THAN ON FILM, WITH THE DIRTY RACKETEER TRANSFORMED INTO WHAT'S CLOSE TO BEING A LOVEABLE ROGUE. THE SERIES WAS BROADCAST ON THE OLD BBC LIGHT PROGRAMME IN THE EARLY FIFTIES, AND THE SHOWS OPENED WITH THE SHARP AUDIO OF A GUN GOING OFF. THE EPISODES TOTED GREAT TITLES – SEE NAPLES AND LIVE, EARL ON TROUBLED WATERS, CHERCHEZ LA GEM. AND I ALSO DISCOVERED THAT, IN THE EARLY NINETEEN SIXTIES, THE BBC PRODUCED A TV SERIES, ALSO CALLED *THE THIRD MAN*, THAT RAN FOR ALMOST 80 EPISODES. I'VE NEVER SEEN IT BUT I DON'T THINK I CAN RESIST GOING OFF TO THE BEEB'S ARCHIVES TO SEARCH FOR IT. DON'T WAIT FOR ME ON THE HARRY LIME FRONT, THOUGH. THERE'S A TALK THIS WEEK ON *THE THIRD MAN* AT THE NATIONAL GALLERY, AND A SHOWING OF A FRESH NEW PRINT OF THE MOVIE. MAKE SURE YOU GO ALONG. TO QUOTE YET ANOTHER TITLE, ART IS LONG AND LIME IS FLEETING. CUE THAT ZITHER.

My piece on *The Third Man* was a means of making amends for being shown up by Bob Crasker. I'd embarrassed myself and felt I needed to find out more about Carol Reed's film before I tackled another viewing of *Greene Land*. I could see where Hegley had taken his cues, but it was clear the storyline had been changed and that he and Crasker had worked hard to big up the original's elements. Overall, *Greene Land* was far grainier, something I felt suited the London location – *The Third Man* was doing Cold

War ambience with its clear antagonisms, while *Greene Land* was shady docks milieu writ large, and it spilled guts and grit. And what Crasker had told me about honing the angles was certainly true. *The Third Man* delivered some truly breathtaking points of view, but *Greene Land*'s perspectives were often so astounding it was difficult to watch the scene and follow the narrative at the same time. And that seemed to me a beautiful take on noir's inherently confusing plot turns. An idea was now beginning to form about what I could do with any film I might make. Of course, that didn't mean I was taking Tabard's word for it on the hotdog media company's intentions.

* * *

I put a call in to Justin.

"I've got something pretty cool for you," I said.

"Tell me, my friend. The way I feel right now I could take on the world."

"A pal of mine's shooting a film. I've read the script, seen the rushes. It's top product. What he doesn't yet have, though, is someone to do the soundtrack."

"Hey, that's big news."

"It's just an indie affair, you know."

"Be major for me, though."

"A chance to follow in your father's footsteps."

"Steady."

"Sorry, I wasn't meaning to…"

"You're right, though. I can't possibly discount my heritage. And it's an incentive."

"To outdo the old man, you mean?"

"Well, he's there to be shot at."

"Sock it to him, I say. Even though he's a nice bloke."

"Easy to say when you're not carrying his genes."

"Let's not turn the pressure up too much," I said. "Have you ever done a film score?"

"I worked up something once for a documentary, though it never got made."

"Tell you what we'll do. I'll put together a package of the treatment, a few pages from the shooting script and ask Abdi to send over some footage on DVD."

"Sounds cracking."

"My advice is to play with some ideas, as many as you can."

"The more the merrier, you mean?"

"One can't be de trop with Abdi."

"Thanks for this, my friend. You're a jewel."

"They all tell me that."

"Harry certainly thinks so."

I saw Justin and Harry, their heads side-by-side on a single pillow, Justin saying something to make her laugh, Harry kissing him on the nose, nuzzling his shoulder, Justin's huge hands cradling her head as the perfect pair began kissing again in all passion…

"She said everyone used to think you two would be an item," Justin said. "But you always had eyes for others."

"Is that right?" I wanted to slam the phone down. Much as I liked Justin, had we been face-to-face, I might well have committed bodily harm.

Chapter Thirteen

I was putting the finishing touches to Roger Huckerby's obituary for Junior, whose offer of two pounds a word had been too tempting to pass up. I'd managed to raise a decent amount of info on old Huckerby and his time on earth, was pretty pleased with the end result. It had turned out far better than the obit I'd put together for Hegley, and I felt I was getting to grips with the form. It was clearly best to open with a few graphs that delivered, in full colour, an incident in the deceased's life, one that captured either the essence of their character, or that summed up what they'd done to even merit an obituary. With Huckerby it had to be, of course, his involvement with the British cinema firmament's current brightest star, Philip Hegley.

I managed to get a gem of a story from Huckerby's widow. With something in it for H&P, Junior couldn't do enough to help out and he patched me through to his mother in Spain. The two of us got on so well we ended up chatting on the phone for an hour. She'd been at the funeral, of course, and though I hadn't presumed to speak to her in her grief, I was able put a face to the voice. And she seemed quite content to talk about her husband, probably felt safe doing so with an anonymous stranger sitting hundreds of miles away.

She told me about the time the cast of *Greene Land* had been shipped to an old Essex manor house for a week on a retreat in preparation for the shoot, and Huckerby had driven out there for the day to see Hegley.

"Roger was beet-faced when he got back," she said. "He went on and on about the shenanigans."

"Did he tell you what had been going on?"

"Well…Roger said he was walking across the lawn with Philip Hegley and there was this couple in full view."

"Full view?"

"In flagrante. He said Hegley didn't bat an eye."

"Sounds like there were tons of affairs on these retreats."

"Oh yes."

"Anything else?"

"The brawling. A fellow named Naysmith broke his finger on someone's head. Roger said he'd run him over to the hospital but he wouldn't have it, even with his finger twice the size."

That'd be the digit that gave Naysmith such an odd handshake. I could almost feel that relic of *Greene Land* jabbing into my palm again.

"I'll bet Roger feared for the film after his day trip," I said.

She laughed. "Over dinner he suddenly threw up his hands. He shouted, '*Greene Land* will be a tour de force … or a complete débâcle."

That was just the kind of quote I was after for the obit, of course.

I asked Mrs Huckerby about the days leading up to the car accident, wondered about her husband's mood, if he'd seemed agitated. He'd been very much as always, she said, working his few hours in the morning before taking her out to lunch down by the port, coming back for a late and long afternoon nap. He'd been nervy about going to Malaga, but then he never really enjoyed driving on the local roads.

I asked her if she'd ever seen Roger with an exceptionally tall man. She couldn't recall anyone quite like that, but they rarely had visitors.

And that wrapped up our call.

I read through the obit once more, felt that the only thing that could improve it would be a quote from Hegley. One dead man's view of another would be something of a progression in the art of obituary writing for sure. With that thought, I zapped the piece over to Junior.

I hopped on a train at London Bridge, got off a few stops later, headed straight for Woolwich Cemetery and moviemaking disappointment. The burial ground was nothing like the one Hegley and Crasker had conjured up for that memorable scene in *Greene Land*. Gone were the broad vistas, the long, unadulterated gravel walkways, the wide sky that had afflicted the scene. Woolwich Cemetery was instead a cosy, grassy place, looking more a local park fit for family outings than a place to bring the departed. I walked the pathways, seeing nothing that belonged to the shots I knew so well in *Greene Land*. Perhaps they'd been filmed in an entirely different spot, were likely a composite of several locations. I felt duped, but also foolish that I'd expected anything more – I obviously needed to be much more on my guard when it came to things Hegley.

On my way out, I came across a white marble Celtic cross commemorating the Princess Alice disaster. In the eighteen-seventies, the pleasure boat went down after colliding with a steamer at Woolwich, and the inscription said more than six hundred Alice passengers had died, a figure that dwarfed the contemporary Thames' one-body-a-week statistic I'd once found so frightening. It was a gloomy thought in a gloomy place.

I left the cemetery and made for Woolwich High Street, searched in vain for the Café Mozart, though its absence now came as no real surprise. And the local street market was nothing more than a smatter of stalls, a minnow compared to the one portrayed in *Greene Land*, though I had no idea whether that was Hegley's and Crasker's historical misdoing or if Iceland, Argos and a succession of pound shops had been busy making over the area.

The river was no great shakes in this part of London either, pooling heavy as it did in a thick and lifeless gunshot grey between the edge of Woolwich where I now stood and Silvertown on the opposing bank. The ferry that had a while ago cast off seemed to be making scant progress, while the planes heading for City Airport appeared to hang in the air forever, ornamented between the tall steel chimneys of the Tate & Lyle sugar refinery. I imagined passengers from the Alice fighting to escape the ship, being dragged down to the bottom of this treacly river.

Then I saw the Thames Barrier. Its plated stainless shells reared from the water, caught and reflected what little daylight there was from a cloud-charged sky. They roiled the surface of the river, too, showed off the force of the incoming tide. I was completely taken by the power of the current, couldn't possibly leave yet. I watched until the sun went down and the Thames turned jet and cold.

* * *

Meaghan and I were eating at the tapas bar by the market. The place had become completely loaded since we'd arrived, our cosy and quiet table by the window now hemmed by a rowdy ruck of City boys that had entered en masse and ordered bloody sangria pitchers.

Meaghan hadn't spoken for five minutes, was concentrating overly on pushing patatas bravas around her plate while I scoffed up a couple of plates of food.

"Something up?" I asked.

"I can't stop wondering about this Austria business."

"What's to think about until you've been and seen?"

"That's just it. They want me to go to Vienna next Tuesday."

"But that's the day of the hotdog party in Brick Lane."

Meaghan gave up on her plate, dropped the fork heavily on the table.

"Ask them to change the date," I said. "If all you're doing is meeting the bods in the office, what difference does it make?"

"I have to visit the Salzburg agency and glad-hand there, too. Everyone who's anyone will be at the Mozart concert the company's sponsoring that evening."

"I didn't know it was a sleepover," I said.

Meaghan shrugged. She seemed far away. I wanted to reach

across and take her hand. But at the same time, I didn't.

"They said you could come," she said.

"You know I'm meeting a bigwig to discuss the film and I really do want you there. This could be a huge deal, Megs. I have a whopping idea."

"Which is?"

"Can't tell anyone right now."

"Not even me?"

"I don't want to hex it."

She grabbed her fork once more, began tapping the tines against her glass. "So, what we're saying is that we both have important irons in the fire."

"I do hate it when you make everything sound so perfectly reasonable."

"Sorry for being too sensible," she said.

The ruck broke out in a loud laugh and I missed what Meaghan said next.

"Sorry, Megs, I can't hear a thing."

She leaned in closer. "Why do I have to come with you?" she shouted.

"Tabard thinks they might offer good money. I need to present a solid image. I have to play corporate for once."

"And me being there with you will lend you respectability?"

"For sure."

"Really?"

"It's a compliment."

"You think I'm some kind of human pinstripe suit."

I grinned at her.

"That wasn't meant to be funny," she said. "You really do believe I'm an acceptable shade of grey, don't you?"

"You're incredibly touchy."

"Well, let's just say you were taking Harriet to the party rather than Meaghan?"

"What on earth does she have to do with anything?"

"I'm doing a bit of supposing, that's all."

I didn't know what to say, was trying to work out what the rules might be in this sudden Megs-versus-Aitch game.

"Come on, Root. What would Harriet do for your fabulous pitch?" Meaghan was furiously gathering her hair, pushing it behind her ears.

"Your suppose doesn't work because Harry's a mover in the industry."

"But if she weren't and you were to take her along?"

"Oh, please." I had the sense that the response that might make this right simply didn't exist. "Harry's too risky. She's…well, she's *too*."

"You mean she's cool and exciting."

"Look…"

"Yes, she's a very sharp lady."

"But…"

"And I'm just a dull edge."

"I never said that."

"Actually, I rather think you did. And I believe you've always thought it."

"That's ridiculous."

Meaghan shook her head.

"Tell you what," I said. "I won't go to the do. I'll head to Vienna instead."

"Sorry, what did you say?" She leaned in closer.

"I'd like to be the dutiful partner and come to Austria with you," I said loudly.

"I don't want you to."

"I've been disinvited?"

"I'm thinking of your career, Root."

"What about *your* career?"

"What about it?"

"The trip's an absolute waste," I said. "It's not as if you're thinking of living in Vienna, is it?"

"I actually think it would be a good move for me."

Meaghan sat back in her chair, a horrid smile on her face that made her lips thin as wire.

"Well, thanks for discussing it," I said. "I wouldn't have liked this news to have been a bolt out of the blue or anything."

The ruck cheered. Meaghan and I were very much in the wrong place for this row. Or maybe it was exactly the right one.

Meaghan jabbed the fork in my direction. "It's rare you give my life the time of day."

"Well, here's something. Up sticks and go to Vienna and you do it alone." I couldn't believe I'd said it flat out like that.

"Is that an ultimatum?"

Tears were beginning to choke her eyes. This was the time to pull back, to make things right once more if that was what I wanted.

"I'm simply saying it would be pointless me moving to Austria," I said.

"Would you go for Harriet?"

"What on earth is all this about Harry?" I asked.

"Funny how you always light up when she's mentioned."

"For Christ's sake, she's going great guns with your brother."

"She'd rather be letting off live rounds with you, and you know it."

"Where do you get this stuff from?"

"It's what Justin tells me."

"But he's besotted with Harry. And she's head over heels with him."

"Her head isn't over *you*."

"Oh, come on."

"And neither is her heart."

"This is insane."

"And I'd think more of you, Root Wilson, if you could admit you felt the same about her."

Meagan tossed her wine in my face. We silenced the City boys for the first time that evening.

*　*　*

119

Daily life after the awful quarrel became thoroughly depressing. The domestic two of us offered each other little more than close-the-door-behind-you-when-you-leave talk. Neither of us tried making up, in part, I supposed, because we both felt we were in the right, but also because we'd never had a row of that magnitude before and were in shock. Meaghan had, of course, been correct in saying I'd issued her with an ultimatum on Austria, and the truth was I knew I didn't care for her enough to give up everything I'd built in London. And especially not right now when some big-ticket items were coming on stream. At the same time, I didn't want to lose her. I was in an odd place.

But I certainly wasn't going to waste my time asking the question whether my decision would be the same were Harry part of the Austrian equation instead of her. What did she have to do with any of this?

The drink in the face before an audience of fools had been a humiliating experience, and Meaghan had left me sitting there dripping wine while I paid the bill. That wasn't something I was going to forget in a hurry. And I was angry at Megs for pulling my best friend into our deteriorating relationship unnecessarily.

I stopped sleeping in the bedroom, spent long nights on the sofa. Sometimes I waited for Meaghan to come to me in the night and make things good again, others I stopped myself from banging on her door and giving her a telling off about poor Harry. I always fell asleep just before it was time to get up. And when Meaghan took off for Austria, I decided not to move back to the bed. It seemed I didn't want to feel too at home in our home any longer.

She left for the airport with no news about when she planned to come back, if, indeed, she aimed to return to the flat at all. I wanted to talk to someone, and normally that person would have been Harry. But I thought it best to hold my fire now that she'd been pointlessly dragged into this affair. I certainly wouldn't be taking her to the hotdog event as my guest. I would never give Meaghan the satisfaction.

CHAPTER FOURTEEN

I arrived at the Vibe Bar for the launch with no one hanging on my arm. Given the stakes, I'd felt the need to spruce up proper, and so was wearing my best – a lightweight Dries Van Noten suit with a subtle herringbone pattern, a plain white shirt from the same designer, a Pucci tie that was yellow and blue in the best way. I was good and ready for the evening's proceedings, I thought.

The venue, a music hang for the Shoreditch cool mob, was full of corporate perks-and-pensions types busy clashing with the contemporary-baroque interior and stainless steel Chesterfields. I scanned the crowd for Tabard, for Tariq, for anyone on the team, but no joy. I began to wonder if any of the faces I could see belonged to the big banana Tabard told me I was slated to meet. But that thought made me nervy – it seemed a possible film deal was hanging on the say-so of someone able to sign off hundreds of thousands of notes like it was lunch money. I needed pluck, lifted a champagne off a passing silver tray.

"One for me, too."

Minona was right by me. I handed her the glass, quickly grabbed another for myself.

"What're you doing here?" I asked.

"You don't sound at all happy to see me. And here I was thinking I'd scrubbed up rather well."

And she had. Minona had on an almost-sheer black top cinched at the waist with a thin leather belt that turned several times around her midriff, bit at her flesh through fetching side vents. She also wore a pair of tight dark satiny pants, the legs finishing just above the knee where they were tied off in bows.

"You're well-wrapped," I said.

"That's a compliment, right?"

"You'd make a beautiful present for someone."

Minona gave me a mock coy look. This wasn't the 'biz ms' I was used to dealing with.

"To answer your opening question," she said, "I'm here for the firm."

"The firm?"

"Ferris Media. The one that pays our wages, remember?"

"Ferris owns the studios?" I asked.

"Plus everything else in-between and either side, of course. You should pay more attention to the business side of your life."

A dense bass chord hung around the room. I saw three guys up on the corner stage. The bald one grabbed the mic. "We're The Former Dictators and we're going to sing 'Judderman'." The band launched into a number that was full of angular guitar sounds and threw off a neat siren riff.

I wanted to tell Minona that I'd been listening to the Dictators for months now, but she'd disappeared. It was the first time I could ever remember feeling disappointed at not seeing her.

I did finally spot Tabard, though, and I made my way through a crush of arms and shoulders towards the back of the room.

"Man of the moment," he shouted above the music.

"You'll tell me anything."

"Fact. You're going to take us all higher, Root Wilson."

"Anyone ever mention you have greater expectations than Charles Dickens?"

He smiled. "Follow me."

"Is this where I get to meet the big guy?" I asked.

Tabard led the way, and we ducked by the Dictators, the lead singer delivering some cutting line about jaws biting, claws catching. We went into the cobbled courtyard and took a few steps into a marquee richly hung with a dozen glass chandeliers in acid colours, the bulbs in them flaring for a few seconds before slowly dimming, blazing once more.

"Root, this is Watson Wyatt," Tabard said.

I held out a hand and Wyatt, an industrial-looking, early-forties of a man, shook it while he clamped my elbow. He wore a row of rings you could have cracked locks with.

"Some tasty words you put together for us," he said.

"Mr Tabard here should be my agent."

"Talent doesn't need salesmanship."

"I reckon freelancers need all the boostering they can get."

"Your show's first-string," Wyatt said.

"I'm flattered."

"Save the false modesty. We like you enough. Which is why we're giving you time. But you still have to work for the money."

I looked around for Tabard but he'd melted away. I was on my own. I looked at Wyatt. He looked at me. The chandeliers toned his face blue, changed it to a light rouge, then suddenly flamed his skin crimson. The atmosphere was that of a seventies psychedelic movie. It had all the makings of a decent scene. To make it a great one, I needed to deliver the pitch of my career, the one I'd been prepping for days. And that's exactly what I did. I picked it up, held it firm and punchy from the tag, then chased it right through to the payoff.

Wyatt stood in an emerald light. He shook my hand again, clamped my elbow once more.

* * *

I left the marquee, went back into a dive bar that had quietened down since the Former Dictators had finished their set. At the counter, I found the stiff-backed Roney and right by him, naturally, stood Naysmith. Everyone who was almost anyone was here, or so it seemed. I wouldn't have been entirely surprised if Hegley had popped up too.

"Don't tell me you're in sway to Ferris as well," I said.

"I work for a chap named Tabard," he said.

"Doing what?"

"Voiceovers for the avatars. At least I think that's what they call those on-screen characters." He spoke in terrific imitation of Bart Simpson.

"Hey, can you do Yogi Bear?"

"Smarter than the average mimic," he said.

"That's excellent." I looked at Naysmith. "What about you, Boo Boo?"

"Steady," Naysmith said, his neck tightening at me. "You've had one too many."

"Actually, I'm only just beginning to celebrate. And I want to talk to your boss."

"Is that so?" Roney said.

"Tell Mr Hegley to stop making those shorts. If he wants to shoot a feature, he should meet me at the London Eye at ten sharp on Thursday."

"He can't come along just like that."

"He can," I said. "And, for once, I think he will."

* * *

I was sitting on the steps outside the bar and was totally chuffed. The deal with Watson Wyatt had opened everything up. Not only was I able to parlay it into a meeting with Hegley, I now believed I had a good chance of being able to make a film with the man. And from what I knew of him, he wouldn't turn his nose up at my offer. It meant the end, too, of all those mysterious messages, the last-minute meeting opportunities and let-downs. I'd finally taken control. The chase was over.

I was shaken from my triumphant thoughts when someone sat himself down next to me on the steps. As I moved over to make room, I noticed a pristine pair of brogues. The wearer also had on a sharply cut piano-black suit.

"I hear congratulations are in order," Nesh said.

Right on cue, here was another individual from the cast of characters that made up the current version of my life. "And where did you come from?"

"I have the knack of appearing to be everywhere at once."

"I'm not a fan of your calling-card games."

"I believe it's polite to let people know when one's dropped by."

"Do you think Roger Huckerby appreciated the gesture?"

"I suppose he had little time to consider it properly."

"Did you top him?"

He laughed.

"Certainly you scared him partially to death," I said.

"I do nothing by halves."

"What portion of your activities do you devote to me?"

"You, you're a full-on kind of character, Root."

"Well, thanks."

"Anyhow, as I said, you should be congratulated for getting money out of Ferris," he said.

"You're well-informed."

"It's my job."

"What is your job exactly?" I asked

"I like to think I steer people in the right direction."

"And where would you like to lead me?"

"I have you exactly where I want you."

"You know, Mr A E Nesh, you're really starting to chafe."

"It's easy enough to stop the friction."

"I'm not giving up on Philip Hegley."

"Dear, dear," he said. "This really isn't the way to live happily ever after."

* * *

I left the Vibe Bar with Minona, and we hailed a cab.

"Is that a film deal in your pocket, or…?" she asked. She edged closer to me on the back seat of the taxi, touched her lips briefly on my neck. "You do it for me."

"Is this a sudden thing?"

"I always got turned on bullying you."

"I never had you pegged for a sadist." I kissed her on the throat,

125

gave her a light bite.

"Ow," she said. "I always loved staying cool when you got mad."

"You used to get off on it?"

"Immensely."

"You did a good job keeping the lid on."

"Now I can barely restrain myself." She ran a fingernail down my cheek. "And when we get to my place, Root, don't feel you have to be at all careful with the china."

* * *

Minona lived on the fifth floor of a redbrick mansion block in Fitzrovia, and her two-bed was decked out as simply and as functionally as a hotel room, with everything in its place, and every expensive thing placed impeccably. There was a Persian rug in the middle of the hardwood floor, a chocolate-brown leather sofa, a narrow tubular lamp that stretched its way to the ceiling.

Minona looked gorgeous in the room's rich ivory light that shone through her top. I put my hands on her hips, pulled her towards me, kissed her.

She pushed me away. "You're not quite ready," she said.

Minona took my hand and led me down the hallway to the bathroom where she unknotted my tie, unbuttoned my shirt, bared my torso. She took a bar of soap from the dish and worked up an extravagant lather with her hands. She painted my face with rich foam.

I saw the razor on the shelf, pink with tiny flowers trailing down the handle. I picked it up, but Minona snatched it away.

"My job," she said.

She cut me on the first pass over my chin. My finger found the spot and a dab of blood.

"I'm not practised at this," she said. "Let me try again."

I looked at the razor in her hand, watched it close in on me. "Are you telling me you don't shave all your dates?" I asked.

"I don't date, I mate."

She kissed me firmly on the lips, got lather on her cheeks. I wiped it away with my thumb.

"Now, pull a face like you men do," she said.

I did what she asked and the razor made a couple of perfect passes over my skin. Minona worked carefully above my top lip, looked immensely satisfied when she'd finished. She moved on to my throat.

I watched her in the mirror. It seemed the best way to take myself away from what was happening, so I wouldn't spoil it by taking hold of her then and there. I noticed the scent of the soap for the first time, something sweet. It was almost overpowering, gave me some kind of high.

"Nice smell," I said.

"Jaqua. Piña Colada."

"I feel spoiled."

"I'm giving you one of my luxuries," she said.

"I'm worth it."

"You'd better be."

"Don't tell me I'm risking my job," I said.

"I'll definitely be keeping a close eye on your ratings."

She ran the razor over my cheek, along my jaw in a long, slow curve, was completely concentrated on the task. This would have been the oddest thing to experience with any woman, with my boss it was practically outlandish. At the same time, though, it felt exquisite.

"What's it like to shave a man?" I asked.

"This," she said, "is incredibly sensual."

"Almost finished?"

She rubbed my chin with her forefinger. "We're getting so very close."

I placed my hand inside one of the vents of her top, ran a finger along the length of leather belt where it ate into her. I jumped as Minona cut me again.

"Let a girl concentrate," she said.

"I want her to focus on other things."

"Don't tell me you're feeling neglected."

She put down the razor, picked up a towel. She wiped my face, neck and checked my skin carefully with her fingertips.

"I think you're done," she said.

"Feels that way."

"Now, didn't you say earlier that I was well wrapped? I think it's time you untied a few of my bows, don't you?"

* * *

Minona turfed me out of her flat early hours, and I walked through one deserted square after the other before managing to flag down a taxi in front of the British Museum. I got it to head south and, as the cab edged from one red light to the next in an endless succession of barren junctions, I began to feel miserably alone. I knew I didn't belong with Minona, didn't belong with Meaghan…didn't belong with anyone.

The driver was silent until we started over London Bridge, the only other traffic a night bus lit like an office block and making its way empty towards us from the far side.

"Don't I know you from TV?" she asked.

"I work on the radio."

"That'll be it."

"Atypical, topical, digital."

She nodded. "I rarely miss a show."

"Glad to have you with us."

I looked east along the river. There was nothing on the water. And the tide was out, muddied banks baring themselves to no one, while Tower Bridge looked tonight to be little more than Thames bling. I didn't want to be here, though the last thing I needed was to go back to what had become half a home.

"Take me to Union Street, will you?" I told the cabbie. "Waterloo end."

"I thought you said"

"I want to make a detour."

I got the driver to drop me outside Harry's building, paid her off with a decent tip. "Stay tuned," I said.

The taxi rode away down the road. I watched it until I could make out only the rear lights which finally drifted around a corner and were gone. I stood by the door, counted the buzzers from the bottom up until I got to Harry's. I spent ages almost pressing the button before I gave up and walked back to the flat. I made it home just before the sun came up, drank a pint of milk straight from the carton. I bedded down on the sofa without even taking off my best suit.

Chapter Fifteen

It was mid-afternoon before I got up next day. I'd woken hours earlier and lay uncomfortably on the couch through a battery of messages as everyone rang to congratulate me on the deal. I didn't pick the phone up once, wasn't tempted even when Harry called. *Absolutely fantastic news. Proud of you, Bro.*

I did, though, keep rereading the letter Meaghan had posted me from Heathrow. I enjoyed looking at the shape of her lettering, the beautiful curlicues that almost sang out. She hadn't written a lot, but I felt the need to put as much meaning as possible into what she'd given me. *Root, I have to get out. Will be in touch about next moves.* Now, *moves* sounded very dramatic, and I imagined her clearing the place, me standing useless as the truck made off, took with it what had been 'us'. But, really, *moves* could mean nothing less than she had decided to take the job in Austria. Now, while I wasn't sure I wanted to be with Meaghan, I didn't want to be without her. If she went to Vienna, I'd barely see her, if at all. I added to the mix the fact I'd spent a few hours screwing Minona – being screwed by Minona? – and factored in my hanging pointlessly outside Harry's place. What the thinking time on the sofa made me realise at last was that En Root Wilson had become horribly derailed.

I spent a day last week on location. The film is called *Gunwhale*, and is one that those in the know reckon will be this year's Brit sleeper. The shoot was over in the southeast on the Gunwhale Estate, a soon-not-to-be set of council flats close to the river. It's not the first occasion that this unlovely part of London has had a role on film, though, because it once served a little time in Philip

130

HEGLEY'S *GREENE LAND*. AND TO SHOW THAT WHAT GOES AROUND OFTEN COMES AROUND, *GUNWHALE*'S DIRECTOR OF PHOTOGRAPHY IS NONE OTHER THAN BOB CRASKER. BOB WAS HEGLEY'S SIDEKICK ON *GREENE LAND* AND HE TOLD ME THE OTHER DAY HOW THE TWO OF THEM WORE THEMSELVES DOWN ON THAT SHOOT. IT HAD BEEN CLEAR EARLY ON THEY HAD SOMETHING A CUT ABOVE, AND THEY WERE DETERMINED TO GO THE LAST MILE, YARD, INCH TO ACHIEVE, WELL, YES, A MASTERPIECE. BOB AND PHILIP WERE IMMENSELY COMPETITIVE, DETERMINED TO OUTDO ONE ANOTHER ON EACH SUCCESSIVE TAKE. *GREENE LAND* ENDED UP CONSUMING VAST AMOUNTS OF CELLULOID, SOMETHING THAT HELPED PROPEL THE FILM WILDLY OVER BUDGET. THEY KNEW THAT. THEY DIDN'T CARE. ALL THAT MATTERED WAS GETTING PRIME PICTURE. PHILIP HEGLEY DIDN'T MAKE ANOTHER FEATURE, BOB CRASKER HAS DONE DOZENS SINCE. HE NEVER SAW THE DIRECTOR AGAIN ONCE GREENE WRAPPED, BUT HE SAYS A NUMBER OF THE INTENSE HABITS HE PICKED UP ON THE SHOOT HAVE STAYED WITH HIM. I CAN TELL YOU WHAT HE SAYS IS TRUE. I WATCHED HIM WORK AND BOB'S A DEMON FOR DETAIL. GO AND SEE HIS EFFORTS WHEN *GUNWHALE* ARRIVES AT A CINEMA NEAR YOU.

The show went pretty well considering my state of mind. And now I was looking for Minona. I'd been texting her like a teenager for hours but without response, and I went up to her office once I'd done my work in the studio. She wasn't there. I asked her PA, who told me she was definitely somewhere in the building. I took the lift down to the lobby. Minona was by the door talking on her mobile. I waited for her to finish the conversation.

"Min," I said.

"Your face is cut."

"Close shave the other night." I rubbed my chin. The nicks still stung.

"You really should be more careful."

"I got waylaid."

"You make it sound like a highway robbery," she said.

"More like a stick-up."

"Bloody crude."

She turned away, walked off down the corridor. I chased after her, grabbed a wrist.

"Can I talk to you?"

She shook me off. "About?"

"How about the blindingly obvious?"

"You're not stuck on me, are you dear? Please don't say you are."

"You flatter yourself," I said.

"You've gone soft, haven't you?"

"While you're back to being the hard nut."

"Ouch, doesn't that hurt?" She threw an ugly grin at me.

"I should have left you all wrapped up," I said.

"Tell you what, Root, let's simply fasten everything back together again."

Suddenly Cushman was standing very close, edging forward almost like he wanted to put himself right between the two of us.

"What can I do for you?" I asked him.

His hand went to his face. He scratched his nose, cheeks, the eye of his tiger ring catching the light. "There are problems with the *Gunwhale* piece. I need you. Now."

"OK, but unbend a bit, will you? I'll come over in a few minutes and take a listen."

He stood there, carried on scratching.

"Why don't you go away, Cush, and do whatever it is you have to?" Minona said.

He scooted off and disappeared behind a door.

"And you," Minona said, "you'd do best to count last night as your fifteen minutes of fame."

* * *

I arrived at the London Eye shortly before ten. Hegley was waiting dutifully for me. We shook hands.

"Root," he said.

"Philip."

We queued without talking. Hegley was as nervous as I remembered him from our first and only meeting at the October Gallery. He kept running his fingers over the top of his head like he was marshalling the unkempt hair he no longer had. He gazed up and down the pathway as though expecting to spot someone he really didn't want to see. I wasn't unhappy he was on edge – I felt I was holding the good cards.

We waited a dozen minutes or so for our pod and, when we stepped onboard, were joined by a band of middle-aged Japanese tourists and an elderly northern-English couple who made straight for the bench and unpacked sandwiches, poured teas from a thermos. Hegley and I stood at the river-end of the capsule. He had his hands pushed past the wrists into his trouser pockets, was peering through the transparent wall.

"What's this about a feature?" he asked. He didn't bother looking at me to ask the question.

"Not so fast. After all this time, I feel an urge to play catch up."

"Straight down to business, I say."

"To be fair," I said. "I think I'm in charge here."

"Mastery is fleeting."

"Come on, Philip, give me some backstory."

"Have it your way and give me the third degree if you must."

He wasn't winning me over. Had this been a ride on public transport, I might have got off at the next stop.

"About your disappearance," I said. "Roger Huckerby was in on it, wasn't he?"

"Ridiculous. It was his conviction of my death that made the whole affair believable."

"Then why was he killed?"

"I'm not so sure he was. I called him when I got to Spain, and I think he was so spooked he just ran off the road in his car."

"Hence your mea culpa."

He shrugged, looked out across the river towards a steadily emerging St James's Park and its green sweep towards Buckingham Palace.

"I think he was on his way to meet Nesh," I said.

"That oik."

"A rather elegant oik to be sure. Who is he?"

Hegley snorted. "Calls himself my agent."

"Who does he work for?"

"Ferris Media."

"Of course."

"Ferris owns the production company that locks me down."

"How do you mean?"

"It's obvious, surely."

"Help me," I said.

Hegley looked me directly in the eye for the first time since we'd become airborne. "It's simple enough. I died my death, then sat back to watch the show unfold."

"You wanted to see what the world had made of you, didn't you?"

Hegley put a hand showily to his forehead. "'Vanity of vanities, saith the preacher; all is vanity.' It was clear I was never going to be allowed to make another film. What I wanted was to read the damn obituaries."

"Well, you got your critical acclaim."

"I'd certainly recommend the experience." Hegley's eyes widened. "But I was absolutely agog when my films became roaring financial successes."

"So you went back to the studio." I was beginning to see the bigger picture.

"Yes, it was to have been the return of the king," he said. "And I was going to make another film at last."

"You reckoned it would be a done deal."

"That new money would easily have financed it, Root. I'd been waiting years for the opportunity."

"But if you flopped it would be a disaster," I said, "and that was a huge financial risk for Ferris."

"I walked in on them, and up went the crucifixes and garlic. They bundled me out of the office and stashed me in a hotel for a while. Then this Nesh character turned up and dictated the terms."

"Terms?"

"A plump percentage of the gross."

"On condition you stayed good and dead, I bet."

"Exactly," he said. "Told them to stuff it, naturally, but the oik made it clear there would be severe penalty clauses."

"He's persuasive that way."

Hegley nodded. "He seems to know a lot of what I'm up to."

"Has he followed you today?" I reached into my jacket pocket, fingered the knuckledusters. I'd thought to bring them on the way out of the flat, felt easier having the weight of the brass in my fist.

"I can give him the slip. I left the house early and hiked across the fields. I had a car waiting."

I looked down, spotted Naysmith leaning into a Thameside railing, smoking a cigarette. I didn't mind the minder. "Where's the house?" I asked.

"Extreme Essex. Ferris's money bought me a couple of delightful oyster cottages in St Lawrence Bay."

"What do you do out there?"

"I built myself a studio. They deliver the footage on a regular basis."

"And you do the new cuts for the DVDs."

"It keeps my hand in."

Hegley was staring at his feet, seemed suddenly frail. I felt sorry for him.

"Tell me something," I said. "There you are living out on the coast, toeing the Ferris line and getting paid. Why on earth did you get in touch with me?"

He offered a pinched smile. "You wrote the best obituary by a distance," he said. "I've seen some of your scripts too. I've listened to you on the radio. You do good things about the river."

"What were you expecting me to do?"

"I thought you were my way back in, Root," he said. "I wanted you to front my next film."

"I'm your ghost director, am I?"

"I wanted a credible name upfront."

Our pod was almost at the peak of its climb, and the Thames at low water seemed little more than a stream from this height. A couple of pleasure boats sailed under Westminster Bridge, made their turns, came back, idled below us. The capsule smelled very strongly of tea, the couple still breakfasting as they pointed out the landmarks. The Japanese tourists occupied themselves digitising Big Ben.

"Funny how things have turned out," I said. "I'm here to offer you a deal."

"Tell me."

"I have money. From Ferris."

"Nice irony there." He laughed. "So, you're going to let me make my feature."

"Come on, I'm not that altruistic."

"Then what?" He seemed genuinely startled.

"I got the coin, so we make a film together."

"I see. Something of a bounty hunter, are you?"

"It's good news for you. Far better than making shorts for festivals."

"I'm a one-man show, Root. End of discussion."

"Well, Napoleon Solo, this is one time when you don't get to roll your own."

"Not a chance in hell," he said loudly.

The Japanese tourists looked worried.

"Anyone ever mention that cinema's a collaborative art?" I asked.

"There's just one director. I put all of myself into my films. Look at *Greene Land*. I did everything to that film except fuck it."

"Bob Crasker will join us."

"Man's no more than a technician."

"He'll give you a run for the money on set."

"Bob only likes to see who can piss the highest." Hegley gestured in front of his crotch.

"A little competition's no bad thing."

"You're a fool if you think I'll compromise."

"You're not in a great position, are you, Philip? Get off the Eye and have your lackey drive you back to Essex, if you want." I nodded in the direction of Naysmith. "But Root Wilson still gets to make a film while Philip Hegley busies himself catching oysters for the rest of his life."

Hegley lashed out at the pod, struck the skin with the toe of his shoe and made the whole caboose rattle. The Japanese gathered by the exit even though we were still good minutes away from landing. The English couple drank more tea.

"You can't be at the shoots, so that's where I come in," I said. "I'll be the one who deals with the crew and the actors."

Hegley was shaking his head.

"The world's moved on since you were last able to call the shots as a director god," I said. "I'm your best option."

"And this is where you tell me you have a screenplay you've been sweating over for years."

"We write this together from scratch," I said. "It'll be easy."

"How so?"

"I'd say the story the two of us are in right now is pretty filmic, wouldn't you?"

I looked into Hegley's face, could see the idea was hooky for him.

∗   ∗   ∗

I watched *Greene Land* again. Part of me had been hoping to be able to tear it to pieces, deliver a damning verdict on the work now that Hegley had lived up to his poor billing. The man was an arrogant shit, and I'd really hated getting his attitude all over my clothes.

But his film was perfectly constructed, beautifully shot, wonderfully acted. I loved the product, hated its maker. Then again,

I had tossed him red meat, so should have expected him to be all animal. I understood the guy's frustrations, him thinking he'd be welcomed with open arms by Ferris only for them to cage him up. His problem now was that he was on good pay but there were no prospects of promotion.

He needed me. And what I wanted more than anything was the opportunity to study with the master. Yes, we were a good match. All I had to do was come up with some way of working with Hegley.

Establishing shot of a terraced house in a Woolwich backstreet.
Cut to:
The interior. Boocock stands in a living room together with Les Lea. We're seeing it very wide angle, everything possible squeezed into the frame. The dimensions look to be that of a ballroom rather than something from a two-up, two-down, the characters Giacometti-like in their leanness. The room's well furnished, with a West End feel to it, has clearly been put together by someone with money and taste.
"He was living it up," Boocock says.
"Thom always enjoyed the good life."
"Must have drawn a fat pay packet."
"He made the most of what he had." Les Lea takes out a cigarette, puts it between her lips.
Cut to:
An extreme close-up of Les Lea's mouth. A glare of light. We see a cloud of smoke that gradually clears to the lip shot.
"You knew he was bent, didn't you?" Boocock asks. We hear his voice, watch her mouth.
"Because I slept with him doesn't mean I knew ev-

erything he did," Les Lea says.

"Which means you really didn't care."

"You some kind of judge?"

"Just Thom's friend."

"Be a friend. Let him rest in peace."

"What if he's not dead?"

We see black for a second, hear her laugh loudly.

Cut back to the wide angle:

"You're funny. Want to join me on stage?" she asks.

"Baron lied to me about Thom's accident."

"And?"

"That means he has something to hide."

She laughs again. "One minute the judge, next minute the detective."

Cut to:

The lip shot.

"I'm just a writer," Boocock says.

"Sounds like you have plenty of stories to tell."

Les Lea puts the cigarette to her mouth, takes a long pull, blows smoke directly into the lens.

Cut to:

The wide angle.

"It's when everyone tries to put me down that I know something's wrong," he says.

"Maybe they're not putting you down, but putting you straight."

More laughter, this time from Boocock.

"If I really thought Thom was dead," he says, "I'd kiss you here and now."

Cut to:

A good fifteen-second shot of Les Lea's lips.

Fade to black.

Chapter Sixteen

Next day when I got home from the cafe, I had a phone message waiting for me. Meaghan had made the most of her knowledge of my morning habits to get in touch at a remove. She wanted some things from the flat, planned to send round a van, could I call the man and arrange a convenient time please, she asked.

My first e-mail of the day was from Theresa Noble. It was short, but not at all sweet. She'd spotted those photos of hers that I'd posted on my blog, wanted them back. I was to meet her that afternoon at Somerset House, and I wasn't to think anything was more important.

I also got a mail from Harry who wanted to take me up on my offer of a game of pool that evening, her chance at last for revenge. *You're about to find out, Bro, that Harry washes whiter than ever.*

I worked my way through a batch of texts, found one from Minona reminding me of our midday meeting at the studio. *Be on time,* she wrote.

Well, it was nice that the women in my life had been kind enough to get in touch. And touching that they all wanted a piece of what was left of me.

I got the van to come immediately, thought it best to get this part of the Root and Meaghan story over and done as quickly as possible. The guys showed up at the door and inside a quarter of hour managed to empty the wardrobe and bedroom drawers of all of her clothes. Then they handed me note in Meaghan's handwriting. The flourishes got to me a little, the curls and coils corkscrewing into that place inside me where the affections I had for Meaghan still lived. I might have been in tears if the movers hadn't been there.

I read the list. She was demanding a mound of things. And a lot of them were gear we'd bought together for the flat, stuff which rightly belonged to the two of us. No way was she getting that print from the Tate, that set of tiny mustard spoons we'd found at the flea market, that... Then again, why not give here everything she wanted? I wasn't going to be as small-minded as she was, wouldn't give her excuses for petty arguments. I told the guys to take everything.

It was only when the last box was being carried out of the door that I grabbed the kilim. Meaghan was rather unlikely to pick a fight over a rug.

I asked the movers for a ride to the studio.

* * *

I waited forty-five minutes in the lobby for Minona. I chatted to the receptionist, to a couple of engineers, read through the film reviews in *Time Out*. Minona's assistant was as much at a loss as I was over her no-show. It was unheard of. He tried her on her BlackBerry, called Ferris HQ. But she'd gone AWOL. With anyone else but Minona I might have thought they'd shied away because of our spat. In her case, I presumed it was some kind of punishment. I told the assistant to ask Minona to get in touch once she resurfaced.

* * *

I arrived way early at Somerset House. On the river terrace, I drank my way through a cappuccino, then another, read over and over the upcoming events on the National Theatre's electronic display board across the river – something from Mike Leigh, from Chekov, a play about Rwanda. After an hour of it, I began to feel I'd actually seen each of the attractions the place had to offer.

Theresa arrived, took a chair opposite me without saying a word. She was wearing a sealskin coat buttoned up to the neck, had on thick woollen leggings. She must have been baking on what was a warm afternoon.

I took the envelope with the photos from my bag and placed it on the table.

"Why didn't you ask me?" she said. "You know you could have had them."

She was right, and I couldn't properly explain it. "Rush of blood?"

"That caused bad blood." She squeezed her eyes shut, opened them once more.

"I apologise."

"What are you going to do about it?"

"Well, here are the photos," I told her.

"You *do* want me to forgive you, don't you?"

I shrugged, wasn't one hundred percent sure why I was putting myself through this. After all, I'd only chased after her to get to Philip Hegley, and I'd managed to do that now. Theresa Noble was spent as far as my mission was concerned, but I would have felt bad simply standing up and walking away. I liked her well enough, felt flattered by her flirting. And I was sorry she was still in love with a guy she believed to be dead, that she went so far as to try and talk to his spirit. Another reason I stayed put was for my own damn good. Meaghan had just walked away. Minona had stood me up. Harry had too little time for me nowadays. I didn't feel strong enough to cast myself free from all these women in one fell swoop.

"You know, Root, I think we can do something about this."

"You do?"

"After all, one does make lemonade from lemons."

"Certainly." I wasn't too sure where she was heading.

Theresa picked up the envelope, pulled out the photographs and studied each one before putting them back. Then she ordered a tonic water from the waiter. She was playing the scene very well, working my discomfort for as long as she could.

"I'm going to give you a chance to make amends," she said. "I know you have a deal for a film. Put me in it.

"It's already cast." It was the only thing I could think to say.

"Then recast."

"I'm not sure there's a part for you."

"Then write one."

"I can't just…"

"But my dear, you can just."

And she was right, I could. I looked at her lips, the ones I'd spent time adoring in stunning close-up in *Greene Land*. Putting Theresa Noble in the film I was planning was a great idea. And an even greater one was to reunite as many of the cast and crew of Hegley's last work as possible. Get them to do what they did once again. Only even better.

*　*　*

Harry was already on the baize at the Bunch of Grapes when I arrived. She was trying out a shot, leaning far over the table and putting an astounding stretch in a maroon-leather jumpsuit.

"Need the practice, Aitch?"

Harry put the ball very cleanly in the centre pocket. "I ought to warn you I'm feeling pretty limber," she said.

"I'm ready for another drubbing at the hands of a woman."

"Trouble at work with The Min?"

"It's a domestic. Meaghan's moved all her stuff out." I hadn't planned to tell Harry anything about the break-up, though it now suddenly felt right.

"Bad news," she said. "But you really ought to have talked to me about this before. I shouldn't have to rely on Justin to tip me off about his sister and you."

"What did he tell you?"

"Only the basics. We can abandon the game, and you can upgrade me if you like."

"I say play on."

"You don't have to be a man about this, you know."

"Seems a good stance to adopt right now."

"Steel in the upper lip, firm jaw and the rest?" She tightened her face at me.

"You've got it."

"You'll let me know if you feel the need to loosen up?"

"First person I'll turn to, Aitch."

"Good to hear." Harry chalked her cue. "Then battle shall commence."

"And let the only man win," I said.

"You're begging for a beating, Mr Wilson."

"You say that because you're in leather."

"Hey, just because you're newly single doesn't mean you can try it on. Just you remember who I am."

"And who are you exactly?"

Harry stared at me with deep kohl eyes, batted her lashes showily. "Your opponent," she said. "Your sworn enemy."

"Then I'll take you on at any game you like."

"Pool will do for starters," she said. "Select your weapon, mortal."

Harry went to the top of the table, broke and freed most of the balls from the rack, was obviously setting up a few possibles for me.

"No need to do any favours because you feel sorry for me," I said.

"I'm only sorry you're about to lose so badly." She prodded me in the back with her cue. "I'd go for that there stripey ball in the corner pocket, if I were you," she said quietly in my ear.

"And if you were a man, I'd ask you outside for your cheek."

"Promises, promises," she said. "Play the game, chum."

I whacked the gimme ball in the pocket but fluffed the next shot, leaving Harry with a host of openings. She put one away at the far end of the table, got back behind the next ball thanks to a perfect dose of bottom spin, potted that, a third and a fourth. Then she missed after mis-parking the cue ball.

"There's a chance for you, Bro. Your last, so use it well."

I messed it up and sat out the rest of the game as Harry cleared the table. I wasn't too disappointed as it gave me the opportunity to do further study of the amazing way she was managing to fill out her leatherwear. I lost track of the game.

"What's with you?" she asked. "Given up already?"

"Sorry, I lost the plot for a while."

"Maybe this really isn't a good time."

"I'm fine."

"You'll take the shine off my victory if you don't play seriously. Don't ruin my revenge."

I stood up, thumped the butt of the cue in my palm. "OK," I said. "I'm ready to assert my superiority."

She gave me a stern look. "I mean it. Play to win, or else."

"I like the idea of the 'or else'. But I'd rather give you a whupping, as they say. Think *The Hustler*. Only this time our hero triumphs."

"Oh boy." Harry broke for a second time.

The next game was nip and tuck, with Harry a little on the back foot following my return to form. Donning the Fast Eddie mantle seemed to have helped because he was playing far, far better than Rattling Root had done. It went to the wire. With little left on the table, Harry missed a tough shot, the target ball catching wickedly in the jaws of the pocket. I went on a run, needed only to sink a simple hanger to win.

"Not worried," Harry said. "You'll flub."

I pocketed, punched the air. "The beginning of the end," I said.

Harry gave me the finger.

"You got me, under your skin," I sang. I couldn't believe how much fun I was suddenly having.

"Rack 'em, Bro."

The next game was tight too, but Harry was clearly in trouble, her play uncharacteristically conservative. In this state, I knew just one error would undo her so I waited, played safe by ignoring some of the percentage balls she was sending my way. She was a better player than I was, that was clear, but I believed I could psyche her out. The only thing capable of stopping me was her leather get-up, but I could feast on that all I wanted once the game was won.

The turning point came when I pretended to sandbag a couple of shots to make her think I was flagging. And sure enough she rushed her game, ended up pocketing whitey. All she was able to do then was stand by and watch me clear the table, which I did as slowly as I could, the phrase milking it not quite doing justice to my lack of pace.

"At least you won the first game, Aitch. But if I can beat you, then I know for sure that everything isn't fine in the world according to Harry. What's up?"

She threw her cue on the table.

"What is it?" I asked.

"Just when I think all my ducks are in line, they start flying away."

"You're talking about work?"

"That's one thing. It's true this business with Philip Hegley shows my career isn't trending well."

"And another thing?"

"Justin and I are spoiling very quickly."

"But the two of you are smitten."

"I'm messing it up, Bro. I've spent a lot of my time separating the chavs from the wheat, and now I'm not sure what to do with it."

"Justin's a good guy." I couldn't bring myself to talk him up any further.

"You know, maybe good's bad for me."

"You have to make this work." I didn't want Harry to take the advice, of course. But I felt too battered emotionally to open up to Harry and make the move I should have made years ago.

CHAPTER SEVENTEEN

"Take a look at this," Bob Crasker said, "isn't she so absolutely beautiful?"

It was the middle of the night. I was back in Rotherhithe, back on *Gunwhale* location and staring at the gear Crasker was hefting. It looked just like a movie camera ought to. The film magazine stood proud on top, curving in and out beautifully like the body of a violin. The viewfinder was as precision-crafted as a microscope's. And Bob had the bellows reined in tight, the corrugations almost begging the run of a fingertip.

"The very first of the lightweight Arriflexes," Bob said.

"It looks oh so sixties."

"Exactly. I wouldn't dream of shooting the scene without the real McCoy." He raised the camera to his eye, panned.

"What does Old McCoy have to say about a car chase?"

Bob dropped the Arriflex to waist height where it looked more like a machine gun. "There's only one way to do it, and that's the way it was done on *Bullitt*," he said.

"They used Arriflexes to shoot the Mustang and the Charger?" I saw the cars flying one after the other over the brow of a San Franciscan hill.

"Now you're getting it. We'll hard-mount one in the car. No cushions. We want to record every shock. Every jolt. Every jerk." He shook the camera hard – it really did resemble a weapon.

*　*　*

We had ages before the rest of the world woke up, and the crew was busy setting up. I started chatting to the film's stunt co-ordinator, a rangy blond-haired guy named Carey Loftin – *call me Lofty,* he said. Abdi had told me he was something of a film vet but he had the look of a kid who'd only just grown out of his skateboard, his flop of hair with the beginnings of its first proper style. He told me he and a mechanic had schlepped over to Canning Town to trawl the scrap yards, shelled out a few hundred on an old Escort and a banged-up Mini, hauled them back to Rotherhithe on a low-loader. Lofty said the cars would be doing a lot of jumping – over traffic calmers, a few stunt ramps they'd laid along the route – so they'd needed work to beef them up.

"We had to rebuild the f'kin' shock towers, rip out the stocks, bolt in some f'kin' Konis and new crossmembers," he said.

Lofty explained that the game plan was to race the Escort and Mini between the Gunwhale buildings, crack over the wasteland where the two cars could bump, barge each other before they hit a narrow strip of road that ran along the river for about a thousand yards into a dead end. Right there in the cul-de-sac, the Mini would do a three-sixty spin and the Escort would slam it into a brick wall. An explosion would burn both of them up, he said, leave nothing for the birds to pick over.

Lofty showed me the cars standing side by side under an awning.

"We cut out all the rotten panels, so there's barely anything to them now," he said.

"They look in good shape to me."

"We put in board and tin where all the f'kin' holes were. Gave 'em both a respray. They're not quite dry to the touch so that's why they're under cover."

"I presume they're way up off the ground because of the new shocks."

"And we pumped the tyres."

"How come?"

"Cuts the friction. Engines were a bit f'ked when we found 'em, cars would barely do sixty, needed all the help they could get. Now they'll fly when they're pushed. You'll see. F'kin' hell."

The plan was to do a dry run at half speed to see if the basic motor choreography worked, and I was to ride upfront in the

Mini with Lofty at the wheel to get some car chase content for the programme. I strapped my audio gear in the back where the rear bench used to be, wrapping it in old seat belts, tying it to a couple of floor mounts to hold it firm. Bob had already fixed the Arriflex between the two front seats.

Lofty and I were fastened into position with a couple of flying harnesses that had been bolted into the car, the crew belting them up tight.

"If they're right, they'll be squeezing your f'kin' nuts," Lofty said.

He took the Mini for a saunter to warm the engine, then parked it at the north side of the estate where we idled. Abdi's voice jumped suddenly from the walkie-talkie taped to the dash and immediately Lofty took off. He slipped the clutch and the wheels spun then caught dirt, the front end of the car swaggering forward for a few yards before boring a straight line. Lofty had barely managed to get the car into third gear before we hit the bend and he had to bang it back down into second to bring the Mini between the two buildings. I couldn't believe this was only a fraction of the pace they planned for the actual shoot.

The Mini tore a zigzag down the strait and I glanced behind me, saw the Escort doing the same just a second or so after us. There was no one ahead. Abdi and Bob were up on the sixth floor from where they'd do a long-shot, follow the cars over the wasteland, while the crew, cast and extras were locking off the entire area to make sure we had a clean run. No one had told the council or the police about the chase – Abdi was sure they'd nix it, or at best get it toned down to the point of nothingness, so he'd decided to go ahead with the full Monty, risk the authorities getting legal on him.

Lofty pulled the car around the bottom end of the estate and onto a broad sweep of land. The crew had marked a route with a series of wooden pegs so that we'd be sure to avoid the worst of the hummocks, dips and major scrap that junked the scrubland. The Mini still bucked like a wild horse, though, pitched us hard to the left, right, right, right again. The car lifted high for a second, banged down with a jolt, the noise like it was breaking apart. During the shoot, the Escort would be gnawing at the Mini from the rear, bending metal, and the racket would be worse then ever.

"We're f'kin' shock jocks, Root," Lofty yelled above the din.

I nodded. I'd planned to do a commentary on the ride but hadn't been able to talk as we'd chased through the estate. Now that we were jumping clear off the planet, a Nescafé-and-croissant breakfast rising in my throat, the only thing that concerned me was getting to the end of the ride without chucking up.

We hit glorious, smooth tarmac as we closed on the river, and hearing the motor once more was pure joy. I turned to see the Escort and there it was, just a few yards to the rear still, the driver doing a great job of staying pally.

"Time to open up, Root boy."

Lofty gunned the Mini, rode quickly through the gearbox, crashed the gears. The engine was screaming as we ripped past the warehouses, the buildings dissolving in a blur. I checked my harness, gripped the base of the seat with both hands.

Then I saw the tall, slim figure ease of out an alleyway. He stepped into the road, seeming to be walking on air.

"Look out!" I shouted.

Lofty steered hard away from the man and the car did a couple of spins, broadsided the kerb and tilted up a few feet on its two offside wheels before slamming back down onto the full four.

The day went haywire for a few seconds, but once I got my life back, I checked on Lofty. He was slumped unconscious in his seat, blood on his face. The Arriflex had been torn off its mountings and was sitting in his lap.

The engine turned over quietly.

* * *

I woke up next day on the sofa, could barely move, the muscles in my back and shoulders as good as solid. I rolled off the couch onto the floor, managed to get myself standing in an uncomfortably crooked way.

I'd felt more or less OK after the accident, pretty shaken up, of course, but my body had been sound as a pound. Like everyone, I'd been worried about Lofty. A couple of crew guys lifted him out of the car, laid him on the road. He came round soon after, was groggy certainly, but seemed to have all his buttons. *F'kin' pedestrians.* He began cleaning blood from his face with a rag, wanted to check the car over. But Abdi was having none of it, and he had Lofty stacked in an ambulance despite his protests. I rode along with him as I was the only one who wasn't needed for the shoot. We blue-lighted it down to the hospital where I hung around for hours waiting for him to get X-rayed. I decided to take off once his girlfriend arrived.

"Good of you to wait, Root," he said.

"Next time look out for the UFAs."

"The f'kin' whats?"

"Unidentified Flying Arriflexes."

On the way home, I picked up a pizza, chowed it down on the sofa where I fell asleep, waking some twelve hours later rigid as a corpse.

Now I walked awkwardly over to the kitchen, got my hands on a bottle of water, chugged most of it down in one pull. I thought of the accident, of the metallic smash, bash and then the sudden hush as the car came out of its wicked spin and jump, was finally resting on all fours. I felt like I'd be able to explain the whole show if only I could properly finger the sounds that I hoped were all safely stored on tape.

I finished off the water, crunched the bottle, tossed it in the bin. I remembered the very tall figure floating out of the alleyway and into the road. Was it Nesh?

The sound of the doorbell startled me.

I buzzed my visitor in.

*　*　*

"Let me take your coat," I said.

"I'm good, thanks." Inspector Callaghan pushed his retro Bakelite-frame glasses into place onto the bridge of his nose.

He was an unsettling presence. As soon as he'd come into the flat, he'd begun poking around. And now he reminded me of a rodent the way he jerked his head one way, then the other. I half expected him to begin sniffing the air. His trenchcoat was belted tight around his midriff, and the dark black of it contrasted severely with his straw-blond buzzcut. He looked to be about thirty but seemed to be straight out of the post–World War Two era.

"Coffee?" I asked. "Tea?"

"Still good."

"Let me know if you want a chair."

He smiled at me. "Are you OK?"

"I must look a real dinger." I still felt twisted ugly out of shape. I rubbed my chin, realised I badly needed a shave and the hot water of a long shower to buck myself up.

"Sleeping on the sofa?" Callaghan nodded towards the sheets and pillows piled up on the cushions.

"I had a spat with the girlfriend."

"She live here too?"

"Just moved out and took all her things. That's why the place looks so bare."

"Can be a difficult time, for sure." Callaghan picked the knuckle-dusters up off my desk, tossed them in the air, caught them.

"I found them by the river," I said.

"Have a license for these?"

"Do I need one?"

Callaghan put the dusters back on the desk. "Where is your girlfriend?" he asked.

"I'm not sure. Vienna maybe."

"You don't even know if she's in the country?" Now he was scanning the shelf.

"We're incommunicado."

He picked up an old stoppered bottle – another Thameside find – and peered through it, put it back in its place. "I'll need to speak to her."

"Talk to Megs? Whatever for?"

"As part of our enquiries."

"How could she know anything about the accident?"

"Is that what you'd call it?"

"What else could it have been?" I was going to bring up Nesh, thought better of it.

Callaghan took off his natty glasses, rubbed his eyes, pushed the specs back on his nose. "Did your girlfriend leave because of you and Miss Turner?"

"Miss Turner?" I asked. "Oh, you mean Minona." How did Callaghan know about the two us? And what did it have to do with the car accident? The man surely had a strange train of thought. "Why do you ask?"

"There are suspicious circumstances surrounding Miss Turner's death," he said.

"Her death?" I suddenly wasn't with Callaghan any longer. I was certainly in the room but felt I was watching him from a distance.

"When did you last see her?" he asked.

"We had a meeting two days ago." My voice didn't sound anything like I was used to.

"Not possible. Her body was found before then."

"Body?"

"You said you saw her two days ago."

"I meant we had a meeting planned, but she didn't show up." Christ, I'd cursed her for not being there at the time. "We weren't on good terms. I was happy not to have to deal with Min."

"Deal with her?" Callaghan picked a book off the shelf, flicked through it, slid it back into its slot.

"It was personal." I could suddenly smell the soap Minona had used when she shaved me. I was sure the floor was moving. I felt dizzy. I sat down on a stool.

"You alright?" Callaghan asked.

"Still shaken up from the accident."

"What accident would that be?"

"The car chase. Though, it wasn't for real."

He shook his head. "Listen. We read the texts you sent to Miss Turner. You were pretty angry with her, weren't you?"

"She was being difficult."

"What do you mean by difficult?" He was walking around me now, circling.

"Impossible," I said.

"You wanted to see her, but she refused?"

"Something like that."

"Exactly like that, Mr Wilson." Callaghan was right in front of me now. "Were you angry with her?"

"Min and I had just had a one-night stand. She threw me out next morning."

"Threw you out?"

"Look, there was nothing between us either before or after that night. It was my fifteen minutes of fame, apparently."

"That what she called it?"

"She was terrific at put-downs. She could be a tough bitch." I couldn't believe I was bad-mouthing her. He said she was dead.

"I can see why you were angry," Callaghan said. "Girlfriend moves out. You don't even know where she is. You're ... intimate with Miss Turner. She tosses you out. Two rejections. Yes, I understand your anger."

"I wasn't angry."

"I've read your texts, remember?" he said. "I'm good at reading between the lines, picking up the nuances."

I was sick of Callaghan's insinuations. I got up off the stool. "That must come in very handy in your work."

"Yes," he said. "I'm a sensitive man." Callaghan tightened the belt on his raincoat a notch. "They say at the station that I know it when a dog scratches his bollocks in the next borough."

Chapter Eighteen

Alida von Altenburger is dead. She was better known as Valli and she played Anna Schmidt, Harry Lime's girlfriend, in *The Third Man*. And En Root contends that the film's shot of her walking straight past Holly Martins at the very end is absolute top-of-the-class killer movie-making. Bad luck there, Holly. I've done some detective work and have found that he wasn't alone in being rebuffed by the beautiful Valli. Frank Sinatra described her as the greatest unrequited passion of his life. Gregory Peck talked about seeing a flash of love in her eyes when they worked together on Hitch's *The Paradine Case*, where she played a deceased actress telling her story in flashback. Hollywood certainly fell for her, naming her Valli in an effort to create a replacement for Garbo. But *The Third Man* was her only major hit. Years before she was doing those Italian costume dramas known as white-telephone films due to their opulence. Mussolini was reportedly a fan. And that was just the start of her being drawn into the sphere of shady politicians. During the war she hid away for a while to avoid being dragooned into making pro-Nazi movies, though that didn't prevent her from being accused of having an affair with Joseph Goebbels. Valli also got tied up in an Italian society murder scandal in the fifties, and that took the shine off her acting career. But, for me, it's enough she was in that shot in *The Third Man*. So, let's use this as an excuse to hear that zither music one more time.

Once I'd recorded the segment I went off to do my Sherlock thing. I could tell Callaghan fancied himself some kind of hot 'tec by the way he dressed up snazzy, played fast and smart in interrogation, and I was as much out to prove him a simple flatfoot as to find out what had happened to poor Min. That's why I took the lift up from the lobby to the top floor and headed for her office.

The cops had already visited, of course, but all I had to do was duck under a flimsy barrier of stripey tape to get through the doorway. I hadn't any kind of idea of what I was looking for, guessed in any case that anything worthy had probably already been carried off in a hundred Seal-it bags. My best hope was that my insider knowledge of the studio might allow me to make sense of something the cops had overlooked.

Minona's desk was as tidy as ever. There was no scatter of papers to search through, just her core hardware – a PC, a telephone, a framed black-and-white photograph of a distinguished-looking older man I'd always taken to be her father, and a white-metal Montblanc pen she'd used to sign off documents. I gazed at her empty leather chair, wished very much that she were sitting in it, would for once have been more than happy for her to be giving me a hard time about absolutely nothing.

Her diary wasn't there, no doubt carted away by Callaghan's mob. I knew they had her mobile, too, so anything that might have provided clear leads wasn't going to come my way. I tried each of the desk drawers, but they were locked, ditto for the filing cabinets. I found a few sheets of A4 at her conference table, but they amounted to nothing more than a few spreadsheets, a single list of the latest audience ratings. I noticed that En Root was still spiking – Min would have been pleased.

I picked up a brochure. It was a Huckerby & Partner publication, a glossy prospectus for the upcoming stock exchange float, the forming of the great PLC. I opened the cover, and there was an image of Junior alongside a jaunty open letter he'd penned to prospective investors. There were pages of biz-speak summoning up honey-tongued praise of the company, charts with rapidly rising curves and slender blocks of colour that soared into white space just like the buildings of the City grew into the sky. I saw a picture of old Roger Huckerby slap bang in the middle of the obit I'd written. And on the inside back cover I read an inky note. *Min, want to see you, need to see you, Rog xxx*

* * *

Min crashed my thoughts as I drove up to Dalston that evening. I wasn't in the least rhinoskinned, and it certainly hadn't sunk in that she had gone for good. At the studio I'd expected her to pop up at any moment and give the whole team a rollicking. Right now I was feeling shaky, and I thought the best way for me to get through this was to find out what had happened to her. And I needed to build my detective muscle to do that.

It took me a while to find a parking space for the Beemer in Dalston. Hackney Council had had a field day digging up as many streets as possible, almost every single yellow disappearing under the pneumatic drill. I eventually squeezed the car in between a couple of empty market barrows, locked up. I wasn't sure it was legally located, hoped it would still be there when I got back.

A drunk mumbled something as I passed him on the pavement.

"Can't stop," I said. "Have to see a man about a dog."

"A girl about pussy more like," he shouted after me.

I had to dodge the buses that tracked fast down Kingsland High Street, looking like they were headed straight into the base of the Gherkin that lifted huge from the end of the road. I was surprised to see the building here. I was so used to viewing it from my side of the river and I felt almost offended that it was showing itself off to other boroughs.

I arrived at the Vortex Jazz Club, hadn't been there since it had moved from its old, cramped location in Stoke Newington. The latest incarnation sat in what looked pretty much like a long glass drawer on the first floor of the Dalston Culture House. It hung above the pavement and threw off a crackling attitude that was everything inner-city. I stood on the road outside, washed by the blue light that seeped from the Vortex out into the neighbourhood. The piazza – one of the ex-mayor's vaunted one thousand open spaces for London – looked eerie in the manufactured glow, but I suddenly saw it as a great spot for an outside broadcast for the show, an opportunity maybe to put local upcoming artists on the airwaves.

Inside was a sizeable crowd of North London jazz addicts, and I had to work my way through them to the front of the room where Justin had reserved a table. He'd told me something about Harry wanting to come down but that she'd had to zip last minute over to Munich, so the place would be my own. I knew he was fibbing, though. I'd just spoken to Harry, and she was still in town.

I sipped a bottle of San Miguel during a short set from a trombone, bass and drum trio. The spindly blonde who surely couldn't have been out of her teens turned out some sweet brass stuff, her instrument nicely understated as it picked its way through the chords. I felt happy with my appreciation of the music, wondered if some of Meaghan's skills hadn't rubbed off on me at last. I suddenly missed her. And Minona too.

Justin came on, lumbering into place wearing a huge sweater that was half-tucked into the waistband of his jeans, the laces of his right boot untied. He launched straight into his first number without a word to the audience. He'd told me he was planning to go it alone, felt he'd really needed the support of the musicians he'd played with for his first outing at the Spitz a few weeks ago, but was ready to take the training wheels off now, be the solo artist. I was certainly no expert but quickly recognised that Justin was in superb form – he tooled each and every note, shaped a mood that reminded me of the streets of Dalston, as if he'd soaked up the ambience on the way to the club, managed to steep his sound in it. I was completely blown away. The audience cheered him off once he'd closed.

Backstage I found him slumped in a chair in the changing room.

"Fantastic," I said, pumping his hand.

"I'm a goner, my friend. Absolutely and completely drained, don't you know."

"No wonder."

"That mean you liked it?"

"You were amazing. Everyone else thought so."

Justin's face was a huge smile. "I haven't had the music take over like that in years," he said.

"Must feel great."

The blonde who played the first set popped her head around the door jamb. "Cool stuff," she said in a voice that was surprisingly deep. "I'm going to make sure I catch you again."

"Thanks." Justin stood, made for the door, but the woman had taken off before he got there.

"Told you," I said.

"I wish Harry had been here."

"Next time."

"Maybe not," he said.

"She's not always and forever on the road." I felt I had to go along with the lie.

"But she might well be going in a different direction," he said.

"Come off it. She's really keen on you." I punched him softly on the shoulder.

"I haven't seen her for ages." Justin picked up the sax, unscrewed the neck, pushed a long brush down the barrel. "You?"

"We played pool a week back."

"And?"

"I won," I said. "Which usually means she's out of sorts. What's up with the pair of you?"

"I don't know. She just says she doesn't want to see me."

"Not like Harry to keep anything back."

"You sure she didn't say anything to you?"

I shook my head. This wasn't my battle. Or rather, it was and I hadn't a clear idea how to fight it.

"She'd tell you, too," he said. "Harry is rather fond of Root."

"Best of friends," I said.

"That all there is to it?"

"Of course."

Justin rested his sax on the countertop, gave me a big hug. I felt like I'd been grabbed by a bear.

* * *

I made my way back to the car with Justin, who was so broken up after our conversation, so wiped from the gig, that I offered him a ride up to Hampstead. He tracked a yard or so behind, his long shadow chasing by me repeatedly as we passed the street lamps.

"It's not right you and Meaghan broke up," he said. "You were good together."

"So people say."

"Well, they bloody know what they're talking about," he said.

"Where is she?" I asked. "Vienna?"

"At my place."

"Jesus."

"Don't worry, I won't be inviting you in."

"I should meet her, really," I said.

"I want to speak to Harry."

"Tell you what, Justin let's talk about something else. We're both in danger of getting messed."

"There's one thing worrying me," he said. "There's no reason for us not to be friends, is there?"

"Course not."

"Even though you're best pals with Harry and I'm Megsie's brother."

"Even though," I said.

We carried on walking, Justin's shadow the only way for me to know he was still with me.

The Beemer turned out to be exactly where I'd left it. The problem was the offside rear tyre was down.

"Not again," I said.

"Again?" Justin asked.

I opened up the boot, grabbed at the floor mat, pulled out the spare and searched the wheel well but found nothing that shouldn't have been there. I realised I was in a real sweat.

"Just a puncture," I said.

"What else would it be?" Justin asked. "Here, give me the jack."

I stood back, watched him raise the car, change the wheel.

Chapter Nineteen

It was just past dawn as I eased out of what I considered London proper, hit the A12 and began to move through a scatter of down-at-heel towns. Redbridge, Romford and Brentwood had little to show apart from their stumps of offices and flats, and it was depressing stuff having to gaze at buildings way past their prime – they were more than ready for the dozers.

The string of urban red lights broke and I pushed the Beemer into longer stretches of clear road, began to leave the ugliness and motor into the countryside. It was good to be free of the suburbs, and I relaxed into the drive, let the car knock off the distance. I turned up the volume on the player, hummed along to the Former Dictators' 'Judderman'. But after just a few miles of open landscape I started to feel uneasy. Dropping Justin off in Hampstead knowing that Meaghan had been just yards away had unsettled me, though I hadn't known for sure whether it was because I wanted to see her again, or simply didn't. And here in the car I realised that the last time I'd been out of town was on that trip to the Cotswolds – the weekend in the hotel where Meaghan had danced across the floor, where we'd made love in the bathroom, again on the bed.

I had to stop the train of thought, didn't need to get drippy. I checked the map, noted the turn I had to make so that I could head east towards coastal Essex. Though Hegley didn't live far from London, on paper it looked like he inhabited almost unchartered territory. The red and yellow grid of routes I was on thinned into a lacework of minor roads which eventually faded into the pale green of country. It was almost scary.

My last meeting with Hegley on the Eye had gone badly, and we certainly hadn't become pals. And here I was headed for his territory, the treatment I'd worked on for the past couple of weeks in my bag on the passenger seat. Though I'd been confident enough on the last read, all its faults suddenly raced into my head. I imagined Hegley tearing into it with relish.

I drove through a chain of small villages full of thatched-and-clapboard architecture until I got to St Lawrence where I followed Hegley's instructions and parked the car at the back of the village hall. I climbed over a stile and hit a muddy path that ran across a ploughed field. A fine rain fizzled on my cheeks. I didn't mind a bit, relished it, in fact. Had someone asked, I'd have been pushed to describe the London weather of the past week, while right here I was almost part of it.

At the other end of the field I saw what I assumed were Hegley's oyster cottages. They were two dead-ringer houses, each of them topped by a trim grey-tiled roof made of four triangular panels and an eight-foot chimney that looked like it had been pinched and pulled into shape. The houses were highly simple structures but no less beautiful for it.

I reached the rear of the buildings, rapped on a door, waited. I knocked again. Nothing. I opened up, stepped inside, called out. Silence. I closed the door behind me and went in search of Hegley. He wasn't in the kitchen, or in the living room, and I ended up in what looked to be his study. He'd kitted it out with stripped-back Danish furniture, the latest Mac notebook open on a long, narrow pine desk, Bang & Olufsen entertainment system slotted tight into a wall of floor-to-ceiling shelves stuffed with books. The room was pristine apart from a noticeboard that was full of scraps of paper about half-an-inch deep. There were newspaper and magazine clippings of reviews of Hegley's works, director profiles, a sheaf of his obits, plus faded cinema tickets, a curled length of celluloid, a programme from the recent Raindance event, a pencil sketch of a young Theresa Noble. And – I couldn't believe it – a snap of Minona signed *Min xx*. I went chill.

"What the hell are you up to?" Hegley stood in the doorway. He was dressed in black shirt, black jeans and black shoes.

"No one answered the door," I said.

"Fucking snoop."

"I was just reading your clippings." I pointed to a review from the *Observer*.

Hegley yanked the paper off the board. "Mr French was the only one who ever gave me good notices."

"They've all come round now." I felt the need to soft-soap after this bad start. But what was Hegley doing with a picture of Minona?

He read through the review, pinned it back up. "What the devil are you doing here?" he asked.

"You knew I was coming."

He looked at his watch. "You're early. Ever heard that punctuality is the virtue of the bored?" He scratched his bald head violently with his fingernails, scored vivid red lines into his bare skin.

"Boredom's something you've been on good terms with over the past twenty years, I'd say." I'd already learned that the best way to deal with Hegley was to give back what he dished out.

"You've got a cheek," he said.

"But I have come all this way to see you."

"You must want something pretty badly," he said. "Now, what have you got for me?"

I wasn't going to give him the treatment immediately. "How about you brew me a coffee?" I said.

* * *

Hegley brought the drinks back to the study and sat down at his desk, let me stand around holding my cup.

"Out of the way doesn't begin to describe this place," I said. "I can't imagine you get too many visitors."

"The odd soul makes his way."

"Like Roney. Like Naysmith."

"For example," he said.

"Must get lonely."

"I need the space to edit. London crowds in on me too much."

164

"Me, I have to go down to the river to think," I said.

"No finer place for it. But when I'm too long in the Smoke, I have to get out. And I'm at my best in the cutting room."

"Care to give me a tour?"

Hegley's state-of-the-art studio was particularly unimpressive. The problem was that, as a one-time media student, I'd seen many an old editing suite full of vintage gear, tackle that looked hands-on practical, like it would do exactly the job for which it had been built and no messing. Modern equipment was nothing more than jumped-up monitors and computer keyboards. Even the high-end get-up on show here in Hegley's oyster haven looked no more exciting than anything you'd find in your local TV studio pumping out dross for the tube.

"They make complicated little boxes nowadays," Hegley said. "They're nice, they're fast, and they do more than you could ever want them to do."

"But they're still boxes."

"All made out of ticky-tacky."

"And they all look just the same," I said sing-song.

Hegley smiled.

"How much work does Ferris give you?" I asked.

"There used to be more than enough for a working week. It's tailed off recently."

"Giving you the time to turn your hand to shorts."

"Indeed," he said.

"I presume you've done all the different cuts?"

"There's talk of taking on *Greene Land*."

"That'd be crazy, Philip. Don't even think of it."

Hegley grinned at me.

*   *   *

Hegley put together a big pasta lunch, said he'd had plenty of time to make himself a decent cook in the past couple of years.

"Tell me what you got up to after *Greene Land*," I said.

Hegley forked a couple of mounds of spaghetti into his mouth. "I worked on loads of scripts," he said. "And I pitched like a madman."

"But no takers." I knew exactly how that felt.

"Almost got there a few times. With the Italians and with the Americans."

"But you couldn't close."

"They all thought I was too much of a money pit." He took a huge slop of red wine.

"You were ahead of your time."

"So they say now, but it's been awfully barren," he said. "I worked a lot on my memoirs."

"I'd love to see them." This was fantastic news, and it played right into my big idea.

"It's a work in progress," he said.

"Just let me know if I can help."

"I'd rather see what you've been up to."

"I want to talk more before I show it."

"Then let's walk down to the water."

"Is it safe?" I imagined the area might be crawling with Ferris heavies.

"Of course it's safe, dear boy. They call off the Baskervillian hounds now and again." He let out a comic howl.

Despite the assurance, Hegley took me on the byways rather than the highways, had us ducking down alleys, dodging through tight clusters of rundown agricultural cottages. We edged the touchline of a school playing field where a bunch of primary-age kids were chasing a football, then passed a circular pond with a rickety wooden jetty that stretched into the centre.

"Ever come across someone called Minona at Ferris?" I had to ask him about her.

"Should I have?"

"She was my boss. Perhaps you met her along with some of the other execs."

"If I did she left no impression."

"I think she would've. She was a bit of a dynamo."

Hegley shrugged. He picked up a stone, walked along the jetty and skimmed it across the water, bouncing it four times over to the other side of the pond where it hopped into the grass. "Takes years of training."

I grabbed a stone for myself, pulled five hops out of it before it died in the water.

We walked on, reached the estuary where the vista opened out dramatically, the land so low to all sides it barely registered in the 'scape. Above us, the early-morning rainclouds had burnt off and the sky was now a cool mid-blue strafed with cirrus. It was spectacular.

"'There is a prospect greater than the sea, and it is the sky. There is a prospect greater than the sky, and it is the human soul.'" Hegley shouted out the words.

"Who said that?"

"Hugo. *Les Miserables.*"

"Do you believe it?"

"Human capacity is vastly overrated. We're born once, live once, die once. That's the length of it."

"Except for the lucky ones like you who ditch one life and get a second shot."

"Lucky?"

"A lot of people would say so," I said.

"Much of the time I feel I'm in a dark prison with no way out."

"I could be about to free you."

"Maybe, Root, maybe."

We followed a vague path through swathes of marshland, the only sounds coming from swallows that dipped and darted a few feet above the bogs. I looked at the river that grew broader and broader as it neared the sea. The surface of it jagged until it ran into a series of wave-breaks just off the shore and after that the water was still as glass. Hegley said the breaks were old lighters – flat-bottomed steel boats – that had been towed up from the Thames and moored here to protect the marshes.

He pulled something from his pocket. I heard a metal click and saw a blade cutting from Hegley's fist. I couldn't believe it. He was holding a flick knife that pointed right at me.

He bent down, lifted a dead fish that was floating in a pool of water, and expertly sliced it down its length, cut out the beast's innards with the point of the knife. "I've become a decent countryman," he said.

I watched him fold up the knife, drop it back in his trouser pocket.

"I can't believe you didn't set up shop further south," I said, surprised he'd ended up so far away from our beloved Thames.

"My first choice, but the area's been ruined by Southend. I can run down to it in half an hour if I need to, so this is a good place to be." He tossed the bits of fish into the water.

"I can see that." I was taken with Hegley's location, could imagine myself scooting off to a spot like this to get work done. We had something very much in common, and I knew I could use it to make this project work.

"Ever seen the Maunsell Forts?" I asked.

"What on earth are they?"

"Wartime defences built smack in the middle of the estuary. They're like squat oil rigs. They were abandoned years ago and are falling apart, have bits of steel hanging like loose threads everywhere. They'd look fantastic on screen."

Hegley closed his eyes. I guessed he was trying to think up the forts, figure possible shots.

"I want Theresa Noble in the film," I said.

He grunted.

"And as many of the cast and crew of *Greene Land* as we can assemble."

"Fine."

Hegley pumped some pace into our marsh march and we moved at a fair lick across the mire. He was clear he did these walks often and that they made him a strong beggar for a sixty-year-old.

"There's an actor I know who will be great for the lead," I said. "Name's Alan Smithee. He's working on a film called *Gunwhale*."

"OK."

"Fine? OK? I was expecting Hegley fireworks."

"What else can I say?" He talked to me over his shoulder, didn't slow or break stride. "You told me last time you have me over a barrel."

"You have a reputation of being a shouter."

He stopped walking. "I like you, Root. I told you before that you pulled off the best obituary. I loved that line you wrote."

"Which one?"

"*When it comes to competing with Hegley, no other British directors have even begun shaving.*"

"But you haven't been lying doggo all these years to simply roll over, have you?" I said.

"*Truth is truth…*"

"*To the end of reckoning,*" I said.

* * *

We were back in the kitchen of the oyster cottage before it turned dark. Hegley took off his jacket, hung it on the back of his chair, looked at his watch. "It's after six," he said. "Which means we're allowed a spot of R and R."

He pulled open the door of a tall cupboard, reached up to the top shelf and grabbed a bottle. He placed two shot glasses on the table, filled them to the brim.

"What is it?" I asked.

"Lime schnapps." Hegley lifted the glass to his mouth. "Here's to it, Bob."

I drank my drink back in one. "You mean Bob Crasker, don't you?"

"We got into the schnapps habit during *Greene Land*. Bob used to break out the hooch every night. It helped smooth things over for the next day. Now, when I've finished up here on my own, I have a tendency to toast Bob."

"He'll be good for the film."

"I have to see this treatment of yours to know that."

The alcohol had done a loosening job on my nerves. I opened my bag, pulled out the dozen pages I'd worked and reworked, handed them over to Hegley.

He read through them once, then again. His face gave nothing away. He laid the treatment on the table, smoothed the top page several times with his hand. "Well, doesn't that take the small, flat, sweet cake?" he said.

"Meaning?"

"You're a clever boy, Root, pandering to a fat ego like mine," he said. "You knew, didn't you, that if you pitched a fictionalised biography of my life I'd be hard pressed to turn you down?"

A long-shot of the Woolwich ferry in midstream.
Cut to:
A medium-shot. Boocock and Les Lea, who looks stun-
ning even in a business suit, stand by a railing at
the stern. The camera has them centre frame. It's
a very straightforward shot for *Greene Land* - and
highly disconcerting for it.
"When did you last see Thom?" Boocock asks.
Les Lea doesn't look at him, gazes instead at the
river. "I told you."
"Tell me again."
"The night before he died."
"You slept together?"
"None of your damn business."
"Let me put it another way," Boocock says, "when
you kissed goodbye the milk was already on the
doorstep, wasn't it?"
"Fuck you."
"I think that was a yes."

"Keep thinking," she said.

"You're not helping yourself."

"As long as I'm not helping you."

"You're not doing Thom any favours either."

"I never pretended I could do anything for the dead," she said.

"Thom's alive, you know that."

Les Lea laughs. "If he were he'd be kicking too."

"Me or you?"

She slaps Boocock on his left cheek. He grabs her wrist. She slaps him on the right cheek. He takes hold of her other arm.

"Thom never hurt me," Les Lea screams into Boocock's face. "Not once."

He keeps firm hold. From the distance we're at, the pair could be lovers, staring into each other's eyes, parting from a kiss, no, wait, surely *about* to kiss.

Boocock leans in close, presses his lips to Les Lea's. She tries to draw away, struggles to free herself from his grip. Boocock keeps tight hold and it now seems the couple is engaged in some kind of dance.

Cut to:

A top-down shot of Boocock and Les Lea. Freeze frame. The couple in endless embrace. A saxophone yowls a chain of intermittent sharps.

Fade to black.

CHAPTER TWENTY

I was waiting for Meaghan in the lobby of the St Martin's Lane Hotel in Covent Garden. Justin had brokered the meeting, was obviously doing his fraternal bit in trying to repair us. He'd told me that the place, public with a muted environment, would reduce the chances of a loud spat. I took that as a measure of what he believed Megs's current temperature was. Forewarned, I'd turned up a quarter of an hour early, was togged out smartly in agnès b – Meaghan always had good words when I wore the label – and I'd also showered for the second time that day before leaving the flat. For all that, I had no clear idea what I expected from the meet, from her, from myself. I was presently in a big no man's land when it came to women.

I got comfortable on a two-seater sofa that gave me a view of the single revolving glass door, so there was no way I could miss Meaghan's entry. The place wasn't particularly busy and, apart from the Armani'ed receptionists, the only people I could see was what appeared to be a trio of ad men sitting on a cluster of Starck stools. I flicked through a score of pages of the latest *GQ*, ignored articles on the new Aston Martin and the latest male grooming products, a double-page spread of gadget reviews, along with half-a-dozen Paris Hilton pics.

I thought back to how totally fired up I'd been driving the Beemer back to London. Hegley had really run with the biopic concept, his mind throwing out one thought after another. One thing he talked about at length was what he was calling his time-scatter narrative, something he'd developed during his long years of film exile. It was obviously a fusion of Isenhour and Kuleshov, and it was clear was that it would come into play during the edit, i.e. the cutter would be king. That was why I'd watched more of *Greene Land* on getting back from St Lawrence Bay, had been busy sussing out just what part the editing played in making that film great.

"Dreaming of Paris?"

I started. Meaghan stood tall above me, her eyes on the magazine open on my lap.

I jumped up, was about to give her a kiss. Didn't. I suddenly had little sense of what was, had been, Root and Meaghan.

She sat. She was wearing an expensive navy blue pleated dress I'd never seen before, along with some seriously pointy shoes. She looked stunning, though I sensed she wasn't toting the outfit for me.

I sat next to her at what I had to guess was an appropriate distance. "Are you moving to Austria?" I asked.

"No pussyfooting, is there?" she said. "Root Wilson cuts to the quick. For your information, Vienna's up in the air."

"They might not be sending you after all?" I was relieved at the thought.

"I mean I haven't yet decided."

"What's it come down to?"

"Well, on the one hand, I don't want to go. On the other, I really do."

"Your indecision is final," I said.

"I borrowed the Root method. You couldn't ever make up your mind between your girlfriend and your old flame."

"Harry and I were never an item."

"Ah, the non-consummation defence."

"Why do you have to make Harry sound like the source of all evil?"

"*Root* of all evil is the term you're avoiding." Meaghan stared at me sharply.

"I've become third person, I see. It's almost like I'm not here." I realised I was shouting in a whisper, that Meaghan had been too.

"A reasonable deduction," she said.

"You're cold, Meaghan." I hadn't called her Meaghan for ages – Megs had apparently tumbled from my vocabulary. "Why on earth did you come?"

"I want the kilim."

I forced out an odd, thin-sounding laugh. "That's absurd."

"Give me the kilim."

"I can't believe this."

"You don't know, do you?"

"Don't know what?"

"See, you don't deserve it," she said.

"Look, I'm not about to argue over a rug."

"Then I can have it?"

"No, you bloody well can't."

We didn't talk for a very roomy two minutes. I watched Meaghan undo and redo the clasp on her bracelet over and over. Then I stared at a knee-high wooden chess set at the other side of the lobby, then studied the buttoned upholstery on a Queen Anne chair.

"I got the finance for the film," I said. I had no idea what else to talk about, and this seemed safer territory.

"That's good news."

"I'm shooting a biography of Philip Hegley, and I'm going to re-assemble the cast and crew of *Greene Land*," I said. "That means your mother and father too, of course."

Meaghan's face was suddenly right in mine. "Are you crazy?" she shouted. "Have you completely lost your mind?"

* * *

I left the hotel and went to a faux Victorian pub off Leicester Square, stood at the bar for as long as it took for me to drink my first pint. I carried my second over to a table next to a games machine that oozed flashing bulbs and electronic sounds. Normally I would have baulked at sitting so close to such a noisebox but the inter-ference was discomfitingly appropriate to my mood.

I spent a lot of headtime railing at Meaghan, was appalled by the volume of her anger, her utter unreasonableness, her desire to club me to death with Harry…Harriet. I tore a beer mat to shreds imagining it was a picture of Meaghan. I felt foolish. Then I raged at her for blowing up about Ben and Rachel. I knew how touchy she was about her parents but couldn't fathom what had caused this outburst. It was obvious to me which one of us was out of her mind.

When I left the pub, I wasn't drunk. Then again, I wasn't completely sober either. To clear my head, I decided not to dive into a cab but instead to hoof it down towards Embankment. I crossed Hungerford Bridge and enjoyed looking down onto a river that was boiling upstream while the trains banged behind me. When I landed safely at the RFH, I set off along the footpath in the direction of home.

It was now a decent stretch past midnight, and I didn't have many fellow walkers. I passed a busker – a Jamaican guy drawing blues tunes out a battered electric guitar – and I tossed a handful of coins into his open case. I sang the refrain from 'I Got My Mojo Working' as far as Blackfriars Bridge.

It was there I spotted the strangest thing. I'd never seen anything like it on the Thames before. There was a swarm of lights a couple of hundred yards away, and it hovered above the surface, hopped and dodged, sometimes joined to make what looked a single beam before breaking apart again. There seemed to be no form to it at all, but I could see the lights were closing on me, and it was getting spooky.

As they came out from under London Bridge, I began to make out cigar shapes skidding over the water, saw the flash of paddles. I laughed. It was a party of canoeists, each one of them with a lamp strapped across their forehead. I sang out a line from Mojo, and they waved at me, shot under the next bridge and were gone. I carried on walking.

It was then I was whacked in the back. The force of the blow knocked me forward, and I lost balance, was soon facing off concrete. I could hardly breathe, my whole body seeming to tighten around the point of hurt. I was lying awkwardly, tried to straighten myself up. Then someone smashed me on the legs. Again and again. What the fuck was going on? Had a crazy canoeist come ashore angry at my singing, chased me down with a paddle? I balled myself up. The attacker was swinging a foot hard at my torso, and each kick sent a flame of pain across my back. I thought I could hear my ribs split. I was ready to throw up. I was going to pass out.

The assault stopped. I stayed tucked in. I could hear feet moving away at speed. Everything went quiet. Suddenly I knew why Meaghan wanted the kilim. The first time we made love was on that rug.

I looked up. There was absolutely no one about.

* * *

I washed up at Harry's.

She opened the door, screamed. "Jesus Christ, Root. You look like you just lost the war."

"I was jumped from behind, Aitch."

Harry took my arm, led me down the hall – on my own I would've been thrown by the flat's latest layout – and into the living room that was now far smaller. She let go of me and right away I tripped over the feet of the Dinky Inky. Harry had to move quickly to stop it from crashing to the floor.

"Sit down, Bro," she said. "Please."

I dropped into an armchair and yelped, clutched my ribs.

"Take off your shirt," she said.

"I'll be fine."

"Don't be getting shy on me."

I removed my jacket. The right sleeve was torn, was hanging on by a few threads. The knees were through on my trousers too. I unbuttoned my shirt, took it off. My rib cage was sickening to look at – it had turned a dozen hues of red, was streaked with nasty-looking welts.

"I hope you gave as good as you got," Harry said.

"Lost every round. Didn't swing a punch."

"Well, so you know, you're still the dog's nuts to me." She tousled my hair. "And now you're in good hands."

"I knew I could count on you."

"You're going to need some running repairs, though," she said. "Stay here while I get my tool kit."

I touched the welts, almost jumped off the chair in agony. The bastard who'd worked me over must have been wearing some serious footwear.

Harry came back toting a handful of wadding, a couple of bandages and an enormous bottle of antiseptic.

"You expect me to drink that?" I asked.

"I'm going to whack you over the head with it so you won't whinge. I just so know you're going to be a little boy about this."

My wounds scorched like crazy as Harry treated them, though she did take care, applied very gentle pressure to the worst-hit areas.

I started as the antiseptic ate into a gouge.

"No pain, no…"

"My thoughts entirely," I said.

I noticed for the first time that Harry was wearing a tight-fitting outfit that was doing it in many of the right places. "Odd get-up for a nurse," I said.

"What's up? I hear yellow skinny-rib sweaters and green bike shorts are all the rage at Guy's."

"You're good at this," I said. "Ever thought of taking up medicine professionally?"

"I wore the gear once."

"Tell me more."

"Your body wouldn't stand it right now."

Harry went off to make a drink, left me to pin up the bandaging job.

She returned a few minutes later with a mug. "Here, drink up."

"What is it?" I asked.

"Hot buttered rum."

"Buttered?"

"Helps it go down. There's nutmeg too."

"What's that for?"

"Erm … good for bad breath, I believe." She smiled. "So, tell me what evil befell you out in the dark."

"It's to do with Philip Hegley."

"Wow, biography writing's a lot more dangerous than I ever imagined." She fell back into the chair opposite, sat cross-legged, looked absolutely gorgeous.

"There's something I should have told you a while back." I sipped the toddy, which was so steamingly hot it tasted of nothing. "Hegley's still alive."

"What? Did you take a knock to the head or something?"

"He faked his death."

"And you're telling me he just beat you up down by the river?"

Harry's face looked more beautiful than ever in its puzzlement. I had the wild idea to go over to where she sat and kiss her. I started to move and my ribs gave me a sharp kick.

"Steady, Bro," she said. "Sit still and tell me everything. You just know you want to."

So, I told her about shaking Hegley's hand in Bloomsbury. And about Nesh's window-breaking antics, the carved tyre. Then came Theresa Noble's seances, Huckerby's Spanish drive-off, Hegley in the Eye, his oyster retreat, our biopic. And there was the ubiquity of Ferris Media. Plus I added stuff I thought might well be part of the big picture. Such as the Arriflex incident. Callaghan telling me about Minona's death. Huckerby's love note.

"Minona? You are kidding. Oh, fuck," Harry said. "The dead are brought back to life, the living are gone forever."

"That's a good summary."

"Was Minona done in?"

"Maybe." I hadn't, of course, mentioned anything about the

close-shave session.

"This beating could be another warning from Nesh," she said.

"Possibly."

"God, I bet they turfed me off the Hegley account because I'm too close to you."

I hadn't thought of that but could see the sense. "Sorry, Aitch."

"Not your fault. But someone has to pay for this. I'm on the case with you now, Bro."

I took a sip of the drink. It tasted vile. I understood now why I hadn't told Harry everything before. Because I knew she would weigh up all the clues quick as a kitten, would be way better at this detective game than me. And I suddenly saw the reason why she and I had never been a couple – I'd been so afraid of her totally running the show, of being buried by the force of Harry.

* * *

I spent a bad night on the couch, even though it was at least a couple of notches more comfortable than my own sofa. It wasn't the pain in my ribs that kept me awake, although it didn't help in the deep-sleep department. I had a series of nightmares that began with me lying on a Thames beach being kicked in the tripes by a crowd of shadows. Then I was sitting naked by the water before Meaghan arrived and wrapped me in the kilim. And I was also up at Harry's where I was attacked by the walls, which were shifting crazily around. Justin appeared, turned the lamps on and made me cook under the hot lights.

* * *

Harry was in pamper mode next day. She brought in a breakfast tray with a mug of tea, bowl of cereal, toast, jams, said she'd pop out and get anything I needed before taking off, no trouble, that I could stay at her place as long as I liked, heal my hurts before heading back into the big bad world.

"Thanks, Aitch, but I'm all set. You're gold."

"Bet you say that to all your girls the morning after."

There was a heavy silence. Harry looked surprised by what she'd said, took off quickly down the corridor. I could still smell her, though, the rose and vanilla along with the smell that made Harry Harry.

I chowed down everything, hadn't eaten at all the evening before and was ravenous. Then I wrapped myself in the towel Harry had put out and set off in search of the bathroom, thought it unlikely she'd moved that particular room since my last visit.

I soaped myself carefully in the shower, my ribs still giving me hell, though the pain started to ease under the flow of hot water. I was slowly loosening up.

Through the heavily steamed glass I saw the shape of Harry come into the room.

"Howzit, Bro?" She was shouting so that I could hear her through the rush of the spray.

"I was just having thoughts of Psycho," I said.

"Hey, has that beating frightened you?"

"Takes more than a little scrimmage to frighten Root Wilson, doll."

"Sounds like your brain went wonky though."

"Just routine sleuth talk," I said. "You're going to have to get used to it working on this case."

"You know, I've decided that the thing not to do is go all grassy knoll," she said. "The situation needs careful consideration."

"For sure." I was surprised, Harry being cool-headed was a rare beast.

"Let's go easy on the action," she said.

"I don't think I'm in any shape to play Batman anyhow." I ducked my head under the flow, felt the full force of the water for a couple of seconds.

"I have to dash off to Paris this afternoon. Lots of affaires à faire," she said. "Will you be alright on your own?"

"Ta for the concern, Aitch, but I don't reckon I'm in grave danger."

"Agreed," she said. "Yesterday's attack is a red herring."

"How so?"

"Elementary, my dear Wilson. If Nesh or one of his pros had turned you over, you'd have been minced rather than mashed."

"You're right." Harry was indeed a clever cookie.

"But make sure you tell that detective chappie you mentioned all about it," she said. "It might well send him off on the wrong trail."

"Why would we want that?" I rubbed the shower screen with my palm. The glass was badly smeared but Harry became more than a mere shape, and I watched her pick her way through her gear on the shelf. She was barely dressed, and as she stretched for a bottle, her T-shirt rode up and I saw she had a large butterfly tattoo on her lower back. *I should've known that already*, I thought.

"I want to leave the field clear for the two of us," she said.

"Aren't you getting a bit melodramatic?"

"Look, Bro, somebody has done me over at Ferris. Am I the type to take it lying down?"

"I'd say they better watch out. I wouldn't want to be harried by Harry."

"No?"

"I'd be afraid." I cleared the glass again. Harry was looking right at me.

"I'm that scary?" she asked. "I thought I'd taken good care of you."

"Bang-up job. Only thing you haven't done is scrub my back."

"You think I wouldn't if you asked?"

I listened to the pour of water as I peered at her through the screen. She was no more than a foot away. Harry.

"Bro…"

I opened the door, took her hand, pulled her into the shower. I waited until the T-shirt soaked through, then I took the longest time peeling it from her body. I ran my tongue over her skin, drank in drops of water, couldn't satisfy my thirst. There was no taste of rose, no vanilla. Just pure Harry.

Chapter Twenty-One

I watched Harry from the sixth-floor window as she ran from the building and hopped into the back of a black cab that took her off to Waterloo. I'd promised to meet her hot off the Paris train in a couple of days, but right now I missed her awfully.

I pulled on my battered suit after a few mend-and-make-dos of the jacket sleeve with some safety pins. The tears in the knees of my trews were another matter – I could only hope that people would think they were cool in some urban kind of way. Luckily the studio was only a five-minute walk from Harry's place, and I planned to get a taxi home once the programme had been put to bed so my public exposure would be light.

The short hike, though, turned out to be way tougher than I'd imagined. I was jittery as a bug once I was on the streets, expected to be jumped on at each blind corner, couldn't stop myself from looking over my shoulder every few seconds. And the pains that had vanished for a couple of hours while I enjoyed the incredibly fragrant and soft universe that was Harry attacked me on every step. By the time I got to the studio I was feeling pretty wrecked.

It was clear I was in poor shape for work, and it was no surprise when the session turned tough on me. The editing part of the afternoon went smoothly enough but I was wrung out by the time the Foley team turned up to record their segment. I'd managed to snag Jason and June, who everyone in know-man's land said were the best sound designers in Soho, plus they'd worked on mixes for hot-off-the-griddle Britfilms like *Saxon* and *London to Brighton*.

The session started off well enough as the Jays ran through a number of stock effects. There was much snapping of celery to mimic the breaking of bones – a seriously painful noise after what I'd been through – and the crunching up of a mess of audio tape to bluff rustling leaves. When June crazily flapped a pair of leather gloves to conjure up birds' wings, I could hear in the sound the footsteps of whoever it was that had given me the beating taking off into the dark. My sore ribs fired up again.

The Jays played items from a library of sounds they'd put together that were waiting deployment in the world of celluloid. Then they gushed engagingly about clips of molten iron being poured in a foundry, ambient street sounds from early-morning Gdansk, cows chewing grass in a meadow and the laying of a yard of cement out in the East End. All of them would be great for creating atmos, they said.

They were great talkers but I was severely out of step. True, I hadn't had the time to put in decent prep but I would normally have counted on knocking off a simple set like this in one go. And the Jays had some superb stuff to share, such as how Foley artists seemed to spend most of their time producing footsteps. They were absolute trade staples, and if you couldn't deliver a believable trudge, plod or stomp, they said, you simply wouldn't be able to cut it in the noise trade.

This kind of chat was meat and drink to En Root, but I fluffed much of it, gave far too much dead air. My mind got busy trying to work out who'd attacked me. If Harry was right and the deed didn't have Nesh's tracks on it, then maybe it had nothing to do with the Hegley business. Maybe it was personal. My thoughts sprang straight to Meaghan, though surely she wouldn't set someone on me for a rug. And then there was Justin…

I simply couldn't keep the conversation flowing, was managing, in fact, to knock my interviewees out of their comfortable strides rather than help them along. Even when June came up with the gem about how Jason was unquestionably the best in class at doing high heels, I took us too quickly off topic, failed to milk the material.

I apologised to them both once we'd finally got everything in the can.

"No probs, Root," the Jays said, completely in sync.

*　*　*

I spotted Callaghan in the studio lobby. He'd switched the post-war mac for a duffel coat of the same era, and his glasses were different, too, with stainless steel frames that looked like they might hold up well in a severe storm. He was a rakish character for a mere plainclothesman from the Yard.

"You should have told me you were coming," I said.

"You'd have changed into something more suitable, would you?"

I looked down at my knees – the holes were gaping. "I was jumped last night," I said.

"They take anything?"

"It wasn't a mugging. And it wasn't a *they*. That guy was out to get me."

I told him about the long rib-kicking. My body hurt again.

"Get a look at the perp?" he asked.

I shook my head.

"I'll read your statement," he said.

"I haven't made one."

"You said it happened yesterday."

"I spent the night with my girlfriend. She lives nearby." I was shocked when I realised I meant Harry.

"Didn't you share a flat with Ms Terry?" Callaghan took off his glasses, polished them up with a cotton handkerchief.

"I was with Harry…Harriet."

"I should talk to her," Callaghan said.

"She's in Paris."

"You sure of that?"

"Why wouldn't I be?" I suddenly feared something had happened to Harry, that I'd dragged her into danger. Was that why Callaghan was here? No, he hadn't known anything about her …

or maybe he had.

"Well, you never seemed to know the whereabouts of your previous girlfriend," he said.

"Meaghan's in Hampstead." I felt oddly proud of my knowledge.

Callaghan put his glasses back on, folded the handkerchief and put it back in the pocket of his duffel. "Maybe you should go home and get cleaned up," he said. "And then report last night's goings-on to the bobbies."

"But I told you all about it." More than anything I wanted to get back to the flat and crash.

"Procedures." Callaghan buttoned up his coat.

"Fine," I said. "Why did you want to see me?"

"I didn't."

I pulled on my jacket, managed to tear the sleeve from its seam.

"Not your day," he said. "Though one thing you ought to know is that we verified you were working in the studio when Ms Turner died. You're not a suspect."

* * *

I taped my ribcage up tight next morning, needed the shoring-up job for the busy day ahead.

In the cab out to Rotherhithe I was full of thoughts of Harry. I re-read the dozen text messages she'd sent from Paris, enjoyed their gushiness, revelled in a side of her I'd never known before. Then I sifted through them for details that might tell me just how she felt about me, then looked for those that actually might mean the opposite. This would be a good way to go crazy, I thought. I was about to hit the button that would delete all her messages, but couldn't bring myself to do it.

Shortly after arriving at the Gunwhale Estate, I was standing coffee and doughnut in hand. I watched Abdi and crew shoot a scene that involved the lead jumping on the bonnet of a moving car and trashing the windscreen with a claw hammer. It was odd looking on and realising I'd be working on my own feature shortly.

It had been a couple of years since I'd directed a drama for TV, and this reminded of how much there was to think about for just one shot. Abdi, Crasker, Lofty and Smithee ran through it again and again, broke it down into as many sequences as they could – first positions, vehicle starts to move, hits the marker, protagonist begins his thirty-step run, leaps onto the back bumper, belly-climbs along the roof, piles the hammer into the windscreen, car veers sharply off, stops inches short of the wall.

Lofty was arguing for more crash pads on the ground in case Smithee tumbled. Smithee wanted none at all, was refusing to wear protection on his elbows or knees. Abdi brokered a deal – no pads, but Smithee ought to protect his legs – so in came wardrobe to undo the seams on his jeans, sew them up around some lengths of thick sponge. It took forever.

There were around ten rehearsals until everyone was satisfied, the basic choreography now seeming a big ask for all concerned. But, after so much meticulous prep, Smithee slipped effortlessly into Method and went into action, did the scene to perfection in all of two-dozen seconds.

Then came the set-up for the next shot. New sugar glass was pushed into the frame, Crasker and camera were fitted onto the back seat of the car.

The more I watched, the more excited I got about the film. And I was determined to put together a crew I could rely on.

* * *

I caught up with Lofty as he was measuring out distances with a tape.

"How's it going, Loft?" I asked.

"Root!" He took me by the shoulders. "You're a f'kin' brother to me, man, d'you know."

"Glad to be part of the family. And to see you back running with the bulls."

"I feel top."

Lofty tapped me in the ribs. It was little more than a gentle knock, but the pain fired up instantly and I doubled up, was filled with nausea.

"Jesus, Root. Sorry."

I forced myself to take a few deep breaths even though each one hurt fiercely. "It's … not you," I said. "I got … beaten up … the other night."

"Never had you down for a brawler."

I managed to stand upright again. "I got jumped from behind."

Lofty lowered his voice. "You want tit for tat," he said, "there's a few boys who will."

"Thanks, I'll let you know." I pulled up my shirt, unravelled the bandages and showed off my wounds.

Lofty whistled. "Good job. We should get photos for makeup. They'll love it."

"Happy to help the cause," I said.

Lofty eyed my injuries. "You got lucky. Your man definitely wasn't wearing toe-caps."

"How do you know?"

"Bruising's too light," he said. "And look here." He pointed to what looked like a series of dots and dashes. "That's stitching – means he was wearing f'kin' moccasins, or summat."

"Great, I got beaten up by a guy in slippers."

"And this big round mark here, that was most prolly a ring did that," he said. "And your boy was a left-hander if he took you from behind."

"You're a pro, Loft," I said as I rewrapped my ribs. "I need someone with skills like yours."

"I'm a free man after we're done here."

"Then I name you stunt coordinator on my upcoming film."

"F'kin' great." Lofty balled a fist, was about to give me a chummy bop, then thought better of it.

* * *

I caught up with Bob Crasker enjoying a cigar on one of the estate's long, empty skywalks.

"How did it go with the Arriflexes?" I asked.

"Got great footage."

"Good as Bullitt?"

"Better." He drew on his cigar, hung a rich cloud of smoke in the air.

"I'm working on a film, Bob," I said. "And I need a good cameraman."

"Can't. I have a chunk of TV work lined up."

"I'm planning to shoot Philip Hegley's biopic."

"I'm definitely not your man," he said, "but I can give you some names."

"I know exactly who I want."

"Why would I rehash Philip Hegley?"

"You respected him. Like he did you."

Crasker ground the cigar out on a wall and tossed it off the sky-walk. "The bastard."

"He used to toast you every day," I said. "A schnapps every evening and a *here's to it, Bob*. He did it to the end."

Crasker giggled like a boy.

"Come on, you're the one I want behind the lens."

"After Hegleyesque, are you?"

"I want Crasker's fingerprints all over this," I said. "Bob, you have to."

"I could chat with the television guys." He pulled another cigar from his top pocket.

"Fantastic." I grabbed his hand, pumped it.

*   *   *

"I hear you've been poaching my crew, Root," Abdi said. He was squatting down by the monitor, watching the rushes.

"Cherry-picking is the term you're after," I said. "Don't mind, do you?"

"Three more days and we're done. So it'd be enormous if you have jobs for the people. Crisp that you're doing a film about Hegley."

"News travels."

"Smithee just told me you asked him to play the man," he said.

"I have to talk to his agent."

"Course. But he'll do it."

"You think?"

He nodded. "And Bob won't pass it up."

I crouched down next to Abdi, watched the shot from inside the van when Smithee had hammered the windscreen. The glass smashed gloriously.

"Nice, isn't it?" Abdi said.

"When do you start the edit?"

"Soon as we're done here. I have so much of it in my head right now I can't afford to lay off."

"Still after cash for post."

"I've got the whole eighty thousand."

"Good job. Who's stumping up?"

"While you were eyeing my crew, I went crawling to your financiers."

"Ferris," I said. "The wheel keeps on turning."

Chapter Twenty-Two

I left Rotherhithe all fired up for my own shoot. I got the cab driver to drop me at London Bridge and went for a stroll by the river where I could see the City all showy in the dark – the Gherkin's lights spiralled into the night, the summit of Nat West's tower hung jade in the sky, the needles of financial district's church spires were lit almost white at the feet of the scrapers.

Hegley had given the treatment the nod, and the two of us were now scribbling up a bare-bones script via e-mail. I was also putting together a decent team, what with having signed up a number of *Greene Land* stalwarts and having grabbed a few gems from *Gunwhale*. I was now getting my hands good and dirty on the feature, and it felt great. Not only was this was what I'd been writing and pitching for, I was going to work with a master craftsman. I was ready to cook this film with plenty of gas.

I took off for home to view *Greene Land* once more.

```
Boocock sits alone in the Mozart Cafe. He undoes
packs of sugar, piles up cubes until he's built a
pyramid. Then he balances a dessert spoon on top,
pushes on the handle so that it rotates slowly.
Cut to:
A top-shot. The spoon's at the centre of a round
table. It does a full rotation. Boocock is motion-
less at the bottom of the frame. A man enters from
the top, sits to face him.
Cut to:
An over-the-shoulder shot of Boocock.
"Get that trick from Boy's Own?" the man asks.
```

Cut to:

An over-the-shoulder of Wark.

"Takes years of training," Boocock says.

The over-the-shoulders continue to mirror the dialogue.

"You'll have to teach me some day," Wark says.

"Once I've cracked the case."

"Case?" Wark asks. You're sounding like one of your paperback detectives."

"My guys always do a good job. Cops, on the other hand, are such blunt instruments."

"You have gripes about the police?" Wark asks.

"Couldn't even catch a cold? That kind of silliness?"

"Instead of following me around you could be chasing Thom's murderer," Boocock says.

"Murdered was he?"

"Any fool could tell you that."

"What kind of fool are you?" Wark asks.

"You're a braver man than I thought," Boocock says.

"Shooting your mouth off without your sidekick."

"You're harmless enough. Physically, at least. But you're interfering with investigations. I'll tell you one more time to drop it."

"Where's your 'or else'?" Boocock asks.

"I'll arrest the girl."

"For what?"

"You know she's a pro, of course."

Cut to:

A top-shot. Boocock swings a punch across the table. Wark dodges it easily.

Cut to:

The first of a series of over-the-shoulders.

"Leave Les out of this," Boocock says.

```
"Take my advice and forget her. If she was with
Greene, then she's one blonde who doesn't prefer
gentlemen."
Cut to:
A top-shot. Boocock and Wark sit motionless at the
head and foot of the frame. The spoon turns slowly
on the sugar pyramid.
```

I met Harry off the Eurostar. She was super sharp in a grey flannel outfit, and I imagined how good she'd look emerging from a platform in a cloud of locomotive steam, heading towards her true love.

"That's a classy suit I'd like to do business with," I said as we hugged.

"Did the job on the French."

"And now on me."

We kissed. Harry felt great under my touch.

"Pity we can't take the day off," I said.

"Duty calls, Bro. But I fully expect you to make it up to me later."

"More than happy to play ball."

We took a cab out to the East End and Harry filled me in on her French trip – the possibility of getting her hands on a Daniel Auteuil pic, of inking a distribution deal with Besson, of getting UK release for a flick she simply wouldn't let go straight to DVD.

"Wonderful to have you back in town, Aitch," I said.

"Wunnerful to be back," she said. "But where is it you're taking me again?"

"As per your request we're off to meet Huckerby Junior. We'll get him to talk about Minona."

"And where will we find this geezer?"

"Bethnal Green Working Man's Club."

"Wow, anyone ever tell you that you know how to make a girl feel special?"

"No, not never."

"Good news."

Harry ran her forefinger along my top lip, sent a delicate tremor across my shoulders.

*　*　*

The club proved to be an inspired choice for the launch of H&P PLC – it was almost hikeable from the eastern borders of the finance hub and had just up and come. Harry and I walked in to be greeted by walls Formica-ed to the max, a stretch of booths down one side of the room lit gloriously by a row of pink and yellow tasselled lamps and rammed with what turned out to be financial hacks from the dailies and money mags. A haze floated below the yellowed ceiling, probably some artificial re-creation of a smoke-and-nicotine fug.

"This place is very cool," Harry said.

"There's a rickety table by the stage with your name on it," I said. "You've got a front-row seat for my first emcee performance."

"My hero." She batted her eyelids, pecked me on the cheek.

I had felt I'd done enough for the company after finishing old Huckerby's obit, had decided not to carry on furthering the corporate cause. But when Junior called and asked me to perform for the float it seemed a good opportunity to see him again, to find out just what it was he'd been up to with Min.

I kicked off the proceedings by ushering on stage the Delecta Gals. The fully bustiered ladies delivered a short, full-on version of 'Big Spender' and the audience, pretty much City males to a body, went bananas.

Once the Gals had closed, Junior stepped onto the boards in premium chalk stripe to dedicate the proceedings to his father, and then asked me to read out the obituary. I gave it my best serious voice and earned long and steady applause from the assembled. Junior went into what I took to be stock-exchange boilerplate before handing the event over to me once more.

I was more than happy to get back to the entertainment. I

introduced some blood-warmingly risqué pole dancing from the impressively garbed Wae Messed before the show was closed by a grey-haired local crooner by the name of Matt Moores, who sang 'Fly Me to the Moon' in a delicious cocoa-powder tenor.

Harry and I went backstage and found Junior in one of the place's tag-rag dressing rooms – bare bulbs and peeling paint were clearly de rigueur in this part of London. He was glad-handing a group of moneymen, showing off a Cheshire grin. I'd never seen him look happier. I waited for the band of guys to break up, then went over and introduced Harry.

Junior was clearly absolutely bowled over by her. "Root's kept you under cover," he said.

"He's a good man, though" Harry said. "He takes me out now and again. And we only go to the nicest places."

"Harry shipped in from France especially for this," I said.

"I hope we were worth it." Junior smiled at her.

"No worries," she said. "Paree has absolutely nothing on Bethnal Green."

Wae Messed came into the room, slipped out of her scarlet spangled corset, gave everyone a good view of her impressive chest. She sat in front of the mirror and carefully untied the extensions from a huge rick of hair.

"A bit different from life at H&P," I said. "Tell me, how did the float go?"

Junior rubbed his hands. "Fully subscribed."

"He means they sold every single share," Harry said.

"Last week a big VC firm took a chunk, and that basically underwrote us."

"Now Roger's talking venture capital," she said. "Some outfit buying and selling stakes in companies."

"Harry here's on the beam," Junior said. "Impressive for a woman."

"Careful," Harry said. "Deadly is the female."

Wae Messed began singing wildly off-key. She'd plugged in her earbuds, was listening to The Former Dictators on her iPod. *I woke up didn't know where I was, didn't know where I was, didn't know where I was.*

"Who's the VC firm?" Harry asked.

"FerInvest," Junior said.

"That wouldn't be part of Ferris Media, would it?" I asked.

He nodded.

"I used to work on the Hegley account at Ferris," Harry said. 'It's me who's responsible for you getting those nice fat percentages."

"The more I hear from you, the more extraordinary you seem," he said.

"You know, I think we can do business, Roger," she said. "I see something coming your way."

"You do? Tell me what kind of deal you have in mind."

"Now that H&P's a PLC," she said, "you need to manage the news very carefully. Anything even the slightest bit odd can send the share price south and be very costly."

"What are you saying? Is this blackmail?"

"Don't get me wrong, Roger. All I want you to do us tell me about you and Minona Turner, or I leak your link with a recently dead woman to the press."

"I don't know what you're taking about."

Harry whipped out the prospectus I'd picked up in Min's office, showed Junior his penned message.

His hands were suddenly in his manga, tugging it into new shapes. "We met just a few times," he said.

Harry pointed to the note on the page. "Judging by this, she made an even greater impression on you than I just did."

"We shared certain tastes."

"So, it was just a harmless spot of S&M, was it?"

Looking at Junior's face, I could see Harry had it nailed. My fingers went to my neck, the Bloomsbury shave feeling closer than ever.

"We never did anything dangerous," he said. "I didn't kill her, for

God's sake. My mistake was to fall in love with her."

You like to surprise me when you can, Wae Messed was singing painfully. She'd dismantled her hair, looked to have been scalped.

✳ ✳ ✳

Harry and I rode in silence in the back of the cab until we hit the City. I was pissed off, couldn't believe how Harry had jumped in and taken over my interrogation of Junior. I'd been completely sidelined.

"Christ, Aitch, you went in heavy," I said.

"You think?" She pretended to look surprised.

"Seems to me you lost it after that silly woman crack of his."

"Hardly," she said. "It went exactly according to plan."

"You nicked the prospectus."

"I can't believe you didn't even think to bring it along."

"Look, my investigations have been going pretty well so far."

"Duest respect to you, Bro, but your approach hasn't got you much more than a duffing so far, has it?"

"That's a low blow."

"Come on, I thought that thumping would have got you going. Where's your manly fire?"

"You have enough of that for both of us."

"Dear, I have put a crease in your style today, haven't I?"

"We have very different ways of doing things."

"Thanks to me we know now what Junior was up to. And that Minona was a true belter. I bet she played musical beds with half the blokes at Ferris."

As we drove past the Tower of London I could hear Wae Messed's tuneless singing. *Didn't know where I was, didn't know where I was.*

What I did know was that Harry was way too much. That I'd made a huge mistake sharing everything with her.

Chapter Twenty-Three

I'm off this evening to a rare event. Angels, the world's oldest movie costumier, is holding an auction out west at Bonhams. Expect some fancy prices – I've been reliably informed that some of the togs on offer could fetch as much as sixty kay. So, pen a cheque for that amount and you could find yourself garbed in Alec Guinness's *Star Wars* cloak. Or squeezing into Michael Keaton's Batsuit. And there are Eva Peron get-ups as worn by Madonna – don't cry for me, gals, if they're not your size. Also up for grabs are Mel G's kilt from *Braveheart* – thanks but no thanks – some spiffy sorcerers' outfits magicked away from *Harry Potter and the Chamber of Secrets*, as well as Indiana Jones's hat recovered from the Lost Ark. And what will En Root be bidding for? Easy one, dear listeners. I have my eye on James Bond's *Thunderball* dinner jacket. That's wool with a cool silk lining for the sartorially minded among you. I'm not feeling shaken by the prospect of wearing such an item. Just everso nicely stirred. So look out for me later when the hammer comes down at Bonhams. Proceedings start at oh-oh-seven pm.

After I'd finished up at the studio I made straight for Al's, ordered a long, strong coffee, settled in for a decent session. The shoot was slated to begin in just three months, with Ferris keen to super fast-track the project so it could ride the Hegley wave before it started dipping. My agent was already dealing with the paperwork.

I had a barrel of work to get through. But luckily I'd already filed loads of copy with Tabard for the Net project, though I still needed to put together a decent bank of stuff for En Root. I was planning to compile a diary that I would feed in from wherever the film took me – I was going to call the segment Filmphile and it would include exclusive audio rushes, interviews and behind-the-scenes content.

I fired up the computer, picked up a local wireless signal and got into my mailbox. Hegley had sent his latest draft of the script, and we were now on a daily back-and-forth, planned to have a very basic draft in a couple of weeks so that we could use it at the retreat out at the Essex manor house in Tiptree, start developing the improvised dialog. We were fortunate we had a rough of his memoirs to work from, were able to build a provisional structure. Otherwise, the timetable would have been way too tight.

In his e-mail, Hegley said he'd been boning up on the Maunsell Forts, now had a massive idea, but desperately needed to go and sound the place out. I had to come along too, he said, Naysmith would pick me up the day after tomorrow. *Crack on with the script, good man.*

The cafe was busying up now in the run-up to midday, and there were plenty of faces that never ever made it to my early-morning breakfast sessions. This later shift was a rougher-looking crowd, a mix of road and construction workers, and those who looked liked they hadn't seen much in the way of hard labour in years. I was feeling a bit of a sore thumb tapping on the keyboard of the laptop as they troughed on plates of lasagne and chips, bubble and squeak. Lard and onion scented the room, the sound of knives and forks clashing sounded almost like there was a battle going on.

I got a message from Theresa Noble. She said she had to see me, wanted to know if I could make that day. *Please, please, for me.* I told her to come over late afternoon, sent my coordinates.

I was about to get stuck into compiling a running order for the next show when Callaghan walked in, came over to my table.

"Mind if I join you?" he asked.

I shrugged.

Callaghan sat down. He was wearing a khaki jacket with epaulettes and tin buttons. It was pressed to perfection.

"You should give me the name of your tailor some day," I said.

Callaghan waved at Al, ordered a tea.

"How did you know I was here?" I asked. He and Nesh were similar in that they seemed to be able to get on my tail at will.

"Thanks for reporting the assault," he said.

"Are you following me?"

"We'll continue to make our enquiries."

"I'll report you if you are," I said.

"We'll leave no turn unstoned, as they say."

"I think this is a case of infringement of civil liberties."

Al brought the tea to the table, gave Callaghan a hard stare. "Everything alright, Boss?" he asked me.

"No problems," I said.

"Let me know if that changes." Al folded his towel over an arm and went back behind his counter.

"Your muscle?" Callaghan asked.

"Al looks after his customers."

"Must be good for business."

"What's your business? Little me, it seems."

"I have bigger fish." Callaghan picked up six packets of sugar and poured their contents into his cup. He took a sip of tea.

"You like it sweet," I said.

"New habits die hard."

"You mean ones like listening out for hounds scratching their bollocks in your borough?"

"Stop playing the witty fuck, will you?"

"It's what my listeners expect," I said.

"Well, listen to me." Callaghan banged his elbows on the table, leaned forward, was huge in my face. "I expect you to stick to your airwaves. Roger Huckerby's reported you, says you and your girlfriend are out to blackmail him."

"What? We were just following a lead."

"Lead? You're a radio presenter not a private dick."

I could feel Callaghan's breath, smell sweet tea.

"I'll admit that Harry did go in a bit heavy."

"She shouldn't be going in at all," he said. "It's dangerous. A woman's dead. You were beaten up."

"We thought…"

"Don't think. Don't meddle. Or I'll have you." Callaghan pointed a finger at me. "Everything that's going on is way above your tree line."

Al was back at the table, standing at my shoulder. "You sure everything's good?" he asked.

Callaghan stood up to face him. "And you, you have no dog in this fight at all."

* * *

Harry's OTT-ness had brought Callaghan crashing down on me. She was a clear liability, and this incident proved I was right in thinking I needed to toss her off the case. I picked up my phone, was about to text her before I realised I had to do a face-to-face. This wasn't a stay of execution, though. Harry was on her way out.

I got back to work, managed to put in a few decent hours on the computer before Theresa Noble showed. She turned the regulars' heads with her outfit – a black, almost sheer chiffon dress with a wired hem that bounced sleekly as she made her way across the room. She held out a hand for me to kiss, waited until I pulled out a chair for her, then sat only on the edge of the seat as if she thought it unworthy of supporting her.

"Drink, lady?" Al asked.

She shook her head.

"I have Earl Grey if you'd like."

"Thanks," she said.

"Yes thanks, or no thanks?"

"Thanks, but no."

I ordered another coffee, slept the laptop and turned my

attention to my latest visitor.

"I have to see the script," Theresa said.

"It's not finished."

"Give me a few pages, Root."

"Can't until it's done," I said. "I'd feel naked."

"Interesting thought. What if I turn my girlish powers on you?"

"Won't work," I said. "Guaranteed."

"Are you going to be as awful as this on the shoot?"

"Depends if the actors play up or not."

"I'll be beating the drum for you," she said. "We had good rhythm the last time we did a scene together."

I could feel her clawing at my back again, biting my neck. The blood rushed to my face. I was saved by Al's coffee delivery. I picked up the drink and sucked at it. Too hot – the roof of my mouth burnt instantly.

Theresa hugged my hand. "Come on, darling, give me a peek of the script."

"No way."

"You know, you're no fun."

"You'll get it at the retreat with the rest of the cast," I said. "Your very own copy."

"I can't wait to go to Tiptree."

"Who said we were going to Tiptree?"

"You," she said, "just now."

"I never."

"Did so." She stood up.

"Oh my God, I can't believe it," I said.

"Can't believe what, dear?"

"Philip's the only one who could have told you about Tiptree."

"That's exactly right," she said. "At the seance."

"Christ Almighty," I said. "You knew he wasn't dead all along, didn't you?"

"Root…"

"And you've been seeing him."

"We are lovers after all."

I shook my head. "Well, I'll say one thing, that was a great performance on your part."

She curtsied for me, the hem on the dress dancing along beautifully to the movement.

"I'll have to go over this frame by frame now to get the story to rights," I said.

"Let me know if I can help."

"Why didn't you ask Philip for the script?"

"You think he would have handed it over?"

Suddenly there was an old man standing next to Theresa. He was no more than five-five tall, hair greased back and showily grey at the temples, looking the picture of a gone-to-seed East London gangster. "I know you," he said. "You're Les Lea."

She glanced at him.

"You was excellent in that film. I didn't 'alf fancy you."

"That's kind," she said.

"Thought you was going to be big, but then you sort of disappeared."

"I'll be back. Actors come and go. It's a fashion thing."

"I get it," he said. "You're like tank tops. Like flares, innit." He let loose a hoarse laugh.

"You hear what I said, Al?" he shouted across the cafe. "I told her she was like flares. You know, flared trousers." He began to laugh again, rocked back on his stacked heels.

* * *

When I got home, the door to the flat was open a crack. I put a hand in my jacket pocket and slipped my fingers into the knuckledusters – since getting the beating by the river I'd got into the habit of carrying them with me wherever. I opened up slowly, stepped into the hall. I took a breath.

"In here," a man's voice said.

Nesh was in the living room, sitting cross-legged on the sofa, head leaning back into the cradle of his hands. He looked well comfortable.

"Fucking hell," I said. "This is breaking and entering."

"I've broken nothing," he said. "But I can't deny I'm right here in your home."

"You can't simply walk in."

"Looks like you're wrong about that."

I put my bag on the desk, kept my hand in my pocket, dusters still on. "Get out of here."

"Charming," he said. "I only came to chat about your breach of our agreement."

"I didn't know we had one."

"It was unspoken."

"Ah," I said. "Remind me what it was we didn't discuss."

"You went to the police."

"I don't like having to pull you up on the fine points, but I think you'll find they came to me."

"Nonetheless, it's a violation. More than one too."

"Minona's dead," I said, "and I was done over. You can't blame the cops for being mildly interested."

Nesh stood up, fastened his jacket, a nice single-breasted black blazer with a red kerchief in the top pocket. "You're attracting far too much attention. This is your final warning." He took a couple of steps towards me.

"And here's one for you." I pulled my hand out of my pocket, made a fist at chest height with the dusters.

"You ready to use them?" he asked.

"You want to find out?"

"They're illegal."

"Like some people I know."

"This is ridiculous." He went back to the sofa, unbuttoned his jacket, sat down again.

"Did you have me turned over the other night?" I asked.

"Oh really. That's not my style."

"Did you kill Minona?"

"Excuse me?" He looked genuinely surprised. "That's plain wrong."

"You had absolutely nothing to do with it?"

"Of course not."

"I suppose you weren't out at the shoot? Didn't almost kill us in that car?"

"Now you're being ridiculous."

"I'm having trouble understanding why you can't understand," I said. "It's not as if your shadow hasn't hung over everything since this affair started."

"I've been advising, yes."

"You call carving a hole in my tyre giving advice?"

"I don't know what you're talking about."

"Come off it. You can't possibly expect me to believe that you didn't follow us out to Oxford."

"Certainly not," he said.

"Or leave one of your calling cards in the boot?"

"No."

I took out my wallet, found Nesh's business card, handed it to him.

"That's one of mine," he said. "But not the handwriting."

"Here's a pen. Copy what it says, word for word. And do it fast."

Nesh scribbled *You shouldn't have gone bothering Huckerby* and handed the card back to me. The writing was nothing like the original. It didn't look to me like he'd faked it, had been too fluid for that. A sidekick could have scribbled on the card, but I had him down very much as a man who worked alone.

"Tell you what, Root," he said, "we'll have a proper talk when you've given up playing with silly weapons."

He stood up again, buttoned his jacket once more. "Here's another card, this one has my number," he said.

I looked at it, then eyed the spot where Nesh had last stood. I saw that the kilim had gone. "Where's the rug?" I asked.

Nesh was heading for the door in that enviously easy fashion of his. "Rug?"

"There was an important carpet right here." I pointed to the floor. "Have you…?" I stopped myself from making a foolish accusation.

"You've lost a rug?" he asked.

"Damn it," I said. "Meaghan's been round. I just know she has."

"The door was open when I got here," Nesh said. "I told you rightaways I didn't break in." He left.

I stood there a long time fingering the dusters. Theresa Noble didn't talk to the dead, Nesh didn't go around slashing roadware or doling out beatings down by the Thames. At least I knew exactly what wasn't going on.

* * *

I tried Meagan on her mobile for ages but couldn't get through. So I drove up to Justin's in Hampstead, hoping to find her there. She opened the door soon after I rang the bell.

"You can't simply go to the flat when you want," I said.

"Fine. Have the key." She let it drop onto the path.

"Great now you've thieved."

"I only fetched what was mine," she said.

"What made you think you could have the kilim?"

"You didn't want it."

"I remembered why it was special."

"Too late," she said.

"It's just not right." I couldn't think of anything else to say. I jabbed the doorstep a few times with the toe-end of my right shoe.

"Look," I said, "it doesn't have to be like this."

"Oh no? This Philip Hegley jaunt of yours has wrecked everything."

"You exaggerate."

"It's torn us apart. And now you want to fuck with my parents."

"I don't understand that."

"You never knew my mother had an affair with Philip Hegley on

Greene Land?" she said.

"How on earth could I have?"

"If you'd talked to me I would've told you," she said. "But you gave up on that ages ago."

I began tapping the doorstep with my foot again. I couldn't shake the image I now had in my head of Philip Hegley porking Meaghan's mother at the back of some set while poor Ben Terry was sitting somewhere in a studio pushing out sax notes.

"And you slept with your boss," Meaghan said.

"Only after you moved out."

"Excuse me for getting hung up on details."

"Anyhow," I said, "how did you know?"

"Dennis told me."

"Who's Dennis?" I asked.

"Dennis Tabard. We're seeing each other."

"How did that happen?" The idea of sorting him out with the dusters appealed enormously.

"We met at a Ferris Media bash," she said.

"You have nothing to do with Ferris."

"It owns half my company," she said. "See how right I was when I said you never listened to me. Just as I was right about you and Harry.

I started kicking the step again, felt four feet tall, maximum.

"You're going to slam the door on me, aren't you?" I realised that was what I wanted her to do.

"Actually, I'm planning to watch you walk away, make sure your tail's tucked well and truly between your legs."

I turned my back on her and spotted Justin coming up the path. "My friend," I said. I was delighted to see him, held out my hand.

Without breaking stride, he caught me with a corker of a right hook, put me down on the lawn in one.

Chapter Twenty-Four

I was working magic with the pool cue, was two games up and sitting pretty in the third.

"Shouldn't you stick a piece of steak over that eye?" Harry asked.

"That's the only way you'll beat me." I slammed the target ball in the corner pocket, set up the next shot wonderfully. The injury looked worse than it was – though the eye was still sore to the touch, I could see through it fine.

"Any resemblance your game has to pool is purely coincidental," I said. I missed the next shot, but only barely. "I'll clean up later."

"You're enjoying this far too much," she said.

"Come on, you're way ahead on aggregate, Aitch."

Harry dropped her stripe easily but gave herself little chance with the next as the white ball spun away from a decent set-up. She stood back and examined the lay of the baize. She was wearing some psychedelic T-shirt in glaring colours that made her face pale. Her distressed blue jeans had ugly bleach stains above the knee. Her hair was tied back with a floral headband but odd curls hung down her neck, fell untidily onto her shoulders. Her face needed a decent paint job. Harry was very much off her game.

"Look, I'm sorry about Justin," she said.

"Not your fault. I might have done the same in his position." That was true, but it didn't mean I wasn't smarting. Life had been very muscular recently, what with the riverside beating and now Justin's zinger of a punch. On top of that, Theresa Noble had been stringing me along, Nesh felt able to walk over my territory at will – Meaghan too – and Harry was intent on spreading herself all over my activities. I knew now that I'd been wrong to put my trust in anyone, especially when it came to matters Hegley. I was about to put some of these matters right.

"Still, I feel bad," she said.

"That why you've lost your touch poolside?"

"I wish." Harry leaned her cue against a chair back, picked up a glass and snatched a sip of her beer. "The last few days I've started to realise I have no future at Ferris. All my projects get nixed."

"It's a blip, Aitch. They're merely resting you."

"Downgrading more like. I doubt there's a way back up either."

"They'd be fools to push you out." I sank my first colour, then the second and third in quick succession.

"I'm beginning to think they're fools whatever," she said.

"Then work for someone else."

"Hard to avoid The Federation of Ferris in this calling. Somehow, I can't help but think we need to solve this case to rescue my career."

I took time over my next move. It was a tricky one with the shot slightly masked, and I could have easily snatched at it because sinking it meant winning the game. "That's what I've been wanting to tell you, Aitch."

"You've got something new on Minona?" she asked.

I half-weighted the shot, and the white glided off the cue, hit the target with a beautiful crack and snapped back cleanly. The ball rode evenly towards the middle pocket and dropped out of sight. "Game, set … and you're no match for Root Wilson."

"Don't be a meanie," Harry said. "Tell me what you've got."

"That's exactly it, I haven't got a thing." I racked my cue. "Things aren't going the way I'd hoped."

"We need to sit down and talk the whole thing through. What I want more than anything is to give Hegley the third degree."

"There you go jumping in wildly again. Like you did with Junior."

"I knew exactly what I was doing."

"You lost your rag more like. Pushed me out of the way so you could tackle your prey. That's so typical."

Harry pulled off her headband. Her hair tumbled everyways.

"Look, I have to crack this on my own," I said.

"I know exactly what you're up to, Root."

"It's far too dangerous for me to involve you."

"You bastard."

"Aitch, listen. This is the best way."

Harry spent time wrapping the headband around her fingers. "I've gone from hero to zero in no time at all."

"Oh, come on."

"Here was me thinking we'd be riding off into the sunset together. I've been swimming around in that happy-ever-after stuff."

"Will probably still happen."

"Yes, let's listen to the sound of pigs flapping their wings," she said. "You're well and truly dumping me, aren't you?"

"Look, let's go quiet for a while."

"You want a softly, softly approach, that it?"

"You've got it," I said.

"Well, Mr Detective, you've solved one mystery for me."

"What's that?"

"Why you've always run away," she said. "You're absolutely scared to death of me, aren't you?"

She grabbed the cue and threw it at me. The tip almost caught me in my good eye.

* * *

I was picked up at around five in the morning by a black four-by-four, all smoke-glass-windowed, fleshy-tyred. I sat in the back with Hegley while Naysmith chauffeured.

"Hell of a shiner you have there, Root." Hegley laughed. "Not sure I know of a makeup artist could do a better job."

"I don't understand why people think black eyes are so funny." I touched the swelling with a couple of fingertips.

"How did you get it?"

"Meaghan's brother didn't like me sleeping with his girlfriend."

"Ouch," Hegley said. "Didn't think you were the type."

"It's more complicated than that. His girlfriend – former girl-friend – is Harry. She was the one running your account at Ferris."

"Ah, When Harry met … Root."

I remembered having to duck the flying pool cue, Harry on fire at me. But I was grateful for that as her anger had made it all easier. In any case, I knew this could easily be sorted later.

Naysmith knocked the wagon down a gear to beat a set of lights, barrelled through them at around seventy. A couple of speed cameras blinked at us but they didn't slow Naysmith – either he knew they weren't loaded, or he simply didn't care. We soon ran out of Old Kent Road, were boldly straddling a couple of lanes, the rest of the traffic nothing more than street candy.

"There is always some madness in love," Hegley said.

"Yes, I only just found out you had a fling with Rachel Terry."

"She was some lady."

"Still is," I said. "She's also Meaghan's mother."

"You're joking."

"Perhaps I'm following in your footsteps. I am about to make my first feature."

"If that's so, my boy, beware the twenty-year hiatus."

I was about to ask him why he hadn't told me Theresa Noble was in on his so-called death, but decided to shut it. I reminded myself I'd turned into a solid one-man show now, and the plan from here on in was to share nothing, keep a decent distance from everyone.

I looked out of the window, saw we were up on a bridge. I spotted scores of white hulls stitched along the banks of a river, guessed we were over the Medway. We were crossing at a lick and I noticed Naysmith was scoping us in the rear-view mirror, his dried-fruit eyes sharper than ever. I began wondering if he wasn't the one responsible for me getting done over – he seemed the type who might jump you from behind on a dark night.

"We'll have ten set-ups a day on the shoot," Hegley said.

"That doable?"

"We won't get more because of all our exteriors."

"Should've written a meticulous drawing-room drama."

"Best work gets done under pressure," he said.

"You're right. And we don't want to manicure the thing to death."

I glanced at the speedo. We were riding at close to ninety, had long since abandoned the Medway. I had no idea what Naysmith's rush was.

"I won't stint on lighting," Hegley said.

"Know that." I thought of all the stunning Les Lea shots. "Any big ideas?"

"I'm thinking chiaroscuro."

"Be great for visual tension." I ran through some of the scenes in my head, could almost feel the hard blacks Hegley had in mind. Everything was suddenly coming very alive.

"Exactly so," he said. "The shadow of the characters."

"Fantastic." I couldn't wait for the shoot to start.

* * *

When we arrived in Whitstable, Naysmith parked the car bang up against the harbour. He got out and disappeared into a mess of huts on the quay while Hegley and I waited in the car.

"He isn't hanging about, is he?" I said.

"Boy's a rock."

"Haven't seen his pal Roney for a while."

"Still out of action with a bad back."

"Will he be OK for the film?"

"You can count on that trooper too."

Naysmith was on the quayside once more and standing next to a man in cobalt blue waterproofs.

"Here they are," Hegley said. "Let's go."

The new guy introduced himself as Dave Catt, owner of *The Sturry*, a cockle boat that Hegley had hired to take us out to the forts. He walked us over to where he'd tied up and we climbed down a ladder onto the deck, Naysmith with a huge black bag strapped to his back.

I stood at front of the boat holding onto the rail alongside Hegley and Naysmith as Catt cast off, then steered us away from the walls. *The Sturry* was lozenge-shaped and butted the water, seemed a clumsy vessel to go to sea in compared to the slick yachts and cruisers that filled the port. But Catt took us gently through the maw of the harbour, swung the boat through ninety degrees and brought a lot more horsepower on stream as we pressed into the waves.

I joined him in the wheelhouse, and he gave me a running commentary of the waterscape as we sailed by a mile-long sand spit tagged with a buoy *The Sturry* set rocking. We passed an old harbour tug blowing smoke from a tall stack, then took a sharp turn when we reached the red-flagged oyster marker. Catt told me we should now consider ourselves in the estuary proper. I leaned out of the window, caught the snap of brine on the sharp breeze.

We weren't long out of Whitstable when Hegley began waving furiously. "Dead ahead," he shouted.

I saw what he was seeing. It looked like someone had hammered a batch of nails into the horizon. The Sturry was headed right for Maunsell.

∗   ∗   ∗

Once we arrived, Catt eased off the engines. He told me we were at Red Sands, the only fort that had all of its seven towers still standing, though the walkways between them had fallen into the sea a long time ago. They were strange constructions – four stout legs tapering up some seventy feet above the surface of the water into huge octagonal platforms that supported what looked little more than enormous cisterns with a couple of storeys of tiny windows.

I looked over at Hegley who had a video camera out, was wheeling around, shooting everything on offer.

Catt pointed upwards. "This was the control tower," he said. "They built the others around it in a semi-circle."

"Wish I could've seen them in their heyday."

"Look up there, it still has the antenna from the radio boys."

I saw the arms of the huge sky wire jutting from the top of the stucture. Down the side of the fort, in faded black paint, I could make out the name Radio City 299. I imagined the broadcasters holed up in the steel tank in a storm, their voices and music batting wirelessly towards the mainland.

The Sturry suddenly bucked, threw us all off balance. Naysmith was holding tight onto Hegley's jacket as he continued filming.

"Have to be careful round here," Catt said. "The currents well up. This wide girl stays steadier than most in this water though." He slapped the boat's wheel.

"Get closer," Hegley yelled.

Catt steered *The Sturry* until it was about ten feet from one of the legs.

Hegley tracked his lens right up the platform. "Come on, right in there," he said.

Catt edged a little nearer, and the boat started to get a proper buffeting. "Daren't go any further," he said.

"Do it, man," Hegley said.

Catt shook his head.

"Come on, lightweight. I want to go up this thing."

I couldn't believe it. I looked over at Naysmith who was pulling a rope ladder from the black bag. He started unrolling it.

Hegley came to the stern, collared Catt. "An extra two hundred quid if you get us close enough to attach a line," he said.

Catt puffed up his cheeks, let the air slowly out of his mouth. "It's a tricky business."

"We have to get up there," Hegley said.

"I'm coming with you," I said. I'd been dreaming of the forts for an age.

"Those places are wrecks and someone could get hurt," Hegley said. "You have to stay on the boat. If anything happens to me, the film still gets made."

* * *

Catt opted for the loot and got us in close. We tied a line from one leg of the fort to the boat's bow, tied a second to another and to the stern. That made *The Sturry* steadier in the water, though not by much. Naysmith threw a rope ladder over a horizontal spar between the two legs and tied it off on the boat's railings.

Hegley went up first, Naysmith holding the ladder for him until he'd climbed onto the spar. I steadied for Naysmith who quickly joined Hegley. They both scaled the tower's steel steps which looked as though they might not be strong enough to support either of them. They disappeared into a square hole in the base of the platform.

Catt and I sat in the wheelhouse and waited.

"You ever been up there?" I asked. I wanted to be inside the fort – it had been my discovery after all.

"Sea's my level."

"Still fish for a living, do you?"

"Gave up a while back," he said. "I make more money knocking off gear at the docks."

"Your dad a fisherman, was he?"

"Family had oyster bed rights going back to the sixteen hundreds."

"Shame to give it up then."

"No cash it in. Quit while you're behind is my motto."

We were slap in the middle of a major shipping lane and I sat back, watched the big ships come by one after the next, couldn't see a soul on the decks of any of them. Catt burned through half a packet of cigarettes without saying another word.

I looked up at the platform, wondered what the two of them were seeing. I wouldn't have wanted to be up there alone with a rough-houser like Naysmith. He hadn't said a word during the car ride, had driven like a madman the whole way. I was finding it hard to shake the idea that he'd been the one who hammered me the other night. Nesh had pretty much convinced me that he was telling the truth about his non-involvement in that, and in everything else I'd accused him of, in fact. So was it such a stretch to think that Naysmith and Roney were the villains of all these disparate pieces, that they had been cooking something up? In which case, was Philip safe up there with him?

Catt looked at his watch. "We'll have to move soon to catch the tide," he said.

I checked my mobile, saw I had a signal. I called Hegley and gazed up at the hole in the platform. That was when Naysmith came out headfirst and dropped into the water.

"Fuck me," Catt said.

He ran from one end of the boat to the other, untied the ladder, the two lines, and then fired up the engine. He took *The Sturry* under the tower, steering to where Naysmith had gone in – I'd been watching the spot the entire time, hadn't seen him come up yet. The swell pushed us too far and Catt had to bring the boat round again. I ran to the other side of *The Sturry*, scanned the water. We were taking far too long.

"There he is," I shouted.

Naysmith was lying face down next to one of the legs, the water banging him up hard against its steel, over and over. Catt edged the boat towards him, managed to get it close enough so that I could lean over and grab Naysmith's sweater. Catt joined me, and we dragged him along the hull to the stern where Catt hooked Naysmith's top to a winch and wound him onboard. We stretched him out on the deck. His lower arm was bent out at an ugly angle from his elbow. The left-hand side of his face was battered, his eye hidden behind an evil red swelling.

Catt went hard at it to save Naysmith, pumped his chest, gave mouth-to-mouth. He must have worked him for ten minutes, probably cracked some ribs. But Naysmith never showed signs of rallying. His eyes were wide open, but I couldn't look into them, stared instead at the water draining from his thick sweater, pooling against the rope ladder lying coiled next to him. Catt finally wore himself out. He went over to the rail and threw up.

I saw Hegley come down from the fort. He climbed onto the horizontal spar and shouted to Catt who ran back to the wheelhouse. He steered the boat over to Hegley who leapt into the water. We helped him onboard. Catt turned *The Sturry* back towards the port.

But we'd missed the tide, had to hang by the sand spit for an age. Hegley told us over and again the story of how he and Naysmith had been filming in the fort. *Had to be careful up there, hard work keeping your footing, couldn't see much by the light of the camera. Making our way back to the entrance, the phone rang, Naysmith standing close to the manhole. The noise startled him, he stumbled, hit his head against a girder and down he went, right into the hole.*

* * *

I sat alone at the bow, couldn't face seeing Naysmith lying at the back of the boat. A half-mile off the shore, I stared at Whitstable, could pick out traffic and people in the streets, wished I was over there with them doing the mundane instead of waiting out the tide on what had become a floating hearse.

Hegley sat down next to me. "I've made an arrangement with Catt," he said.

"What kind of arrangement?"

"For a few grand he's prepared to say he took just you and Naysmith out to the fort. And he likes the idea of putting one over on the cops. He has the story down already."

"I don't get it."

"I'm persona non persona, Root. It's time for me to disappear."

"But…"

"It makes no difference to what happened," he said. "And the narrative doesn't have to change much."

"Fuck, you think you can direct everything, don't you?"

Hegley slammed the heel of his shoe hard into the railing. "Look, I go to the authorities and the shoot's over," he said.

"So we postpone it for a while."

He laughed. "You think you've got your film deal with Ferris when they get wind of this?" he asked.

"It was an accident."

"One that becomes a major news story once I'm involved," he said. "The corporates will stamp on this little project, no doubt about it."

I knew he was right. But we'd be taking a hell of a risk.

"Come on, Root," he said. "We have to do it for the good of the film. For your film."

*   *   *

I picked Hegley up in the four-by-four in the car park of a pub on the way out of Whitstable. He jumped into the passenger seat.

"How did it go?" he asked

"They bought it," I said.

"Good man," he said. "How did Catt do?"

"He's a pro." I'd just come out of a four-hour talking shop with the police, had little left to say.

Hegley smiled. "Come on, Root, we did it. We saved the film."

"At what price?"

"Like I told you, it makes no difference to anything this way."

I found a gear and pulled away from the harbour.

"We can come clean once we've done this thing," he said.

```
The sun is throwing diamonds of light off water.
The image turns grainy. It darkens, breaks up. Dis-
solve.
Droplets spatter the lens. We hear the sound of
splashing water.
Cut to:
A medium-shot. An oar bats the surface of the wa-
ter. The camera pulls back. We see a boat. One man
rows, faces another at the stern. Both oars hit the
water.
```

Cut to:

A long-distance top-shot. The boat's alone at the centre of a lake. The shape's familiar. It's the Serpentine, Hyde Park.

Cut to:

A series of arc-shots. Boocock continues rowing, Greene watches.

"Middle of the lake's not such an odd place for a dead man to fetch up," Boocock says.

"West End's my neighbourhood nowadays."

"No one knows you in the nice part of town, that it?"

"That's about right, pal."

"I'm no fan of ponds, though," Boocock says.

"Still can't swim?" Greene asks.

"Never got the taste for it. You were always a bit of a fish, if I remember right."

"Why I ended up in the docks perhaps."

Boocock stops rowing, pulls up the oars. Greene trails a hand in the Serpentine.

"How's the writing business?" Greene asks.

"I'm working on a story about a man who dies, then comes back to life."

"Jesus."

"Not him. This chap can't quite walk on water," Boocock says.

"No miracles then?"

"Just the odd surprise along the way."

Greene shakes his head.

"Who was it who was killed that day?" Boocock asks.

"Some bloke who didn't matter."

"We all matter."

"Point of view," Greene says. "Look, pal. See all these people around the lake? One of them falls in and drowns, who cares?"

"They do."

"Most would be very happy it's not their turn."

"So, was the man at the docks murdered so you could disappear?" Boocock asks.

"The sweetest of sacrifices."

"Fuck, what happened to you?"

"Only thing I did was grow up. Where did you go wrong?" Greene asks.

"I'm one of the good guys."

"No one ever tell you they're the ones who lose."

"The game's not over," Boocock says. "Wark's onto you."

"You know Wark?"

"We have regular conversations. Are friends almost."

"Be careful who you cosy up to, I say."

Greene stands up, starts rocking the boat from side to aide.

Cut to:

A bow-shot. The prow rolls violently, Boocock's head and shoulders sway. There are sharp counter-movements from the camera. Suddenly it's a sickening ride.

Cut to:

A side-shot. The boat's steady once more. Greene is still standing. Boocock has his head in his hands. The camera travels full circle around Boocock and Greene, comes to a stop.

"It's important you know who your real friends are, pal," Greene says.

"Tell me. Do you love the girl?" Boocock asks.

"Like the man said, women should be obscene and not heard."

Boocock jumps up, takes a step towards Greene. The boat rocks again.

"Take it easy, good guy," Greene says.

Boocock sits.

Fade to black.

Chapter Twenty-Five

Back in London, I spent a few hours in bed, slept only fitfully, waking up each time with a start, my mind replaying the footage of Naysmith's deadly dive. I got up and viewed *Greene Land* the whole way through. I was only half watching it, was happy for the comfort it provided – I knew exactly how the narrative would play out and felt all the more secure in that. Plus, of course, Naysmith, or at least a younger version of him, was alive once again.

When the film was over, I went to the bathroom, stood under the shower until the water ran cold, then dressed and left the flat. The river was the only place I wanted to go. I picked up a cup of coffee and a few newspapers, and as I waited for the ferry I scanned the news, wondered if there might be articles about a drowning, even though I knew it was far too early for the story to have got into print. I finished off my drink as I walked down the gangway, felt slightly more of the world.

The boat was jammed with commuters until it reached Canary Wharf, but after that I pretty much had the run of it for the remainder of the trip, aside from a teenage boy who was sleeping along a length of seats in the cabin and a blue-haired girl who hung near the exit, a phone shoved in her ear.

Greenwich was as far as the ferry went, but I hoped the return trip would give me enough time to think things through before I got to the studio. I made my way to the stern where I could feel the even bass of the engines in my bones, watch the propellers thrash the water, taste the metal of the river spray on my lips.

Hegley had been absolutely right when he'd said that presenting himself to the police would kibosh the film. And it was true that we could fess up once the shoot was over for all the difference that would make to poor Naysmith. Yes, we'd be in serious trouble, but the film would be a done deal. They couldn't take that away from us. It was a rational enough argument. But…

I saw a police inflatable cast off from a jetty in Rotherhithe, pick up pace and rush in the direction of the ferry. My first thought was that they were onto me, my second that there was nowhere to hide. But when the launch was about thirty yards away, its bow twisted away and the craft bounced off towards Tower Bridge, disappeared below its span in under a minute. Life felt very hairy right now.

Maybe if I'd kept better watch when Naysmith had hit the water then we might have got the boat to him in time, pulled him quickly on deck. It could have given Catt some kind of chance to bring him round. I shuddered. Fuck, I'd never seen anyone die before.

But Hegley, he'd barely stuttered, been able to quickly work up a plan to keep the shoot in the frame. Then he managed to persuade Catt and me to go along with it. Was that the kind of man it took to make a film? If so, I wasn't sure I was up to it.

I got off the boat at the Greenwich turnaround and spent half-an-hour nosing through piles of second-hand books in a shop close to the pier. I found a set of imported pulp novels on the same imprint, all with rakish fifties covers and in great nick. I picked out a small lot that included a Thompson, a Hammett and a Polito, then hurried back to the ferry. I managed to get through the first thirty pages of *The Grifters* by the time we tied up the Royal Festival Hall. Thompson quickly nailed the story. I really got the characters. I got what they were in the game for. I got that Hegley would always do what was needed to make the film.

The tide was out. I went down the steps to the edge of the river. I picked up a pebble, skimmed it across the water. Got myself another. Hop, hop, hop. I tossed one more. It was now very clear that you had to be as hard-boiled as possible to get the job done. It was time for me to do some heavy lifting if that was what I wanted.

Today I'm sad. And that's because the news is in that Roger Deakin is dead. In the dailies, you rarely saw his name above the fold, and his obits are unlikely to deplete the nation's ink reserves. But Roger was big. First of all, there was that book of his, *Waterlog* – think Burt Lancaster in *The Swimmer*, and add a green twist. Its full title was *Waterlog: A Swimmer's Journey Through Britain*, and Roger actually did travel the country, swimming every river, canal, lake and lido he came across on a trip that started in the Scillies and washed up in the Hebrides. He wrote the aqua-jaunt up as an environmental travelogue in which he made the case for wild swimming. Well, you all know I'm a bit of a water baby, so that played absolutely straight to me. But I was also a devotee of Roger's filmmaking, and he made super documentaries of places along the Thames, so make sure you look out for them in the next couple of weeks on Beeb Two. I've been assured they will pop up late nights. Roger was recently the subject of a fantastic radio programme that included segments of the creaks and groans of his old Suffolk house. Plus there's audio of him swimming in his moat that I think is pretty choice. On that splash, I'll tell you that I was actually at the launch of *Waterlog* at the Oasis open-air pool in Covent Garden a few years back. Like all invitees, I was asked to dude up in swimwear, and I went along in a nifty Victorian one-piece I'd picked up from a charity shop. I remember the band played Loudon Wainwright III's 'The Swimming Song', and so you're going to hear that piece of music right now. Then I'm going to give you a clip of Roger doing his moat float. Fitting tribute.

I came out of the studio feeling pretty ropey. Recording the Deakin piece got me thinking about Naysmith once again, and I began wondering how his chum Roney might be taking it over in the Jam Factory. I hadn't heard a thing from Hegley since getting back from Whitstable, and I needed him to get in touch, tell me we were doing the right thing, that nothing was more important than getting the film made.

I had a ton of work to do with Cushman. I'd come across lots of overmatter of Roger Deakin in the swim in the BBC archives and had decided it would be a good idea to deploy some of it, make a bed for the entire piece that we could fade in and out. Cushman had sorted through scads of tape for me to listen to, so I went off to find him in his soundshop.

I wasn't too far into the task before I realised that a lot of what I'd dug up was sub par, that it was going to be tough finding stretches of clean audio more than a few seconds long. It was obvious Cushman would have to do a huge amount of stitching to make this thing work. I pulled off my headphones. "Maybe this is a bad idea," I said.

"We're doing it now." Cushman twisted a couple of knobs on the mixing board – water sounded loudly in the speakers, bar graphs spiked.

"It wouldn't be so bad without it."

"Bit half-arsed, though," he said.

I nodded, enjoyed that I was working with a pro, even if it was Cushman. "What you mean is, it'd be like black-and-white instead of colour?" I winked at him.

"You say so." He pushed the slides around a bit, got rid of some of the white noise that was hanging around us.

"But you'll be doing this for hours," I said.

"Don't mind."

"Work is the new leisure, hey?" I clapped him on the back.

He shot me a look. "You think I need to get a life, that it?"

"Just joking, Cush."

"Not bloody funny. And don't call me Cush."

"Sorry all round," I said. "Tell me, though, why do you have it in for me?"

"Don't then."

"Come on, you get all amped up whenever I'm around. Is it the show? You think it's crap or something?"

"Bit slick."

"The material, you mean?" I asked. "Or me?"

"You reckon you're part of the media-ocracy."

"Just doing the job," I said.

"Think yours is so big it drags."

I laughed. "You're a nut."

"Don't you fucking call me."

Cushman was up out of his chair, standing right in front of me. His hands were almost in my face. I got an extreme close-up of his tiger-eye ring, thought what a bad deal it would be to get belted with that. Then I remembered Cushman was a lefty. I felt my ribs. I looked down at his shoes. They were thick leather, the uppers tied together with heavy-duty stitching. Almost like moccasins. The idea was starting to fit very well.

I stood up. "You live close to the river?" I asked.

"Bankside."

"Ever go out for late-night strolls? Ever see canoeists out on the water?"

Cushman was watching the floor.

"It was you, you fucker, wasn't it?"

He grabbed the ring with a finger and thumb, twisted it around his finger, ground it into a knuckle. "Minona," he said.

"What about her?"

"She's dead."

Fuck, Cushman was about to confess that he'd killed her. Then he'd surely sort me out. He could do me easily, as he'd already proved.

"I loved her," he said.

He did it. I wondered if I could squeeze past him, pull open the door and get out before he grabbed me. Unlikely. He seemed pretty light on his feet. Perhaps the best I could hope for was getting the first one in, though the last time I'd hit anyone and meant it I was probably still in short trousers. What I really needed to do to come out of this still breathing was to play Cushman a little so that he'd drop his guard. Then I could make a move.

"I'm sure Minona loved you too," I said.

"Fuck off."

"Just because she never told you."

"I knew the two of you had a thing," he said.

"That why you were always so antsy?"

"Tell me you didn't hurt her."

"Why would I hurt Min?" I said. "Jesus, you don't think I…?"

"The cops were asking about you. I couldn't believe they didn't arrest you."

"So you turned vigilante, that it?"

"I was watching her. That was how I knew it was you. Though I did think for a bit that it might be old baldy."

"Baldy?"

"That wiry guy who visited her. He always had that bloke with him. Looked like a bouncer."

"Hegley. Naysmith." I was finding it hard to take in what he was telling me.

"Who?"

"Just thinking that she was certainly putting it about."

"Shut it. You're lucky I didn't take you out by the river."

"Know what? You clobbered the wrong guy."

"You telling me you never, ever … with her?" Cushman began clubbing his thigh with his fist.

"I'm not saying that at all."

"What then?" he asked.

"Just that I was one of many."

"Fuck you."

"And that a one night stand was all she was worth."

"You bastard." He was punching the back of the chair.

"She was asking for it, Cush. And I never say no to a lady."

226

He stared hard at his feet.

"So I let her have her fifteen minutes of fame," I said.

"You cunt."

Cushman threw a huge haymaker that I dodged easily. And then I stuck a firm one right in his gut. He stayed upright for a half-second before going down.

The knuckledusters felt good the way they sat in my palm. I hadn't been able to put them on properly in my pocket but wrapping my fingers around the brass had done the trick, had given my punch the weight it needed.

Cushman was lying curled up at my feet. He moaned.

Well, now I knew why I'd been worked over. But Cushman certainly hadn't done Min, had he? Otherwise he wouldn't have had me pegged for it.

* * *

I left the studio, went down to the river. I took in a lots of deep breaths, realized I was on a bit of a high. Dealing with types such as Cushman was good for body and soul, no doubt. And it was time I started hitting back. I was ready to make that film.

The problem was, Cushman likely still thought it was me who'd done for Min, and that meant he'd go to the police once he got his wind back. I had to go to ground.

I went home, squeezed a bag full with clothes. On my way out, I chucked the car keys on the hall table – if Callaghan and Co started hunting for me they'd certainly be on the look out for the Beemer.

On the concourse at London Bridge Station, I put in a call to the only person I could trust. I asked him if I could lie low at his place for a few days before heading out to the retreat.

"Stay a f'kin' year if you have to," Lofty said.

I bought a single to Blackheath.

Chapter Twenty-Six

Lofty put me in the spare room of his top-floor flat in Blackheath. The place was crammed with cinema collectibles. There were scads of books about movie stunts and a stash of stuntmen biogs, plus what looked to be a car crash manual. He had a whole shelf of six-inch lead figures that included likenesses of the likes of Harrison Ford as Rick Deckard and Jack Nicholson as Jake Gittes. There was also a collection of miniature studio sets in balsa – I recognised the bank lobby from *Dog Day Afternoon* right off – which Lofty told me he'd bought as a job lot at a flea market during a dream gig in Tinseltown a few years ago.

I thought of the Union Street loft full of lamps and flags I hadn't seen in a while. "If Harry knew you had this gear, she'd crack right on over," I said.

"Another buff is she?"

"A certified film freak."

"Get her round here."

"Another time." Truth was I missing Harry like mad.

* * *

Next morning I went to work on the latest version of the script. I read through Hegley's rewrites and notes, redid some of what he'd written, added some remarks of my own. This to-ing and fro-ing between us was laborious stuff, and when I did the rewrites of the rewrites it felt like we were merely inching along, like we couldn't possibly get the draft together in time for the retreat. I far preferred crafting brand new scenes, streaming one idea after the other before going back and doing creative edits to make those thoughts hang together in some kind of structure that made sense. That was when I felt real progress was being made.

But today I wasn't even beginning to cut it, and after a couple of hours I'd merely pushed a few hundred words around and certainly added nothing to the whole. I needed to do something pretty drastic. I copied and pasted a scene so that it landed ten pages earlier in the script, believed that would add a new dynamic to the section I was trying to develop. I read through the changes, went over them again. Damn, it was a no-go, threw up far more problems than it solved. I put the scene back where it had started out.

I needed to leave the space. I went to the kitchen, boiled up a mug of coffee and drank it as I looked around Lofty's place. I leafed through some of his books. *The Secret Science Behind Movie Stunts and Special Effects* was far too technical, really didn't fire me up, but I got a kick out of *Stage Combat: Fisticuffs, Stunts and Swordplay for Theater and Film*, wondered where I might find out more about something called katana-style fighting, which sounded like it might prove a useful tool in all the scrapes I was getting into nowadays. I looked over the balsa studio sets – the bar from *Casablanca*, *The Great Escape's* Stalag, the mission from *Vertigo* – and marvelled at the detail that went right down to the stitching on the protagonists' clothing. And, of course, that was it. These were true labours of love, and that was exactly what this script was meant to be, while what I had been doing was treating it as a mere grind. I went back to the screenplay with new appetite.

But whatever I tried, I still couldn't make the writing sing out as loud as I wanted it to. Maybe the length of the thing was intimidating me. After all, I had so far been largely a short-form man, the TV dramas I'd completed never running beyond thirty minutes, while now I was having to reach out to an hour and a half. Could it be that I was overstretching myself here?

"Come on, man," I yelled. "Male up and do this thing."

What I really needed was a powerful dose of what I was aiming for. I took the DVD of *Greene Land* out of my bag, slotted it into the laptop and, when it had loaded, fast-forwarded the action until I got to what for me was the highlight of the film. The final scene.

A blurred, low-key shot. Pale shapes move from left to right, right to left. The imagery becomes increasingly surreal. White drips off black, then dissolves. There's no sound.

The focus burns in. Water, ships. We're in the docks. Men walk by pushing trolleys. We hear the roll of metal wheel across pavement, now the bawl of heavy machinery.

Cut to:

An extreme close-up of Boocock's face. His skin is powder, eyes onyx. He strikes a match. The flare destroys the shot.

Cut to:

A close-up of Greene's face. He's smoking. He steps into shadow and disappears.

Cut to:

A standard two-shot of Greene and Boocock.

"Didn't think I'd be back in the playground for a while," Greene says.

"Boys never could stay away from their toys," Boocock says.

"Talking of which, where's the skirt?" Greene asks.

"Les is safe."

"Odd word for her."

"Not if you treat her right," Boocock says.

Greene laughs. He tosses the cigarette away. "Come on, where's the lady?"

"Sends her apologies." Boocock says. "Couldn't make it this evening."

"You've got me here under false pretences."

Cut to:

A close-up of Greene's face. There's a loud click.
A smile breaks on his lips.
"A gun's some plaything, even for you," Boocock
says.
"It sounds pretty when it goes bang-bang."
"You wouldn't."
"You brought some friends along."
There's the clean sound of a gun going off. A long
reverb. Green's still smiling.
Cut to:
A top-shot of Stranks sprawled on concrete. Greene
stands over him.
Cut to:
The two-shot. Greene throws the gun at Boocock,
hits him in the chest. Greene turns and runs. The
camera tracks him until he disappears around a cor-
ner.
Cut to:
A hip-shot. We're moving with Greene. There's mu-
sic. A sax. A series of dissonant bass notes. We
jump onto one barge, skip onto another, another.
We lose footing, just make the next leap but then
stumble. We run more slowly. Now we're back on the
dockside.
Cut to:
A long-shot. A silhouette of the legs of a skele-
tal structure. A man scales one side. Gradually he
climbs out of the frame.
Cut to:
A top-shot. Greene moves up a ladder. Over his
shoulder we see a group of four men on the ground
below him. Boocock. Wark. Two cops in uniform.
Cut to:
A medium-shot. We see Greene is up a Thames crane.

The gantry is raised, lords it over him. He suddenly looks powerless.

Cut to:

A top-shot. The camera gawks down a long length of
ladder. Boocock steps on a rung, starts to climb.
Long sax notes.

Cut to:

A medium-shot. Greene tries the door of the crane
cab. Locked.

Cut to:

A top-shot. Boocock climbs and climbs. A succession of glissandos from the sax. Boocock passes the
camera. We see Wark thirty feet down the ladder and
coming up after him.

Cut to:

A medium-shot. Boocock stands next to Greene in
front of the cab.

"Do me a favour," Greene says. "One push and it's
over. Hanging's not good enough for me."
Boocock looks down the ladder at Wark. "I've got
him," he shouts.

"Come on, pal. I tumble in there and drown and who
cares?" Greene says.

He runs at Boocock, Boocock fends him off, Greene
topples backwards and off the crane.

Cut to:

A top-shot. Circles spreading slowly outwards on
slippery dark water

A saxophone slur.

Fade to black.

As I watched the credits roll, I almost couldn't believe what I'd
just seen. I whacked the keyboard with my fist. What had I been
thinking? All the time I was waiting on the boat out at Maunsell

I'd been worried about Hegley being alone up there with old raisin eyes. But Naysmith was the one I should've been concerned about.

And all of a sudden I was able to spell out a very different story. Hegley had insisted that I stay on the boat with Catt. That was because he was planning all along to deal with his long-time henchman. It could have been that he hadn't meant to kill him, but certainly he had some kind of rough intent. And after the act, hadn't he oh-so-coolly got Catt and me to go along with his get-out? He sussed that Catt had a strong weakness for sterling. He was certain I'd do the necessary to keep the film rolling.

But what about motive? Surely it had something to do with Minona. Come on, Root Wilson, think it through from the beginning. Hegley had lied to me about not knowing her. Unnecessary if there'd be nothing to cover up. And I knew for sure he'd seen her because Cushman had spotted him going to her flat. She worked for Ferris, so it had to be linked somehow to his need to get back behind the camera. How on earth could I slot Min into that?

I was obviously looking at it from the wrong angle. What I needed to work out was how I fit into the narrative. Hegley had sought me out in the first place because he'd wanted to use me to make a film. As he'd said, even before I got a deal of my own I would have been useful fronting for him. And it looked as if he'd played me, had sucked me into some confection of Ferris as evil empire, Nesh as the corporate hit man. I had been well duped.

It wasn't beyond the bounds of possibility that the well-connected Minona had found out from company high-ups that Hegley was still alive. Had she perhaps tried her hand at blackmail? It wasn't something I'd have put past her. And perhaps the two of them had got together as well – I could see how Min would get a sexual kick out of sleeping with a dead star. And if she had tried to put one over on him, there was no way Hegley was going to let her stop him shooting the feature he'd been waiting two decades to make. So he'd killed her.

And Naysmith? He'd been sticking to Hegley like a piece of gum for ages, would have known everything about what had happened to Minona. Perhaps he'd been threatening to go the police. That could explain why he'd been so hepped up on the drive down to Whitstable. And why Hegley needed to sort him too.

The picture I was painting was pretty compelling.

Chapter Twenty-Seven

I left the flat, and, as Lofty had instructed, I walked to the church and then cut a strict diagonal across the heath. As I slogged my long way across an eerie spread of green that was way short on tree, I realised exactly what it was I was saying. That Philip Hegley, director of *Greene Land*, was a double-killer. Much as I didn't want to believe it, I was now convinced it was the truth.

When I got to the Hare and Billet, I bought myself some courage. I ordered a vodka and knocked it back, wondered if I should get a second, maybe just go for the bottle. I couldn't though – I had a plan and needed to stay sober to see it through.

I found a corner of a long oak table and booted up the computer. Lofty'd said there was certain to be a free Wi-Fi signal to ride, and he was right. I got into my mailbox and wrote to Hegley, told him I was still working on the pages, would send them over short-short, worst case I'd bring them to Tiptree, either way no worries, they'd be in decent shape. The idea was to keep him on the simmer until the retreat. I was now mentally writing up a big scene in which I would nail Hegley in front of his beloved cast at the retreat. It would be pure theatre, and utterly appropriate.

I was relishing the thought when the phone rang again. It was Meaghan.

"Harry was in the office," she said. "She interrogated me about my parents and about Hegley. What's she up to?"

"Haven't the faintest."

"I got security to throw her out," Meaghan said.

"Is she OK?"

"As if I care. But you listen to me. Make sure you keep that pet of yours on a tight leash."

Then she was gone.

Junior had phoned while I was on the phone with Meaghan and left a message. He was angry as hell. Harry had collared him somewhere in the City. *The two of you keep this up and I'm going to get very, very legal.*

I discovered more about Harry's moving and shaking a few seconds later in an e-mail from Theresa Noble. Harry had been round to her house and given her what sounded like the third degree over Hegley's whereabouts. Theresa thought she might just have let slip that Philip lived in St Lawrence Bay.

Well, wasn't Harry busy laying a breadcrumb trail?

I called her. To my surprise she picked up immediately.

"Sounds like you're getting all Rambo-ed up." I said. "You've scared up half of London."

"I've been doing the necessary footwork, visiting all the basic ingredients," she said. "That's what real detectives do."

"I told you to back off the case."

"I'm doing this for me now."

I could hear the sound of an engine building up revs, a gear change. "Where are you?" I asked.

"On the road."

There was music. I could just make out the lyrics. *It's everybody's truth that they've just been used.* It was the Former Dictators – Harry was in the Beemer.

"You stole my car," I said

"Mr Melodrama. I went round to your place and saw you'd put the keys out for me."

"You're heading out to Essex, aren't you?"

"Maybe."

"Don't go anywhere near Philip Hegley."

"Unbend a bit, won't you, Bro? We are on the same side after all."

"Which is why you have to turn around."

"Say please."

"Please, Aitch."

"Sorry, no can do."

"You have to come back to London."

"I'm going to say goodbye now."

"Wait," I shouted. "Hegley killed Min."

"I think you're a bit off beam there, Bro."

"You have to turn around."

"You know, a girl's gotta do, etcetera," she said. "This is Harry's game now."

The phone went dead.

∗ ∗ ∗

I quickly dug up a rental car in Blackheath, then got caught in a snarl of trucks and cars low-gearing towards the Blackwall Tunnel. I kept hitting the phone's redial button but was getting nowhere. Harry had clearly gone dark. I imagined her working the Beemer hard ahead, was afraid she was closing too fast on St Lawrence Bay. I reckoned that at best I was some sixty minutes to the rear, and I badly needed to eat into that time.

I called Hegley but couldn't get through to him either. I tried Nesh but only got a voicemail welcome. I reeled off a brisk message, told him to head to St Lawrence Bay at the double-quick.

I checked the time, realised I'd been on the road for almost an hour, had only put a handful of clicks on the dial. Shit, now I could imagine Harry parking outside the oyster cottages.

It was a relief to exit the northern side of the tunnel and to find the traffic far less sticky. I went at it like a madman, made Naysmith's recent spin down to Whitstable seem like a master-class in controlled driving. I prodded the car into every gap, flung myself ahead of the pack at traffic lights, was out of the blocks at the merest blink of amber.

Harry must be in the house by now. I couldn't bear the thought of anything happening to her. Why on earth had I just cut her loose when I'd been so completely sold on her for years?

∗ ∗ ∗

In St Lawrence at last, it took me far too long to find Hegley's – I needed a couple of tours of the town before I saw what looked like the cottages. As soon as I spotted the Beemer, I jumped on the brakes and hopped out.

I pushed open the front door to Hegley's house and checked out the nearest rooms. No one. I went into the studio. Empty. But there was something showing on the screen. It was *Greene Land* and Les Lea was on stage at the Shirley Ann in Peckham. The sound had been turned off.

I went to the back of the house where I heard voices. I caught sight of Hegley through the window. When I saw he was with Harry I almost shouted out with relief. The two of them were sitting at a table on the patio eating strawberries and cream. I went outside.

"Root." Hegley jumped up. "Harry said you might join us."

"Hi," Harry said. She was perfectly fine, looked very pretty got up in some floral dress that shouted summer. I went over and hugged her.

"Harry, you OK?" I asked quietly.

"Everything's dandy," she whispered. "Just follow my cues and we've cracked this."

"Tea?" Hegley asked.

"Yes, have one, Root," Harry said. "Philip's made a fresh pot and broken out his best silver."

I shook my head. I didn't know what Harry was up to. But I was pretty sure I had Hegley cold anyway.

"Philip showed me the screenplay, and I like," she said. "I'm going to get Ferris to put me back on the portfolio. I can cut the best deals ever with this puppy."

Hegley laughed. "Harry could talk the bubbles out of a glass of champagne," he said. "I can see why you fell for her, Root."

"And what was it about Minona that did it for you?" I asked.

"Who she?"

"Min worked at Ferris. I asked you about her before, remember?"

He shrugged. "Can't say I do."

"I saw her photo on the board in your study."

"There's a ton of crap on there. Don't know what half of it is."

"Not even signed pictures of beautiful ladies?" I said.

"Wait a minute … ah yes, Minona. Another wannabe groupie, I'm afraid. I do get lots of fan mail."

Hegley picked up his cup in all calm, took a sip of tea, placed the cup back on the table. The guy seemed totally composed – or he was a damn good actor.

"A pile of mail for a dead man?" I said. "You're going to have to do much better than that."

"Root, what's the matter with you?" Hegley asked.

"You claim you never met Minona, but there's a picture of her in your study," I said.

"Does this tell us something really important?"

"You went to her flat several times," I said.

"You say." He smiled at me like I'd just wished him good day.

"You were seen there by some guy at the studio who had a crush on Min. He used to follow her around."

"I see. And all this adds up to big news, does it?"

"She wanted money from you, so you killed her," I said.

Hegley looked over at Harry. "Your boyfriend's cracked under the pressure, I think."

"I know you did it, and it's time the police found out." I pulled out my mobile. I found Callaghan's card, began tapping out the number.

"You wouldn't," Hegley said. "What about the film?"

"It's waited twenty years," I said. "It can hang on a little longer."

Hegley knocked the phone out of my hand, and it hit the flag-stones, broke into pieces.

"Root, he didn't kill Min," Harry said.

"Of course he did."

"Listen to Harry," Hegley said. "She knows what's what."

"Yes, and speaking of taking note of girlfriends," she said, "I went to see one of yours, Philip. Theresa had loads to tell."

"Ha, woman barely leaves the house. She lives in some fantasy world." He picked up his cup, tossed the tea away, poured himself some more.

"Thing is, she's your listening post, isn't she? I'd say she's a Philip Hegley compendium."

"You can't believe a thing she says."

"And because you told her you were sleeping with Minona, she's incredibly angry."

"Even more reason to ignore her."

"I was a perfect ear," Harry said. "She explained that Minona was about to go to Root and tell him what you were up to. All that business about big, bad Ferris you concocted."

"Come off it, Harry," Hegley said.

"And when you couldn't stop her, you set your henchman on her," she said. "But Naysmith's only used to playing with the boys, isn't he? He overdid the physicals and killed her."

"Don't listen, Root," Hegley said.

But I was listening. And I realised that Min had taken the biggest hit of all. For me.

I grabbed the dusters from my pocket, took a stride towards Hegley. Harry jumped in my way.

"Naysmith was a tough nut on screen, but no criminal," she said. "A real-life, real-death thing like that would've played on him. Did he tell you he wanted to turn himself in and confess? Was that it, Phillip?"

I squeezed the knuckledusters tight, had a real ache to go for him.

"The state he was in, you couldn't rely on Naysmith any longer," Harry said. "So you killed him."

"He fell from the fort and drowned. Tell her, Root."

He was right. Naysmith was a long, long time in the water. I helped fish him out.

"He was dead before he hit the river," Harry said. "Ergo, you killed him."

"Now I know you're absolutely crazy," Hegley said.

"I went to see Roney," she said. "The poor guy's a bit of a mess right now. But he was together enough to be able to tell me that the police have confirmed Naysmith was stabbed to death.

"The flick knife," I said.

In one easy move, Hegley pulled out the knife, grabbed Harry's arm, and snapped out the blade inches from her neck.

I wanted to use the knuckledusters.

"Let her go," a voice said.

I spun around and saw Nesh standing tall in the doorway.

I looked at Hegley. His hand was shaking, the knife far too close to Harry.

"Drop it," Nesh said.

Quick as grease, Harry stamped a sharp heel down hard into Hegley's foot. He yelled and she grabbed the teapot, swung it. The hot tea hit him in the face, and he dropped the knife, put his hands to his eyes.

I pulled Harry away, put my arm around her.

Nesh walked over to us, bent to pick up the knife. That was when Hegley made his move, snatched the dusters from my hand. I was sure he was about to go for Harry and pushed myself in front of her, was ready to take the blow. But Hegley tossed a vicious punch at Nesh's head and put him down hard on the ground. He dropped the knuckledusters, took off into the house.

Harry and I checked on Nesh. He was face down. We turned him over. The dusters had cut a cheek open from jaw to ear, bone broke out from raw flesh. Harry cried out.

* * *

By the time I'd searched through the house and was at the front door, Hegley must have had five minutes on me. The four-wheeler was still parked in the road and that meant he was on foot – the obvious place for him to have gone was the river. I remembered the path alongside the school playing field, ran by the pond and came out on the water.

I couldn't see him, but I thought his best bet would have been to cut across the marshes where he knew the way, so I headed out after him as quickly as I could. There were no landmarks, nothing I could recall from the last visit, so I stuck as close to the river as possible. Running was difficult in this terrain, and it was tiring. But Hegley must have been feeling it too. I wasn't going to give up on the chase yet.

I spotted him by the shore. He was simply standing there. As if he were waiting for me.

I heard the call of sirens back in St Lawrence.

"Hegley," I shouted, "it's over."

He kicked off his shoes. He dove into the river, was far away from the bank when he broke surface. He was a powerful swimmer, each stroke taking him yards out and closer to the old Thames lighters. I thought that was where his strength would give out, that he'd climb up onto one of the boats, wait until the police arrived to haul him off into their launches. That was how this was going to end.

But Hegley swam right past the boats, kept on swimming further out into the estuary. It had been easy enough to track him on the shore side of the lighters where the water was flat, but beyond, the wind kicked the river up, made it dark and noisy. I thought I saw him. But then he was gone again. I kept on searching. Was that him? I walked on, called out his name over and over. But I was kidding myself. I'd lost him. Or he'd lost me.

Chapter Twenty-Eight

I came out of New Scotland Yard and headed for St James's Park, sat on a bench in the sunshine and enjoyed watching the tourists feed the pelicans.

I was happy to be outside. Callaghan had put me through it all right. He'd led me down to the basement, showily unlocked a heavy steel door, slammed it behind us, turned the key, slipped it into his pocket in a solid performance of bad cop. He was togged up in full uniform, looked odd all blue-coated. Out of his usual garb he'd lost a good measure of cool.

But he gave me a hard time. What the fuck had I been playing at, he asked. If I'd told him about Hegley from the off then maybe lives could have been saved. What kind of fools were you and that girlfriend of yours, jumping into everything that moved? Hegley got the chance to whack Naysmith, take out Nesh, and do himself in it looked like. How did I feel about that?

Bad was the answer. It could be argued that Philip chose his walk-off, but Naysmith was nothing more than the over-loyal lackey who threatened to bite back the once and was made to pay for it. And Nesh? Well, he'd simply been doing the job Ferris had asked him to do in minding Hegley, and Hegley had taken it all out on him at the very bloody end. The poor guy.

Callaghan had been keen to bring charges, he told me, obstruction of justice for starters. Just how many times had he warned me? I didn't deserve a let-off. I'd earned a really hard lesson. But the chief had told him to let it drop. While that business down in Whitstable was technically prosecutable, a caution was the only thing they could reasonably dish out. And that was what I got.

I left the park bench, bought a soft drink from the kiosk, walked

243

up to The Mall, watched the skaters wheel over the red macadam. The thing about Callaghan was that you needed to take what he'd said with a huge dose of sodium chloride. Truth was, he was pissed off I'd solved the case, had gone and done his job for him. The reason he'd kept warning me off was because he'd been chasing the glory. A gumshoe too big for his fancy boots, was how I rated him. He hadn't reckoned with En Root Wilson, had he? On-the-air, online, on-the-ball.

I looked at my phone, was waiting for a message from Harry. I'd arranged to meet her. What teammates we'd turned out to be.

I strolled over to Trafalgar, enjoyed thinking about what kind of sexy outfit she might be wearing. I flagged a cab and got the driver to take me to the river.

A long-shot of St Paul's cathedral.
Cut to:
An out-of-focus image with multiple shades of grey.
There's a steady sharpening of the picture and we
make out a riverscape. The water shimmers unnat-
urally. The film's running at faster than normal
speed. A ferry enters the frame from the right,
leaves it jerkily to the left. A series of boats
skitter from one side to the other like pond in-
sects.
Cut to:
A long-shot taking in the length of the Millennium
Bridge. People race across it and towards us before
peeling off to either side of the camera. Gradually
the pace eases, returns to the everyday.
Cut to:
A medium-shot of the back of a man standing in the
middle of the bridge. He looks down at the river.
He turns around. We see it's Root. He glances at
his watch.

Cut to:

A medium-shot of a crowd of people walking away from St Paul's towards the bridge. We see that Harry's among them. She's a total standout in a long crimson coat with a black boa hem.

Cut to:

A close-up of Root leaning with his back into the railing of the bridge. His hair's untidy. He wears three days of beard. He looks to his right and then he smiles. He's spotted Harry.

Cut to:

A medium-shot. Root's waiting right of cen-tre-frame. Harry's walking steadily towards him. She hits what's surely her mark right beside him…

Cut to:

A long-shot. Harry keeps on walking. She stays in frame until she gets to the end of the bridge. Then she dissolves into the mass.

Cut to:

A medium-shot. Root Wilson stares down into the river.

Cut to:

A top-shot of the bridge.

Cut to:

A long-shot of St Paul's.

Cut to:

A top-down shot of the Thames. The focus slides to a monochrome mix.

White out.

Acknowledgements

There are many people who deserve my thanks for helping me get this far. It's impossible to name you all, but I want to say thank you many times over.

For their input over many Tuesday evenings, I am indebted to the ZenAzzurrians, namely Anne Aylor, Aimee Hansen, Roger Levy, Annemarie Neary, Sally Ratcliffe, Richard Simmons and Elise Valmorbida. And once again to Anne and Elise who ploughed through the manuscript. Plus thanks to Laura Morris and Andrew Emerson who helped shape the final book. And to J David Simons for his input over the years.

The Former Dictators lyrics are reproduced with the kind permission of The Former Dictators/Mark Terry.

About the Author

Steve Mullins is a journalist who has freelanced for newspapers including the *Financial Times* and *International Herald Tribune*, specialising in music and digital media. He is a former advertising agency copywriter and has more than twenty-five years' writing experience, working mainly in London, with spells in Paris and San Francisco. *Fade to Black* is his first novel.

CONTRABAND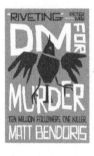

Saraband's distinctive crime, mystery and thriller imprint
www.saraband.net

LITERARY PSYCHOLOGICAL THRILLERS

His Bloody Project
Graeme Macrae Burnet

'A truly ingenious thriller' EXPRESS

'Gripping...a tour-de-force' HERALD

The Disappearance of Adèle Bedeau
Graeme Macrae Burnet

'A captivating psychological thriller'
ALASTAIR MABBOTT, HERALD

CRIMINALLY GOOD READS

DM for Murder, Matt Bendoris
SHORTLISTED, Bloody Scotland's
Crime Book of the Year 2015

'Riveting' PETER MAY

'A murder mystery for the digital age,
#GreatFun' MASON CROSS

Oh Marina Girl, Graham Lironi
'A book you could become obsessed
with' ALASTAIR BRAIDWOOD

COMPELLING CRIME & DETECTIVE NOVELS

Falling Fast & The Storm, Neil Broadfoot
SHORTLISTED, Bloody Scotland's Crime Book
of the Year 2014; FINALIST, Dundee Int'l Prize

'The real deal' CRIMESQUAD

Cracking pace, great characters, satisfyingly
twisty plot. A great read.' JAMES OSWALD

Beyond the Rage, Michael J Malone
Glasgow's answer to Tony Soprano.

'Redefines the term unputdownable.' CRIMESQUAD

The Guillotine Choice, Michael J Malone
The moving story of a survivor of Devil's Island.